11806

To
(I

my Sen
Boyfriend a
Prom Date, who has
the great life and family
he deserves!

Love from
Debora
"the hat lady"

A Ghost Among Us

By Debora Eliza Beth Hill

JAQKAR Publishing
1705 Poplar Place
Forest Grove, Oregon 97116

ISBN: 1-58550-017-8

Dedication

This book is dedicated to Christine Lawrence

and Natasha Laughlin

The ghosts of the past haunt us still

Character List

Dierdre: The television interviewer (present day)

Charlotte: The fashion photographer (present day)

Natalie: The fantasy artist (present day)

Jerome: The ghost (present day)

Vladimir Rochovsky: The filmmaker (present day)

Robin Herald: The rock singer (present day)

Paul Harkness: The biologist (present day)

Sir Jerome Kennington:(1811)

Lady Alicia Mannerly: Sir Jerome's bride (1811)

Richard Foxworthy: Jerome's friend (1811)

Charles Brent: Alicia's cousin (1811)

Lady Sarah Mannerly: Alicia's aunt (1811)

Chapter 1

June.

Dear Charlotte: It's finally happened! Do you believe it, I'm on my way to London! I've landed the job with TV4, and they want me there in September. Is there any chance you can put me up until I find a place of my own? I remember you telling me your place wasn't large enough for more than one person, so I guess there's no chance of our becoming flat-mates. Could you please send me some info about finding a flat or house? I'm not worried about the cost of rents and such -- let's face it, it certainly couldn't be more than they're gouging me for here. Have you heard anything from Natalie? I saw Brice's novel on display at Waldenbooks the other day, and wondered if she was ever able to get her share of the advance-money out of him. What a lizard.

Speaking of real men -- the last letter you wrote me you mentioned you were seeing someone new. I have, of course, lost the damned thing, but I seem to recall his name was Paul? Is he still part of the action? I am, alas, sleeping alone these days -- but then, so is most everyone in Manhattan. Who has time for a relationship, and who can one trust, anyway? I'm ready for some old-fashioned hand-holding, so I hope things aren't quite so drastic in London.

Also hoping things are going well for you, and that your showing at the gallery was a great success. I will telephone you in August.

Love and Kisses . . .Dierdre

Chapter 2

"3209."

"Hi, Chari! This is Natalie -- I'm calling from California!"

"Hey, girl -- I'm glad you called. This must be my day to hear from friends far away. I just got a letter from Dierdre, and she's coming to London. She landed that job with TV4; she'll be here in September."

"Oh, I'm so damned jealous! I want to come, too."

"I wish you would. I showed those paintings you gave me to the Director of the Camden Gallery and he loved them. I think I could get you a showing there, when they have the Camden Arts Festival."

"When is that?"

"Late October and early November. Maybe you could ship me some stuff."

"Or I could bring it myself, and stay with it."

"Are you serious?"

"You know, I think I am. Brice finally couldn't avoid me any longer, and I got half of his advance and royalties as a settlement. The money from the advance won't last forever, but it would get me settled over there and keep me going for awhile. Maybe I could get a job there, or connect with some people in the gallery scene. Northern California is the deadest place on earth. At least, for me it is."

"You used to love it there."

"When Brice and I were married. It's the pits for men - - if they're not gay, then they're farmers or cowboys or something equally revolting."

Charlotte laughed. "One of the things I can recommend about London is the men -- as long as you stay away from the Arabs. No woman in her right mind would go out with a man who's a Moslem."

"Doesn't that include Pakistanis, too?"

"Yep. Listen -- can you come over when Dierdre does? I was thinking of looking for a flat for the two of us. Why couldn't I find a house, instead, and we could all share it?"

"I don't think I'll have the money by then. The court has subpoenaed the records from William Morrow, but the editor is really dragging her feet."

"A woman, and she's keeping another woman from getting money she earned? What an asshole."

"When it comes to corporate women, they have no loyalties to anything but their paycheck. I'll get it, though -- I've gone too far to let him get away with it, now. But I think a month is too optimistic."

"Well, if you're certain you want to come, then I could get the place anyway. Didi and I could settle in and wait for you."

"Will that cause a monetary strain?"

"Be serious -- we're talking about Didi here. Why don't you think about it, and I'll see what she says. Give me a call and drop me a line soon, and let me know your decision."

"OK. Now, are you still seeing that guy you mentioned the last time? Paul? I can't remember his last name."

"Paul Harkness. I sure am -- he's definitely the most special man I've met in a long time. Well, since . . .you know."

"It's been a few years, darling. You should be able to say his name by now."

"I've gotten so used to not saying it in public that I never say it at all. I'd much rather no one knew I was ever his lover."

"You shouldn't be ashamed of it. It ended, just like a lot of relationships do. Just like my marriage did. Well, not just like -- Martin was a lot more generous than Brice ever was. And you weren't even married to him."

"That's because he defined our relationship as one of mentor and protegee. And, he's still a good friend. I know, if I ever had a problem, I could go to him. Oh! Honey, I've got to run -- I'm late for a shooting as it is."

"Then take a cab rather than the underground -- spend some of that money you hoard so well."

"My hoard will come in handy when I'm saving a third of a house for you. Bye! Hope to see you soon . . ."

In the end, Charlotte was forced to relent and take that cab. Even though it was a beautiful spring day and Charlotte's rule was to take cabs only when she couldn't see a foot in front of her face because the rain was in torrents, or she couldn't plod through the snow, that afternoon she was just too late to make it on the underground. And she needed her job as a fashion photographer -- Martin had gotten it for her, and another would be difficult to find with her limited experience. It had been a shock, upon arriving in London nearly a year before, to learn that she wasn't considered so very young -- in New York, a photographer in his or her early twenties was still a novice. There were no novices in London -- either you hit early and peaked at thirty, or you went into another line of work and gave up on the glamor professions. It was hard-edged and no-nonsense, and youth was the absolute ruler of the hip scene. Charlotte wouldn't have liked it if she had been one of the people shut out or just plain left behind; as it was, she had reason to be grateful for her ex- lover's influence. Charlotte fretted through the afternoon, photographing models on Blackfriers Bridge for an American fashion magazine.

Nothing went right; the models were late, the clothes didn't fit, the wind blew everything about. At six she was on her way to New Cross and The University of London, where Paul would be waiting. She wanted to tell him about her friends, and the possibility they would be coming to London. She hoped he would have friends to take them out -- good-looking, nice friends, she amended -- if they worked for the university they were probably intelligent, so that was a given.

She then hoped he wouldn't be more attracted to one of them than he was loyal to her -- it was Dierdre she worried about. Those men who weren't intimidated by her were invariably attracted to her . . .redheads seemed to have an unholy hold over mens' minds. She told herself not to be foolish -- that Dierdre would never take a man away from one of her friends, anyway. But if Paul was attracted to Dierdre, Charlotte would know . . .and that would ruin it for her. Just the way it had when Martin had seen the French girl in Berlin . . .

They were eating fish and chips at *The Seashell* in East London. Charlotte hated to admit it, since it was Paul who introduced her to the place (she liked to think she knew the best spots herself) but they made the best cod in London. Their salads were fresh and their chips weren't soggy. Charlotte popped an entire malt pickled onion into her mouth and glanced over at Paul. She had often wondered why such an outstanding man would choose her as a lover, but she had wondered the same thing about Martin. Rock stars usually had their choice of women, and Charlotte didn't consider herself beautiful. Paul and Martin, and a number of other men, would have disagreed with her. Just her eyes were enough to send a man into daydreams of slow, langorous sex in front of an open fire. They were large, and slightly turned up at the ends, which gave them an exotic quality. And the shade was so unusual -- a vibrant turquoise-blue -- that more than one model had asked Charlotte if she wore colored contact lenses.

"Paul," Charlotte said, swallowing her onion, "Do you like redheads?"

He watched her suspiciously, eating chips with a steady rhythmn. There was no telling what Charlotte was up to, now -- in

Paul's experience, she was always up to something. And frequently her questions were loaded.

"Are you thinking of dying your hair, little ragamuffin? It would be a crime. Too beautiful the way it is, and you don't have the complexion of a redhead." Paul pushed his own chestnut brown hair off his forehead, and ate more chips.

"No, I'm not. You never answer a question, do you?"

"Sorry. I can't say that I ever thought about it -- I don't like or dislike them. I like all women."

Charlotte wasn't terrifically pleased with his answer, and frowned. He smiled, and reached over to squeeze her hand. He had the most devastating smile, she thought.

"What is it? Obviously blondes are my favorite -- one blonde, at least."

"My friend Dierdre is moving to London. You know, the one who hosts *Below Manhattan*."

Paul nodded. "You told me she was thinking about it. Have you heard from her again?"

"Yes; she'll be here in September. And Natalie, our friend in California, is thinking of coming, too -- she's not sure when. You remember I told you about her? Her husband wrote a best-selling book, and she sued him for some of the advance and royalty money."

Paul had switched to eating his fish. He nodded, his mouth full. After a decent interval of chewing and swallowing he said, "And did she get it?"

"Yes, half. Can you believe that guy allowing her to support him all those years and then not wanting to share his good fortune with her?"

"Hey, girl -- there are opportunists everywhere. Where will these two friends be living, and which one is the redhead?"

Charlotte's gaze flashed up to meet his, and she started to laugh self-consciously. "Why do you always have to be so discerning? It drives me mad."

"Dear girl, if I wasn't, where you're concerned it would be me who was driven mad."

"You know, I've been thinking I might be able to rent a house large enough for all three of us."

Paul stared at her in horror. "A photographer, a television interviewer and a . . .what does your friend Natalie do? Nothing normal, I'm sure."

"She's a painter."

"And a painter, together in one house. Will there be enough closet space? Enough rooms? I can see it now . . .you'll need to rent Hampton Court."

"I don't think I can afford it. Not to worry, though -- I'll find something."

"That's what worries me -- don't rent anything until you tell me where it is. I don't trust you; you might rent a house around the corner from Pentonville Prison."

Charlotte glared at him resentfully, stuffing chips into her mouth.

Chapter 3

Charlotte Lewis knew she was a very lucky girl, and she thought she just might feel that way if she could get out of her one bedroom flat in Queensway. It wasn't only the place itself she hated, though that was enough. It was the whole area of Queensway and the Bayswater Road -- filled with Arab men and tourists; the latter didn't bother her much, but the former were the bane of her existence. Twice she'd been arrested for assault when the harassment got to be too much and she took a swing at one of the swaggering, splashily- dressed young bucks who paraded Queensway. The charges had been dropped both times -- what self-respecting Moslem male would admit to having his nose broken by a woman? But Charlotte knew it was just a matter of time before she wound up dead or killed one of the assholes.

The problem was that Charlotte was a beautiful girl. Not beautiful like the models she photographed -- she was far too earthy and substantial for that. The models, even though they liked her, never would have considered her to be competition -- she was too heavy. Too heavy for their world, that is . . .but in the real world, Charlotte was a head-turner of the first order. If her hips were a little too wide and her legs a little heavy, Charlotte was clever enough to disguise it and accentuate her tiny waist and attractive shoulders.

But if Charlotte's beauty made her popular with men, there were certain drawbacks. In London, a natural blond was also a natural target for an entire subspecies of men who had never seen a blond before setting foot in Britain. Once there, they continued to treat women with the same arrogant disregard they had been taught in their native culture, and most of the English women were too timid to fight them. In the year she had been in London Charlotte had tangled with them enough to know they were basically cowards who sought out what they considered to be the weakest prey -- and Charlotte was anything but weak.

Her start in fashion photography had come while she was still a student at the prestigious Arts Academy of New York -- and from an unlikely source. After maneuvering her way backstage at a rock concert one night Charlotte was introduced to Norwegian heavy metal rock star Martin Waaktar, and began a tumultuous two-year affair that ended when Martin married his childhood sweetheart and returned to Oslo to raise future rock stars. But during those two years he had introduced Charlotte to anyone and everyone who might be able to assist her in her career, and so her start in fashion photography had been an assured success while most of her classmates were still working for Kelly Girl or delivering pizzas.

After her break-up with Martin they remained friends, and Charlotte dated a lot of men in New York before finding her way to London, where she was offered a job with Vogue magazine. She met Paul Harkness at a benefit for the homeless, and was instantly attracted to him. But she was surprised when he asked her for a date -- somehow she hadn't imagined she was the type to attract a Research Biologist from the University of London. If she thought it was ironic that Paul was also Norwegian, she didn't allow it to bother her much. She was generally attracted to Scandinavians, and there were a lot of them in London during the summer months, particularly Swedes and Norwegians. Paul's salary as a Research Biologist, even one who had garnered awards in his twenties (he was now in his early thirties) was less than what Charlotte earned as a fashion photographer. He was also living alone, in a second floor flat in Paddington, and his place was, if anything, worse than Charlotte's. She had visions of finding an enormous house with lots of bedrooms, where she could live with Dierdre and Natalie, and maybe eventually Paul . . .it was a charming fantasy that she never imagined would come to pass, because an enormous house in London was practically unheard of.

What it was that took her to Hampstead one day in August she wasn't certain, unless it possibly might have been desperation. If she didn't find a place soon, Dierdre would arrive in London and rent a horribly expensive suite at The Ritz Carlton without a second thought. Then she'd come to Queensway to visit. And if the Arab men in Queensway had problems with Charlotte, she didn't even want to see them come up against Dierdre, the most out-spoken woman she knew. Charlotte had never been to Hampstead, even though she was celebrating her first year anniversary in London that month. But most of her travels involved her work, and she had never been assigned to do a fashion shoot in this most fashionable suburb.

She was immensely impressed with the area, and the houses . . . but she also knew that they were mostly owned by millionaires who used them as retreats from their inner-city townhouses and flats, and even if she did find one for rent, it was unlikely they would have been able to afford it. Well, she amended, Dierdre could, but it wouldn't have been fair to ask her friend to pay rent for Natalie. Not that Dierdre would have minded -- she was one of the most generous rich people Charlotte had known, and in her profession she met her share. But Natalie would mind, and they'd all wind up hating one another.

When Charlotte went into the Chesterton's office, she wasn't even sure that Dierdre and Natalie would agree to share a house with her. But it felt right, and Charlotte had always done well by acting on her feelings.

Chapter 4

"Hello."

"Dierdre! It's me, Chari -- I've found the house!"

"Good thing, girl -- I'm surrounded by the biggest mess I've ever seen, and wondering how I could have accumulated so much junk. Maybe I should leave some of it here."

"You should, but you won't. Don't you want to know about this house, after all the trouble I went to?"

Dierdre laughed. "Of course I do! Tell me, before you burst a blood vessel."

"It's in Hampstead -- five bedrooms, and it's absolutely beautiful."

"Five bedrooms in Hampstead? Honey, even *I* don't have that much money. How did you swing this?"

"Well, it is a little run-down."

"I knew it! You're moving me into an old council house that's falling down and has the ghosts of previous tenants living in it."

"There are no council houses in Hampstead; any ghosts would have to be aristocrats or rock stars. And it really is in pretty good shape -- we can make it look wonderful. Do you know, during the year I spent in that rotten place in Queensway I never put a photograph on the wall."

"Not even your own?"

"Not even. That's the point -- I refused to admit I lived there. But this place -- I have an entire wall in the reception room staked out for my work. Actually, there are two reception rooms, so Natalie can have one to hang her paintings."

"And what about *my* work?"

"What are you planning to do, hang strips of videotape?"

"Not a bad idea -- definitely Art Nouveau. Listen, I'm not bringing my furniture with me. I figured we could always buy more -- and I don't think, now you've told me about this house, that my stuff would suit it."

"Rented houses come furnished here, Didi. And would you believe it, this place is filled with antiques -- some of 'em look really old. It was originally part of an old country estate that's been divided into townhouses. The man who owns the house hasn't been advertising it because he wanted to be careful who he rented it to. This week he finally listed it with Chesterton's, and I was the first person to see it. Shall we take it?"

"Honey, if you say it's right for us, I trust your judgement. I'll be there in a week -- is the place ready?"

"I can get it the day before your arrival -- is that perfect timing, or what?"

"Shall I send you a check? I get the feeling that first and last on a place like that could be astronomical, even if it is 'reasonable'."

"Well, I was planning to use my savings, and have you and Natalie reimburse me when you arrived."

"Forget it -- let me pick up the whole thing. You two haven't got that much money to spare. I'm bringing the most important things with me, and the rest is coming by ship. Do you believe it takes four to six weeks! By then I won't remember what I'm sending."

"What *are* you sending?"

"I'm not sure -- it didn't seem like so much until I started to have it boxed-up. Now it keeps growing, and there are sixteen full cartons already."

"And you're not bringing your furniture? Are you sure you didn't put it in the boxes by mistake?"

"Very amusing. It's mostly clothes."

"I was afraid of that. Be sure to bring your winter stuff with you. It looks like it's gonna be another cold one. August's been too nice -- that's a bad sign, here."

"So says the girl who's spent a big one winter in London."

Charlotte laughed. "You get used to it quickly. Tell me when you're arriving, and I'll be at the airport with a van. You are coming to Heathrow, aren't you?"

"Of course -- do you think I'm a heathen? Don't answer that. September 9th, United 526, and it arrives at 4 in the afternoon, your time."

"Why didn't you book a seat on the Concorde?"

"It doesn't fly from New York to London."

"I should've known you'd check."

"I didn't need to -- you forget I flew to London three times last year. I have to go -- the people are here to pack the rest of my boxes. Oh! Does this place have lots of closets?"

"Well, no. You see, they didn't build them with closets in the 18th century. But the bedrooms have little dressing rooms attached to them -- the owners never had them converted into closets, but I don't see why we shouldn't."

"Perfect! We can have it done by one of those companies that specialize in custom closets. Why don't you call them and have them come in before I arrive? Can you get into the house now?"

"Yeah, I guess. They're having it cleaned and the carpets and drapes replaced."

"Don't let them put in anything that's beige or brown. The two most depressing colors in the world for decorating. I'll call you the night before I'm coming, shall I?"

"Yes; I'm having the phone disconnected, but not for a few weeks. I won't let it go until the new phone is connected in the house, and the phone company is the pits here. They could take forever."

"I hope not! Bye -- I'll see you soon."

Chapter 5

Dierdre Hall's flat on the Upper East Side of Manhattan was small and chic. Small because everything on the Upper East Side had to be, and chic because Dierdre had an engrained sense of what looked good, and the money to execute the most pleasing design. Although she was perfectly willing to have a custom-closet firm design the framework for her closets, she never would have hired an interior decorator. Her mother was a rare specimen for a wealthy woman -- she numbered amongst her hobbies gourmet cooking, interior decoration and clothing design. Dierdre had inherited her talents, in addition to a striking beauty and flaming masses of auburn curls (enhanced now by Clairol "Torch Crimson" haircolor)

It was through her connections that Dierdre had first entered television from the far end of the camera, reporting social events at a New York network. A mere 23 at the time, Dierdre's only claim to fame was her family name and plenty of money. And plenty of people who resented her for it, and attempted to trip her up every step of the way. Although she remained stoically steadfast during her rise to the position of talk show hostess, Dierdre remembered those people. She rarely had to engineer a revenge herself -- fate always seemed to step in before her and deal with the job. But if she was given the chance, Dierdre Hall could be an implacable enemy -- the moreso because she wanted very much to be everyone's friend.

At the age of 28, Dierdre was now one of the most famous talk show hostesses in the U.S., her show *Below Manhattan,* was nationally syndicated and had spawned a myriad of local copies. Because she refused to be cast into any of the molds that had gone before (and she had the money to walk out of any situation she didn't like), Dierdre was able to maintain the show in the original concept, and it lasted through three years of network battles. But finally, when Bush was elected president, the television market began to shrink and tighten. They made it through eight years of Reagan, but Reagan had been an entertainer -- that was his bottom-line. Conservative he might have been, but he knew how to play a crowd. As soon as Dierdre saw Bush's tight, cramped, mean little face for the first time, she knew it was time to think about moving on.

And now she was moving right out of his jurisdiction, across the sea. America was beginning to scare her -- she wanted to become an expatriate, and watch it thrashing about like a whale on the sands from as long a distance as possible. It hurt her to realize that the freaks and the fanatics were taking over, and soon she wouldn't even be able to decide on her own whether or not she wanted to have a baby . . .but she had the money to get out, and she didn't apologize for running. She would hurt for those left behind -- those at the mercy of the women-hating, power-hungry bigots who longed to have women under their power again -- she would hurt for them, but she didn't intend to become one of the victims. She knew she was getting out just in time; every day the headlines were worse, the stories more grotesque. What a travesty the 'land of the free' had become.

Dierdre didn't realize it, but it was her money that had kept her from having a really important love relationship in her twenty-eight years. Or perhaps she did realize it, and didn't want to acknowledge the problem. Men seemed to want her money, or they hated it . . .or they ran from her, knowing they'd never have as much. But no one just didn't care about it, and she wondered if anyone ever would. Perhaps in London, he was waiting -- the one who wouldn't care -- the one who, if she was lucky, might not even know. Because she had no intention of broadcasting her wealth --

that was why she had agreed to share a house with Charlotte and Natalie. Wealthy women didn't have roomies, did they? Perhaps people would see her as just another career girl in a glamour field, who made enough to buy nice clothes and furniture, but who still had to share a house because rents in London are so high . . .as long as she managed to avoid people from her own social set, Dierdre thought she might be able to pull it off . . .

Chapter 6

Several days before Dierdre's arrival in London, Charlotte went to visit her house. She wore her favorite dress, a turquoise shirtdress of jacquard cotton that suited her hourglass figure and was long enough to disguise the fact that her legs were a little thick to be fashionable. She further camouflaged them by wearing black leather ballet slippers -- she had these in all colors and fabrics, and wore them most of the time. They were particularly useful when she was working (unless it was raining or snowing; then she wore low-heeled boots) because she was often climbing or crawling around somewhere not conducive to high-heels. There was also the problem that Charlotte couldn't walk in heels any higher than an inch, even though she frequently attempted to when she went out at night.

Hampstead Heath was beautiful in the June sunshine, and Charlotte walked from the tube stop up the hill, emerging into the park-like atmosphere, her gaze going instinctively down to the corner of the side-street where her house resided. Well, she amended, it wasn't really *her* house -- she would be sharing it with Didi and Nat, and none of them would own it. But she already thought of it as hers', and had chosen her bedroom.

As she approached the house, her eyes were drawn to the upper story window that belonged to the master bedroom. A double French-door opening onto a small iron balcony, it was framed in new pale rose drapes that Charlotte had chosen herself. The master bedroom was for Dierdre -- that only seemed fair to Charlotte, since she knew that Dierdre would be paying the largest share of the expenses involved in the upkeep of the house. She and Natalie would try, but Dierdre always overwhelmed everyone by the sheer logic of her bank account. So, she got the master bedroom. The rest of them were smaller, but the house had so many rooms that they each had an extra -- she would have a darkroom, Natalie would have a studio (Charlotte had given her a ground-floor room overlooking the garden for that; and she had taken another ground-floor room, next to the laundry room, for herself) and Dierdre could use hers as an office if she wanted to. Charlotte wasn't certain Dierdre had a home office, but it was best to be prepared. That left only one guestroom, but they should be able to manage-- Charlotte's feeling was one guestroom was best; it didn't encourage too many people to stay too long a period of time. She was thinking of her own family in Tennessee, of whom she only wanted her maternal grandmother or her youngest sister to ever visit London.

Charlotte's eyes narrowed behind her black sunglasses, and she put her hand up to shade the sun. She was certain she saw a man standing in the upper window of the house, but there wasn't supposed to be anyone there. She started across the street at a run, narrowly avoiding being side- swiped by an Austin Metro. That reminded her that her car was still in the shop, two weeks longer than they had said it would be . . .she was going to have to see about getting another vehicle. British mechanics couldn't fix American cars, particularly something as intricate as a Trans Am. They'd probably destroyed it.

Her eyes went up to the bedroom window again as she saw the drape move slightly. With a shock, her gaze met that of a man attired in what appeared to be a theatre costume. He wore a long, fitted coat of burgundy velvet over black satin knee breeches. She couldn't really see his legs, but underneath the jacket he wore a white shirt with one of those strange, high collars Charlotte had seen in old drawings, with a cravat tied around it. His dark eyes met her's for a second, then the curtain fell again. She blinked, and when she looked again, he was gone.

Taking her new key from her purse, she rushed to the door and fumbled to unlock it. No one was supposed to be in the house but the people who were cleaning and replacing carpets and such . . .and no one would be doing that kind of work dressed in a velvet jacket! She stumbled slightly over the carpeting in the hall, and dashed up the stairs to the second level. She wasn't afraid of being attacked, but she curled her fingers around the handle of her bag in case she needed to use it as a weapon. She reached the master bedroom and threw the door open, stepping into the room and looking around; behind the door and in the corners. There was no one there. She approached the window slowly, and checked behind the drape. She hadn't really believed a man could hide there, but it didn't hurt to be certain. How had he disappeared so quickly, and what had he been doing there? She descended the stairs more slowly, and gave the rest of the house a cursory look-over. She didn't expect to find anyone, though. Perhaps it was a ghost, she thought, as she locked the door again. An old house like this one should have a resident ghost, after all . . .

Chapter 7

Didi was excited to be in London, but it didn't really register that she was there to live. She had made various trips to this, one of her favorite cities, over the years she had been a television celebrity, but never remained there more than a couple of weeks at a time. Now she had all the time she wanted to get to know both London and the rest of England, and in her mind she was already planning trips to explore the more obscure parts she'd never had time to visit before.

Didi had been surprised when Natalie turned up on her doorstep two days earlier, but not terribly so. When Natalie decided to do something, time and circumstances weren't really a barrier. Although she had initially told Charlotte she wouldn't be able to get to London until after Didi's arrival, they knew their friend well enough to realize that her imminent departure would have dwelt on her mind every day until she discovered a way to hasten the date.

Natalie Merchant at thirty had finally grown into her body and her hair. If that seems like a strange comment, it's because Natalie had always been too tall and Amazonian of build until she reached an age when she became striking rather than gangly. With a Russian mother and a Scottish father, Natalie was six feet tall and had masses of dark- blond hair that made Charlotte's lighter tresses seem skimpy. Natalie had intimidated most of the boys and men in her life until she met Brice Merchant and married him. That was when they were both 22 years old, struggling artists ready to take on the world. Unfortunately, the world they took on was the one in which he planned to become a best- selling author of horror/fantasy novels; Natalie's world of painting would have to wait. For seven years Natalie worked as an insurance reconciler while Brice wrote his first novel, *The Blood Ruby*; (that took five) and sold it to Ballantine (that took two). When he received his astonishing advance of $250,000 Natalie was floating on her own private cloud. No more horrible office on Bush Street in San Francisco where she was one of a hundred people who did nothing but attempt to reconcile insurance accounts all day long with other reconcilers they never met but talked to on a telephone a thousand times. No more hour-long commute only to find that she was too tired to paint at the end of the day, so it had to be postponed yet again. No more watching her friends and Brice's make what seemed to be more positive steps in the direction of career advancement. Now Natalie could paint, Brice could write his follow up novel, and they would live happily ever after.

The reality hit three weeks after the arrival of the first advance check, when Natalie found a note from Brice telling her that he was leaving her, and taking the money. Actually, no mention was made of the money at all -- Brice seemed to assume that because he had written the book, Natalie wasn't entitled to any of the advance. He conveniently forgot that she had been supporting him for seven years, and went to live with a nineteen year old airline stewardess he met on a flight to New York, on the way to visit his publisher. It took Natalie a year to get her share of the money. But get it she did -- $125,000 plus the lawyers fees she put out in taking Brice to court. When Brice agreed to the first initial payment (his advance was being paid in two installments of $100,000 each and one final for $50,000) but made it clear he didn't intend to stick around for anymore, the judge (a woman, Natalie thanked God, wherever she was) changed the ruling, and had Carl's editor at Ballantine flown to California and brought into court. When the editor was directed to pay Natalie half of Brice's royalty payments, she attempted to demur, claiming the publisher shouldn't be brought into marital disputes. The judge was adamant, however, and the editor finally agreed, reluctantly. She seemed to be of the same opinion as Brice -- he had written the book, he should get the money. But Natalie won -- she'd lost seven years of her life, but she'd won the chance to try to make it for herself.

She was hoping that chance could come to fruition in London. Charlotte had done very well for herself there, thanks to Martin; now perhaps she could, too. And Dierdre would have an instant bank of contacts on which to draw; everyone would want to get close to her and be seen with her -- surely amongst all those trendy airheads there had to be some serious artists and gallery owners.

At least, Natalie hoped so. She had received her first two installments, $50,000 each, and she still had all of it except what went for taxes (far too much, in Natalie's opinion) -- that should last a long time in London, if she was careful. Surely the money could last three or even four years, and by then she should have established herself enough to make a living. Natalie's style of painting was something along the lines of modern impressionism; she had painted several large pieces from photographs Charlotte took of street people in London. She was working on several more, and had originally planned to finish them before she arrived in London.

What it was that made Natalie decide to go to London with Dierdre she couldn't quite pin down or remember. One morning she decided that she was ready; she had her money, and the final payment wouldn't be available until the novel came out -- that wouldn't be for another six months. It didn't matter to the publishing company if she was in California or Berlin -- they'd use her moving as an opportunity to delay the payment if they could, but Natalie was going to make certain not to give them the chance. She'd see an attorney (didn't they call them solicitors, there?) as soon as she arrived in England, and arrange for him to tell Brice's editor about her relocation. Natalie was quickly learning about the duplicity of men, and their tendency to club together against the common foe, women. If she had looked for a sympathetic masculine soul when this whole mess started, she had soon learned there wasn't one to be found. They all thought she was a grasping, castrating bitch for insisting on her share of Brice's money -- the fact that she had supported him for seven years seemed nothing but irrelevent to them.

Natalie wasn't as well-travelled or as savvy as Dierdre, and sold most of her possessions before she left for London. What she kept, however, was far more than the airline wanted her to take, and they attempted to charge her more than the cost of her ticket to transport the extra pieces. It was Dierdre who came to the rescue -- domestic flights are more lenient than international ones, and Natalie was horrified when it came time to leave J.F.K. Airport for Heathrow, T.W.A. wanted $457, cash. Now, Natalie would have paid them -- she couldn't leave her painting supplies and canvasses sitting in the airport. But Dierdre didn't believe in paying for anything she didn't have to. She figured out that it would be cheaper to bump Natalie up to first class (she'd tried to convince Natalie to fly that way to begin with, but Natalie's money was too hard won to squander it) and bully them into taking the extra pieces. The TWA people hated her by the time she was finished, and she hadn't even noticed -- it never occured to Dierdre that many times people didn't like her because she robbed them of their tiny bit of precious power.

Charlotte arrived at Heathrow an hour early and drank too much coffee. What if the immigration officials gave them a hard time? Charlotte disliked and distrusted civil servants of almost any kind, unless she wanted something from them. In her experience, they were likely to give people as much trouble as they could get away with -- it went back to that little bit of power. The less real power people had, the more they wanted to flaunt their bit in everyone's faces.

Her powder blue wool circle skirt and short, white angora sweater looked like a portrait out of the 1950's -- Charlotte planned her wardrobe around what she thought of as 'theme events', and this week she was heavily into the 50's. Ballet slippers (white satin today) strangely seemed to go with the clothes of almost every era, except the 30's.

By the time the plane finally arrived (over an hour late) Charlotte was jumping up and down in excitement and anticipation, and attracting appraising looks from a number of men who were waiting for the same plane.

When she saw Natalie come through the doorway from Customs, pushing a luggage trolley piled high with suitcases and a large basket bound with elastic cords, she began to leap about in earnest, waving and screaming.

Natalie was dressed conservatively, as she always was -- Charlotte decided she would have to change her wardrobe, if she wanted to make it as an artist in London. She wore a grey wool jersey dress, tall grey boots with nearly flat heels and enormous designer glasses with turquoise and gold frames. Those definitely had to go.

As Natalie neared the barrier, the basket began to topple from her luggage cart. Charlotte slipped under the ropes and caught it as it fell, pushing it back to the top of the pile. Then she threw her arms around Natalie and hugged her, as people attempted to pass around them, cursing them and urging them to 'get along then, won't you'.

Dierdre appeared, with a porter pushing a slightly less laden cart. Charlotte admired Dierdre's style -- she always looked like one of the less outré plates from *Vogue*, without appearing as if she ever tried to. She laughed and waved them through the ropes before her.

"Welcome to London, ladies!" Charlotte caught the basket again, and lifted it down, hefting it onto the top of Dierdre's trolley. The porter looked as if he was going to take offense at this. "You take this, honey -- it won't stay on top of Natalie's mountain. Are you sure you didn't leave anything behind?"

As Dierdre embraced Charlotte, Natalie said, "Seven cartons, coming by ship."

"Oh, good. With Dierdre's cartons, they should just about fit in the house."

"Don't listen to her," Dierdre yelled at them as they made their way towards the exit doors. "From the description, a hundred cartons would fit in that house."

"Which should be just about how many arrive," Charlotte

retorted. "Ready to go home?"

"Are we ever! Lead the way!"

On the way home, a hunger attack hit Dierdre and Natalie, who had been forced to endure airline food. When Charlotte expressed skepticism that first-class food could be a hardship, she was amazed to learn that it was so rich and over prepared that it produced the opposite result coach-class did -- both women were nauseated by it. So they stopped in Queen's Park for fish and chips. Next to **The Seashell**, which was too far to go and out of the way anyway, Charlotte's favorite place for fish and chips was an unprepossessing little fast food restaurant across the street from the Queen's Park underground station. Since she had driven up the perimeter road from Heathrow rather than face going through the center of the city, Queen's Park was on their way to Hampstead.

Dierdre stared down at her fish dubiously. "The English eat too much fried food," she stated, taking a small piece on her fork. Natalie and Charlotte were happily eating chips at a furious rate. "You two had better watch it, or you'll get fat."

"I won't," Charlotte retorted. "Too much sex and exercise."

Dierdre ate the fish. "Hey, this is good! I didn't trust you when you brought us to this place. The sex part I believe, but since when did you start to exercise? I don't believe *you* doing aerobics."

Charlotte swallowed a piece of fish. "Of course I don't! Do you think I'm an airhead with time on my hands? I get plenty of exercise just chasing around after people with my cameras."

"Well, that's all right for you," Natalie said, regarding the remainder of her chips with some suspicion. "I can hardly say I get exercise by lifting a paintbrush. Am I going to have to resort to the aerobic nightmare?"

"I was kidding!" As if to prove her point, Dierdre ate some chips. "I can't believe anyone in London needs to do that -- too much walking just to get from one place to another. I mean, there are lots of cabs, but I try to walk as much as possible when I'm here. I'd do it at home, too, but you never know when you'll run into a psycho on the street. I feel safer here."

Charlotte toasted her with her glass of ginger-beer. "Hey -- you are home! And I can find you lots of psychos to make you feel as if you are."

The other two girls lifted their glasses. "Gee, thanks Chari -- I feel more at ease already." The cheap glasses clanged together.

Chapter 8

By October, the house in Hampstead looked as if it had been home to the three Americans for two years, not two months. When she saw the size of the house, Dierdre started making telephone calls to cleaning services until she found Dorinda, an East Indian girl who stated that the house was haunted as soon as she stepped over the front threshhold. This didn't bother her -- Dorinda was nineteen years old, a student at The London Technical Institute, and attracted by the salary Dierdre was offering. It was approximately double what most people in London paid their cleaning women or men -- Dierdre was horrified by the amount of money people were expected to live on in such an expensive city, and decided she could at least compensate in this small way. It didn't occur to her at the time that there might be more she could do.

The large reception room, originally one of the parlors of the manor house before it was divided into six townhouses, had been painted pale rose and hung with slightly darker silk drapes. The darkness of the house was alleviated by this color scheme -- and the furnishings, which were mostly pale grey and white with touches of rose in various shades. A white leather couch and loveseats, which should have looked incongruous in an old mansion, were instead stunning and original, and the glass and marble coffee and side tables were the perfect accompaniment.

When Charlotte surveyed it the day she hung her photographs, she was glad she had waited for the arrival of Natalie and Deirdre -- if Dierdre knew anything, it was how to furnish a house.

One wall of the room was French windows, leading out into a brick patio and beyond that, a garden shared by the six townhouses that had comprised the original mansion. On one of the remaining walls were hanging three enormous oil paintings of horses -- horses out of a fantasy. They were flowing and prancing, one with a body of silver and a mane of pink and black; one in blues, silver and black; the last in purples, pinks and gold. All three were signed in the lower right hand corner in a flourishing script -- the name "Natalie". The second remaining wall was intersected by a doorway, but the remainder was covered with an assemblage of large black and white photographs of people on the streets of London, or more specifically, of people living on the streets (and in some cases below) of London. They were humorous, pathetic, sad and innovative, and captured a spirit that was made all the more striking and poignant by the beauty of the surroundings and the fact that the subjects were largely ignored by the people shown passing them by.

The last wall was dominated by a large white marble fireplace, flanked by free form, black lacquered bookshelves from ceiling to floor. The bookshelves contained, in addition to a large number of books, several shelves of videos. One entire shelf held a series of black video cases labelled "Channel 20", and a series of dates.

One rainy evening in October (only in London could it be so cold when it rained), Dierdre and Charlotte were seated on the couch together, waiting to be served dessert. It was Natalie's night to cook (they each took turns about once a week; the rest of the time they ate out), and it was the first dinner all three of them had been there on the same night. Joining them for the first time also was Paul Harkness. Although Didi and Nat had met Paul on numerous occasions before, this was his first 'dinner' visit -- they hadn't invited anyone over the first month after they moved into the house. Now he sat on the carpet, leaning back against the base of the couch. Charlotte's legs, draped over his shoulders, looked remarkably dainty against his chest.

At 33, Paul Harkness was incredibly handsome in an almost unreal way, and held the promise of growing old gracefully. Because his looks were unimportant to him, they became even more attractive to others, and he had his share of willing women. Until he met Charlotte at a benefit for the homeless, however, he had drifted from one semi-love affair to another, only touching down long enough to realize he and his latest love were communicating on different channels.

Paul and Charlotte were a strange couple, and any of their friends would have said that they were *definitely* on different channels. But they liked the way they were together, so they stayed. Paul was icy looking, in a way -- Dierdre and Natalie wondered if most Norwegians appeared as if they had just come in from cross country skiing and some of the snow had penetrated their system. His eyes were a frosty blue, and his face was chiselled, strong, and hard. He had longish, wavy dark-brown hair that didn't look Scandinavian but somehow added to the aura of iciness surrounding him. Dierdre understood his appeal -- women wanted to thaw him out. Only Charlotte seemed able to do so.

As Natalie came in from the kitchen pushing a black enamelled drink trolley, Paul looked around the room. "This is really nice," he commented with a slight accent. "Looks as if you ladies are finally getting settled in."

Didi laughed. "You mean there aren't clothes and papers all over the living room."

"That's a good indication, I guess."

"Not necessarily," she retorted. "We could've moved all the stuff into the bedrooms. We didn't, but that's thanks to Dorinda, not us."

Paul frowned. "Couldn't you have found an English cleaning woman?"

"We tried," Charlotte said, "but there don't seem to be any. Strange, since we're willing to pay a lot more than most of them make working in shops or offices. Besides, we like Dorinda. What's wrong with her?"

"Nothing, she seems like a nice, intelligent girl. But England's in trouble from all the immigrants pouring in -- the English won't be able to get jobs, soon."

"I wonder if there's an English person wandering around jobless, because you're working as a research biologist for the University of London. Go back to Norway, you foul interloper!"

Paul stared at Natalie for a moment as she halted her trolley, not certain how to take this exaggerated comment. When all three women began to laugh, he did so, also. "Oh, all right! I get the point. Since there aren't any English people in this room, I guess it's a moot point."

Natalie had a pitcher on her trolley, containing a whitish-beige drink that she poured into wine glasses with different colored pastel stems. She handed a pink glass to Dierdre, a green one to Charlotte and an aqua one to Paul. He sipped his tentatively while Natalie took the last glass, a yellow one, and sat cross-legged on the floor next to Dierdre. "So," Natalie said, "What'cha think?"

"Delicious," Paul replied, a moustache of foam on his upper lip. "What did you call it?"

"A Pina Colada. I can't believe you've never had one."

In a heavy, phony accent, Paul said, "Ve be very backvard in Norvay, yah."

Charlotte put her drink on the coffee table and pretended to strangle him. He started to choke and laugh, and Charlotte said, "Do they have a clue, down at the university, that their most brilliant biologist has a screw loose?"

Paul seemed to consider this as he drank some more of Charlotte's drink. "I don't think they've even realized I'm the most brilliant."

"Obviously a case of intellectual blindness," Dierdre put in. "Or color blindness."

Paul turned to stare at her uncomprehendingly. "You just drank Chari's drink."

They all laughed, and Paul handed Charlotte her drink. "When do you start your new show, Didi?" he asked as he now drank his own.

"Wish I knew. They were so antsy to get me over here, and now they can't settle on a premiere date."

"I guess a new TV show is like a new anything . . .it never happens as planned."

"I'm just happy they agreed to pay me from the day I arrived."

Paul was looking around at the room. "I wonder what the history of this house is. Do you know, Chari?"

She shook her head, finishing her drink. "Not really. But the owner told me the land has been in his family for about a hundred and fifty years."

Natalie frowned. "This house couldn't be anywhere near that old."

"Oh, no," Paul added. "The architecture is definitely this century."

Didi dismissed it cavalierly. "Then something must've been here before."

Charlotte laughed. "Honey, this is London. There was always something here before. I know -- let's go the library tomorrow and see what we can find out. Hampstead was a village, 150 years ago, not a suburb of London."

"I'll go with you," Didi put in, finishing her own drink. "I've got nothing to do but spend money and try not to gain weight before my premiere show."

"If you spend enough money," Paul told her, "You won't have any left for food."

Didi shook her head mournfully. "Somehow it never happens that way. I'll keep working on it, though."

Natalie scrambled up and began collecting the Pina Colada glasses. "Speaking of which, is anybody hungry? Dinner's almost ready."

Paul nodded, grinning. "I'm starving!"

"From what I've heard, that's hardly a revelation. I'll check and see how it's going. There's more booze if anybody wants some."

As she headed toward the kitchen, Paul enthusiastically retrieved his glass and filled it with more of the liquid from the pitcher. He offered it to both women with a gesture of his hand, but they shook their heads. When Natalie's scream was heard, Paul was glad he had already deposited the drink pitcher back on the trolley, but his now-full glass fell crashing down, splattering the creamy liquid over him and the trolley. With a curse he scrambled up and headed for the kitchen at a run. Dierdre and Charlotte were soon after him, although they were a little cleaner at this point.

Paul collided with Natalie as she ran out of the kitchen, and caught her in his arms. Charlotte noticed with amusement that they were nearly the same height, though Paul was noticeably larger. "What's wrong, Natalie? What happened?" He was attempting to peer over her shoulder into the kitchen.

"There's a man in there -- wearing funny clothes!"

Paul ran by her into the kitchen, but returned a moment later. He didn't look amused, and Didi thought she wouldn't want to get into a battle with him. His blue eyes turned to chips of ice, and his jaw looked like it was carved from marble. "Very funny, Nat," he spit out, "There's no one in there! Now I'm covered with gook, and I've broken one of the glasses."

"But there was!" Natalie was pale, and seemed incredibly distraught for a woman who was usually so calm. "A young, good-looking man in old-fashioned clothes!"

Charlotte considered this, and looked around for a camera. "Like an old movie from the thirties?"

Natalie shook her head. "More like a Regency novel." Didi started to laugh, as much from Paul's disgust at the condition of his Intarsia sweater as at Natalie's vision of a Regency cavalier. "Right, Nat -- pretty good."

"He was there!" Natalie was screaming, and Didi stopped laughing -- that wasn't like her, either.

Charlotte shook her head in mock disgust, then stopped for a moment. She remembered the man she had seen in the bedroom window. "Wait -- I've seen him, too."

They all looked around, but she shook her head. "No, not now -- one day when I came to see the house. He was standing in the window of the master bedroom, but when I got up there he was gone."

"That resident ghost, maybe," Dierdre ventured, laughing.

Paul was trying to brush the 'gook' from his sweater. "I'm willing to risk a ghost," he stated wistfully, "If it means getting some food."

He pushed Natalie firmly in the direction of the kitchen, overruling her protests. None of them saw the figure in the corner of the room, next to the window. He stepped away from the wall as they disappeared into the kitchen, and watched them go. He was tall and slender, with a narrow waist, broad shoulders and muscular calves -- all of which attributes were enhanced by his clothes. He had very dark, wavy hair and white skin, that looked as if he didn't know the meaning of the word 'tan'. He wore tight knee breeches, hose, a white shirt and cravat; and the tight-fitting black satin dress coat of the late Regency period.

Chapter 9

Dierdre found the North London Regional Library the following day. A large, old building filled with books that seemed to be filed according to no system known to man; it took her an hour of searching through their card catalogue just to find the section she wanted. Eventually she located the books from the correct time period and lugged an armful to one of the carved tables she was certain must be an authentic antique. Taking out a stenographer's notebook, she began to look through the first book.

An hour passed, and she was wondering with some irritation where Natalie could be. Several minutes later she looked up to see her dash through the double doors at the front of the building and past the circulation desk, looking around in some bewilderment. Her hair was windblown, and she looked out of breath. As Natalie's gaze scanned the room, Dierdre held up her arm and waved, attracting her attention. Not even pausing for breath, Natalie ran to the table and threw herself into the chair next to Dierdre's, plunking her large canvas bag down next to the books.

Dierdre was staring at her in some amusement. "Boy, you're really out of breath. Are you taking up marathon running?"

"Not a chance," Natalie panted. "I was late. I ran from the tube station. I was up at The Camden Arts Center, and met the most wonderful guy there."

Dierdre regarded her skeptically. "Oh, no . . .first Chari, now you. Succumbed to the power of the 'y' chromosome. You know how one of those can screw up a perfectly good human being."

"Spoken like a woman whose divorce won't be final for another month."

"But whose marriage has been over ever since her husband discovered she wasn't going to support him for the rest of his life," Dierdre replied bitterly. "So . . .tell me about this wonderful man. Is he English?"

"Russian." Natalie laughed at the look of disbelief on Dierdre's face. "Well over six feet, thin and with a receding hairline."

"Well, I guess there are princes in Russia, too. Where did you meet this paragon?"

"At The Arts Centre. He works for the BBC. A filmmaker. He's taking me out to dinner this weekend."

Dierdre raised an eyebrow. "These Russians are fast workers."

"How're you doing on the house research?" She glanced at the stack of books. "You sure have a lotta books."

"There are so many books on that period." She picked up her notebook. "The house we're in was built in 1925, on the sight of what had once been Arden Manor, the country house of the Earl of Arden."

Natalie seemed not to understand this. "Country house? In Hampstead?"

"In the seventeenth century, Hampstead *was* in the country. Arden Manor was built by the third Earl of Arden in 1668. The history of the Ardens continues in fairly boring fashion until 1811. Then, in June of that year Jerome, the fifth Earl, was murdered on his wedding night."

"Jesus -- poor guy. Was his wife murdered, too?"

"No; she disappeared for over a year. When she reappeared in the society of London's top ten thousand, she was again a widow -- she'd been married again in the intervening year!" Natalie seemed to be pondering this. "Wait a minute -- she disappears on her wedding night -- the night her groom is murdered -- she's gone for a year and when she turns up again, she's been married to someone else and now he's dead, too? This sounds more than a little suspicious to me."

Dierdre laughed, pulling one of the books from the pile and opening it to some colored plates. "No kidding. Look, there's the original house." She pointed to a large manor house that only vaguely resembled the house where they were now living. It was the green expanse of the heath across the street that convinced Natalie. Dierdre continued. "The house and the Earldom passed to Jerome's cousin Ian -- the present owner is the descendant of Ian, who became the sixth Earl."

Natalie was flipping through the pages of the book, looking at the colored plates of houses. "And the murder was never solved?"

"No. Do you think we can do it now?" Natalie looked up at her in amazement. "It only happened 175 years ago."

"I guess the statute of limitations has run out." Dierdre laughed. "I think so. Let's go home -- I'm starving." She stood, pushing the steno notebook into her bag. Natalie watched her as she gathered up an armful of books. "Take the rest of these, would you?"

"Are you taking all these books with you?"

"Just these on the table -- now I've really gotten interested in the history of the house."

Natalie picked up the remaining books and followed Dierdre through the library.

Chapter 10

Late the following Saturday, Dierdre, Charlotte and Paul were waiting for Natalie to return from her date with 'Prince Vlad the filmmaker'. Charlotte and Paul were sprawled on one of the couches, entwined in a rather strange twist of arms and legs. Dierdre was lying on the carpet, surrounded by her library books. On the coffee table was a litter of coffee cups, plates of cookies and small cakes, and a tray containing a coffee server, cream pitcher and sugar bowl. Paul was munching on cookies as Dierdre read to them.

"And the original manor house, which was destroyed by fire in 1925, was replaced by six smaller townhouses. The manor house had over fifty bedrooms."

"I wouldn't have wanted to clean it," was Charlotte's only comment.

Paul said, "I'm curious about the story of Sir Jerome and his bride. Is there any information on what happened to her?" Dierdre picked up another book and opened it to a page marked with a piece of pink paper. "She was gone for nearly a year; when she returned to London she had remarried and was again a widow. To a minor member of the gentry." She put the book down and sat up, plucking her steno notebook from the coffee table. "His name was Charles Brent. They had only one child, and there was some question regarding his age. At least; I can't determine, from what I've read, exactly when he was born."

"So," Paul swallowed his bite of cookie, "he could be the son of

Jerome and Alicia."

Dierdre nodded. "Good guess." She looked up from the book at the sound of the front door opening. "There's Nat and the Russian prince."

Paul reached for another cookie, and Charlotte slapped his hand away. "Did you meet him before they left?" He asked, sliding in when she moved back and taking the entire plate from the table.

"No," Charlotte replied, attempting to retrieve the cookie plate from him. "We didn't want to scare him off. How many Russian princes are left?"

Paul reached over her head and put the plate, with two remaining cookies, back on the table. Charlotte glared at him and he grinned back. "You mean genuine ones?"

Before Charlotte could retort, Natalie and Vladimir entered the living room from the foyer. Vladimir was very tall, and very thin. His dark hair was starting to recede, but he was handsome in a vague way -- none of his features were perfect, taken separately; but they achieved a pleasing synchronicity. His nose was long and slender, a match for his body, that resembled nothing more than a well-bred greyhound. His eyes were a clear hazel, and seemed to take in everything about his surroundings in one sweep of the room. His mouth was, perhaps, a little thin; and his cheeks a little gaunt, but he had an overall aspect of intelligence and sensitivity.

Natalie grinned at them, giving evidence in her face of a pleasurable evening. "Hi, guys! What's happening?"

"We're discussing the history of the house. It's fascinating." Paul fixed his smile on Vladimir, obviously waiting for an introduction.

"Oh, tell me all about it," Vladimir replied. His accent was stronger than Paul's. "I'm really interested in architectural history."

"Don't be shy, Vlad," Natalie admonished him, "Jump right in."

Vladimir grinned, but colored slightly in embarrassment. "Please excuse me -- I'm Vladimir Rochovsky."

"Sit down and have a cup of coffee, Vladimir -- ignore Nat; she knows she should have introduced you right off and she's trying to get us to forget her bad manners."

Natalie stuck her tongue out at Dierdre, but Vladimir didn't see her, as he was seating himself on the couch opposite Paul.

"Call me Vlad," he replied, "It's a lot easier to say."

As Dierdre poured him a cup of coffee she said, "I'm Dierdre Hall. This is Charlotte Lewis and Paul Harkness. Cream or sugar?"

"Black, please." Vladimir took the cup of coffee from Dierdre and looked up expectantly to where Natalie was still standing, regarding him uncertainly. "Aren't you going to sit with me, Natalie?" The way he said her name sounded like a song lyric.

"OK." Natalie seemed uncertain of Vladimir, and didn't sit too closely to him on the couch. She poured herself a cup of coffee.

Vladimir said, "Pleased to meet you all. Paul Harkness. Aren't you a biologist at the University of London?"

Paul stared at him in amazement. "Surely I'm far too obscure to be a celebrity."

Vladimir took a cake from the platter Dierdre offered him. "Maybe in some circles," he replied, "but I make documentary films for the BBC. Last year I made one about the university, and you were in it."

Paul reached for one of the cakes as Dierdre replaced the platter on the table. "I remember now!" He laughed, taking a tiny bite of the cake icing. "I'd only been there six months."

"But they figured you were the prettiest face they had," Natalie put in drily. Vladimir turned to fix her with his disconcerting gaze, and she stuck her tongue out at him again. He laughed; a deep, bass, booming sound, and popped the little cake into his mouth whole, ending with a grin.

"Don't tease my pet," Charlotte told Natalie with mock-severity. "Did you have fun?"

Paul choked on the remains of his own cake. "Pet!" He roared, and tackled Charlotte, bearing her down to the couch and tickling her. Screaming, she attempted to retaliate, and Paul dragged her into his lap, imprisoning her arms within his.

"We had a wonderful time," Natalie replied, when her voice could be heard. "We went to a restaurant in Elephant and Castle that serves West African food."

Paul seemed impressed. "Wow; that's exotic."

"Foreign cultures are my hobby," Vladimir explained. "I can tell you where to find just about any kind of food you want."

"In London, what we mostly want and can't find is good food," Charlotte retorted acidly.

"More coffee, Vladimir?" Dierdre held up the pot.

"Yes, thank you. Black, please." He held out his cup as Dierdre poured coffee into it.

"Black!" Paul was staring at him in horror; he hadn't apparently noticed the first time. "No cream? You must be American."

"Russians drink it that way, too," Natalie told him. "What progress have we made on the story of Sir Jerome and Lady Alicia?"

"Well, we don't know much more," Dierdre told her, as she replaced the coffee pot on its' cordless warmer, "but I'm of the opinion Alicia must have married her kidnapper."

"Why would she do a crazy thing like that?"

"Who says she had a choice? We're talking about a period in history that had a pretense of civilization, but was really very wild and with little law enforcement. If Alicia was kidnapped and held prisoner for a year, being told she would only be allowed back into society if she were to marry the man who held her prisoner; what else could she do?"

"Kill 'im," Charlotte stated unequivocally. "Let's see the book."

Dierdre handed Charlotte one of the books from the pile beside her. Paul remained beside her so he could look, also; apparently he wasn't bothered by her cold blooded avocation of murder as a solution to one's problems. But even though they spent the next several hours discussing the mystery of Sir Jerome and his bride, they came up with nothing approaching a solution or answer to who had murdered the former or kidnapped the latter and then conveniently died himself.

Vladimir made his goodbyes around one in the morning, promising to telephone Natalie the following day and leaving her wondering, as millions of women had before her, if he actually would -- and if he didn't, if she would be able to summon the courage to call him.

Paul and Charlotte retired to her bedroom, as they did nearly every night now. Dierdre and Natalie were expecting daily announcements of their forthcoming co-habitation (they hoped Paul would come to live in the house -- it would be a strange arrangement, to be sure, but neither of them wanted Charlotte living in Paul's little hole of an apartment in such an unsavory area as Paddington).

Chapter 11

A week later, Dierdre was finally researching her first show. Her guests were to be a British rock group known to be politically active and extremely left wing; something she hoped wouldn't turn out to be just another load of rock star drivel. She had a stack of magazines and clippings beside her on the reception-room coffee table, and she was busily making notes in her steno pad. The lead singer, Robin Herald, was the most interesting of the group -- the rest seemed to be the usual types. But this Robin was unusual, to say the least -- she picked up a color close-up shot of the singer. He was tall (or he seemed so, Dierdre amended - - miracles could be done with photography, and he could turn out to be Dudley Moore's twin) and slender (now that was a little harder to disguise), with nearly black hair and very pale skin. His hair was long and waving in the front, falling over his forehead. His face was thin, sculptured and aristocratic; his eyes a deep, piercing blue. Dierdre knew the photograph was airbrushed -- no one was *that* good-looking. Even the heavenly Paul Harkness suffered from occasional acne.

Dierdre didn't see the man emerge from behind the curtain. He could have been Robin Herald's twin brother, without the heavy eye-makeup the singer affected, and somewhat shorter hair. He moved into the room tentatively, as if he wanted to approach Dierdre but was afraid to scare her. He stopped a few feet away as she looked up at him in amazement, her pen falling to the table with a clatter and bouncing to the carpet.

"My God -- who are you?"

"You can see me?" The man's accent was rich and drawling, and sounded out-of-place and affected beside Dierdre's American twanginess.

She watched him out of narrowed eyes, leaning sideways to retrieve her pen from the carpet. It wasn't much of a weapon, but it would put out an eye. "Of course I can -- and you're one hell of a strange sight, too. Why would you think I couldn't see you? Are you some kind of a weirdo who thinks he's invisible, or something? How did you get in here, anyway? I'll bet Charlotte forgot to lock the front door again."

"I couldn't say. I've always been here. I'm a ghost." Dierdre started to laugh, but it sounded slightly hysterical. When he didn't respond she stopped, and leaned over to look at him more closely. He didn't look like a ghost -- at least not what she had always believed a ghost would look like. In fact, he looked sort of familiar. "You're serious. You're Sir Jerome Kennington."

Jerome came closer slowly, as if he was afraid she would run from him. When she didn't he sat on the couch across from her and crossed one shapely leg over the other. Dierdre thought he looked like he belonged in that room (perhaps not with that particular furniture), more than she did.

"I've been watching you and your friends since you came to the house. I don't know why you can see me, but I've been waiting for someone who could . . .for over 150 years."

Dierdre regarded him skeptically. "And in all this time, I'm the only one who could?"

Jerome smiled. "I think your friends may be able to. At least -- the big blonde saw me once."

"Of course -- the night in the kitchen. She was certain she had, and we thought she was hallucinating. Chari thought she saw you, too -- standing in the window of the master bedroom."

"Dierdre -- that's such a beautiful name, by the way . . .and you're all such beautiful girls." He sighed. "Girls weren't nearly as lovely when I was alive. And so much less of them showed." He glanced over at Dierdre's shorts and little tank top with emphasis. Now she knew he was a ghost, however, she didn't mind so much . . .but she hoped he didn't come into their bedrooms at night. She was about to mention it, when he again spoke.

"I need your help. I'm bound to this house until I can discover . . ."

Dierdre interrupted him excitedly. "The identity of your murderers!"

"Yes. I know you've been studying the history of the house. Can you tell me anything?"

"Very little, right now. But I'll show you what we've discovered -- and if you tell me your story, that might help. You could have clues you haven't considered."

"I'd be happy to."

Before he could continue, the front door opened and slammed closed again. Charlotte's voice came into the room from the foyer. "Where are you, Didi? Anybody here?"

"There's Charlotte! Let's see what her reaction to you will be."

"Maybe she won't be able to see me."

"She already has once -- why not now?"

Charlotte came running into the room a moment later, carrying a large, paper carryall bag from Harrod's. She stopped on her way to the kitchen to speak to Dierdre. "Hi, Didi! What'cha doin'?" Her eyes widened at the sight of Jerome. "Wow -- who's your friend? You going to a costume party?" She dropped her bag on the carpet, and a round of brie wrapped in cellophane bounced out of the top and rolled over to Jerome.

"See?" Dierdre asked Jerome smugly. "I told you she'd be able to see you."

Charlotte took the cheese from Jerome, who had retrieved it when it hit his foot. She replaced it in the bag and plopped down into a chair, putting her feet in their turquoise suede boots on the coffee table. She regarded Dierdre with suspicion. "Are you two on drugs? Of course I can see 'im -- he'd be pretty hard to miss, don't you think?"

"Chari, this is Sir Jerome Kennington." Dierdre was unsuccessful at keeping the excitement from her voice.

Charlotte smiled at Jerome. "Hello -- I'm pleased to . . .wait a minute. Jerome Kennington was that guy who was murdered here. Are you two putting me on?"

"No, Charlotte," Jerome replied. "I'm a ghost."

She narrowed her eyes at him. "Oh, sure. Prove it." Jerome laughed. "How, my dear lady?"

Charlotte thought about this for a moment. "How the hell would I know? I've never met a ghost before."

"I know!" Dierdre was bouncing up and down -- Jerome expected her to clap her hands in delight at any minute. "Disappear and then re-appear!"

Jerome nodded, and slowly faded from their view until he was no longer visible. Charlotte sat and stared at the now-empty chair in disbelief. Jerome's voice came from the air where his head had been. "Am I gone?"

"I'd say definitely," Dierdre told him. "Now if most of the men I know would only be so obliging." Jerome began to reappear again, and Charlotte thought how extremely strange it was to be able to see the back of the chair through his chest.

"Look, he came back, though. They always do." The two girls giggled at their joke.

"You ladies have some strange ideas about men," Jerome replied repressively, removing an enamelled silver snuff box from the pocket of his coat. He flipped the lid of the box open with his fingers and took a tiny pinch of the tobacco blend in his nails. Putting it to his nostril he sniffed delicately. Both girls were now staring at him in horrified fascination. "Jerome," Dierdre replied, "You've been dead almost two hundred years. Your ideas about women must be somewhat outdated."

"Not to mention your ideas about what to do with tobacco," Charlotte added. "Nobody puts it up their noses anymore -- disgusting! As bad as chewing it."

Jerome looked faintly nauseated. "Chewing it? Now who, pray, would do that?"

"Actually, there are still people who do that -- but only extremely ill bred, lower class ones. They come from The Midwest."

Jerome was eager for knowledge about the people of the present day. "The Midwest of what?"

"The United States."

"Oh . . .that. You two come from there, don't you? But not from The Midwest, one would assume?"

"Certainly not! They're all Mormons, or Fundamentalists -- and they wear polyester!" Charlotte delivered this as her coup-de-grace, but Jerome just stared at her uncomprehendingly. "Well, never mind -- just take my word for it that you wouldn't want to know them."

"Accepted," Jerome said faintly. "I thought I understood the changes in society -- I've been watching the people who lived in this house for a long time."

Charlotte snorted derisively. "I can imagine the type of people you've watched. Married, upper-middle class types, 2.5 kids. The wife didn't work and the husband hardly knew his children."

Jerome turned to her in surprise. "You knew some of them?"

"I didn't need to. We don't live that way, anymore. Men and women are equal now." Her tone of voice was belligerent, as if she was daring him to contradict her. Instead, he laughed. "I always thought women were superior. Alicia was certainly superior to me."

"You're an unusual man," Dierdre replied. "Why don't you tell us your story? It could help us find your murderers."

"Well, yes. I'll start at the beginning, shall I?"

"How dreadfully clever of you." Charlotte stretched her legs out in front of her, crossing them at the ankle. "I can see eighteenth century men have it all over their modern counterparts."

Jerome glared at her, but Dierdre said, "Ignore her -- go ahead with the story."

"I had been invalided home when I first saw Alicia, during the season of 1811. Napoleon was the master of Europe, and I was a Major in the Fourth Cavalry. I had come into the Earldom three years before, when my father was killed in a hunting accident. I was twenty-three years old at the time . . ."

Chapter 12

London, 1811

The West End of London glittered in the splendor of the Season, and all of the fashionable "ten thousand" were out in force to establish their position. But Major Jerome Kennington, recently invalided home from the European wars with a bullet wound in the thigh, had little interest in his old, familiar haunts. His three years battling the "Corsican Monster", as Napoleon Bonaparte was called by the British, had sharpened his sense of awareness and heightened his feeling that all was not right with his world.

Jerome's upbringing had been the usual upper class education given to the sons of earls. He was expected to take his place as a leader of society, sit in Parliament and above all protect the rights of his peers. Since Jerome had joined His Majesty's Service when he was twenty, no thought of politics had entered his head before -- now, upon his return to London, he found himself in a very different position. His father had died three years earlier, and his family were now expecting him to take-up the mantle of Earl- hood and look after their interests. His wound would preclude his returning to the war for at least a year, and there was hope that "Boney" would be routed before then.

The signs were there, but Jerome felt out of place in London -- it didn't seem to be such a pleasant city anymore. He realized it wasn't the city that had changed; he had. Beneath the glittering world of the privileged and rich, there was a teeming, festering cesspool of humanity that hung onto survival by the barest margin.

Everytime he spent money (which seemed to be constantly, he thought with irritation), went to a ball or dinner party, he found himself calculating how many people the clothes, the furniture, the food, would support for a year. The totals staggered his imagination. He had stopped going, recently, simply because he couldn't bear the calculations and their outcome.

This evening he had been coerced into attending the Duchess of Rutland's ball with his friend Richard, and as soon as their carriage began inching along Park Lane he knew it was a mistake. The black satin knee breeches and white silk stockings, coupled with a burgundy velvet jacket and tapestry waistcoat, somehow made Jerome all the more aware of his limp and the need for his gold-headed cane. By the time their carriage finally reached the steps of the house, he wanted to tell Richard's driver to keep going and take him to White's. He didn't, however -- instead he endured the long, slow climb up the steps and into the foyer of the house, and on into the over-crowded ballroom. The combined smells of human sweat, too much perfume and unwashed bodies hit him with the same force that bullet had, on the battle-field in Austria, and he held a linen handkerchief to his nose with one hand. While the smells of London couldn't compare to the stench of a horse camp or battlefield, they were unsavory enough simply because they seemed to be so unnecessary. If these people would just take baths more often, Jerome though irritably. They certainly had the money and the facilities for it -- not like those poor unfortunates in the stews of the East End, or Tottenham . . .they had no choice but to be exactly as they were. He shook his head, attempting to drive the thoughts away. They clung tenaciously, as always.

Jerome and Richard paused at the edge of the dance floor to watch the couples involved in a country-dance. Men and women flew past them, the pastel silks and muslins of the womens' gowns flashing intermittently with the dark coats and breeches of the men. A few dandies with yellow or fuschia coats tripped by on their high-heels, but for the most part fashionable attire for men had taken a wild swing to the conservative side when Brummel became the leader of the fashion horde. Jerome was glad of that -- he hated ruffles and patches, and the overdone fussiness of his father's generation. It was true that they had been no less men because of their attire -- his father was an accomplished swordsman and duelist, but it was all so tiresome. Jerome liked things to be simple.

The women blurred as they passed him, circling. Debutantes in white and pastels; young matrons in bright, rich, jewel colors. Most of the mothers and older matrons had arranged themselves in the armchairs along the wall; they were dressed more soberly, in darker colors. There were a few exceptions, of course -- one middle-aged woman floated past in an alarming red dress cut so low in the bodice it displayed nearly all of her sagging charms. Jerome watched her as she made her way back down the room, and shrugged. She seemed happy with herself; so what else mattered? His eyes moved slowly back to the front of the room, and opened in astonishment at the girl who appeared before him, like an apparition from a dream. She was young, certainly no more than eighteen, very pretty and porcelain-pale with golden-blond hair in a short, curly crop. She wore a dress of white silk adorned with small ruffles and flounces, and a garland of white silk flowers in her hair.

Jerome took the quizzing glass that hung on a velvet ribbon from his collar and raised it to watch the girl as she danced by him. She turned her head and met his gaze, and smiled at him; a dazzling, sunbeam smile that was a hammer-blow to his heart. "Richard, who is that divine creature? The little blonde with the wreath of flowers in her hair."

Richard glanced over from his perusal of a young, dashing widow, just out of mourning and enticingly clad in a violet dress that clung to her voluptuous form. After a moment he located the girl, now half-way down the ballroom. "Ah. Lady Alicia Mannerly. This is her first season -- her father was Lord Kelsey Mannerly."

"That old reprobate? She's a beautiful girl."

"Mmmm. A little green for my taste, but pretty enough ne'ertheless. No portion to speak of, of course. Lord Kelsey was an inveterate gambler."

Jerome snorted in disgust, and allowed his glass to fall back into his jacket. "Is there anything more disgusting than a gambler who loses?"

"Spoken with the arrogance of a man who never does," Richard laughed.

"Nearly lost this leg," Jerome retorted calmly.

"Nearly doesn't count. Any other man would have."

Jerome was still studying Lady Alicia. "Who is that man she's dancing with? What an appalling waistcoat he's wearing -- puce and yellow stripes. How very . . .singular."

Richard's bored gaze went to Alicia's partner. The man was indeed a somewhat ludicrous figure -- particularly if compared to the two who were surveying him. He wore a purple velvet coat with extremely padded shoulders and a nipped-in waist that made the skirt of the coat flare out (Jerome suspected the skirt had boning in it). His waistcoat was, as Jerome had observed, comprised of broad stripes of puce and yellow silk, and his cravat was tortuously wound around a collar so high it impeded his peripheral vision. His sparse brown hair had been teased into what Jerome assumed was supposed to be a "Windswept" -- it looked more like a "Storm-tossed".

"That's Charles Brent," Richard told Jerome. "Something of a mushroom, actually -- smells of the shop, I'd say."

Chapter 13

Jerome stared at Dierdre, who had exclaimed in horror at his mention of Charles Brent. "What ails you, lady?"

"Charles Brent -- the name of the man who married Lady Alicia after your death!"

"Are you certain?" Jerome seemed thunderstruck.

"Absolutely. I remember the name, and they had only one child -- a son."

"I suppose I should have realized, but he seemed so ineffectual . . .he *was* her most ardent suitor until I arrived in London."

"Go on with the story," Charlotte urged. "Maybe there'll be some more clues."

Jerome shook his head. "It all seems very clear, now. Though I would swear Brent was not one of the men who came to my house -- they were rough and strong, obviously hired bully-lads. Brent was a weak, posturing fool!" He hit his fist into his palm, as if he was wishing it was Charles Brent's head he was smashing. He took a deep breath, and continued his story. "I didn't see Alicia for about a week after the ball. "Then, one day in Hyde Park . . ."

Chapter 14

London, 1811

It was a mild spring day in Hyde Park. Men and women walked in pairs or groups; the women wore wide-brimmed straw bonnets, and brightly colored muslin dresses with matching parasols. Lord Jerome and his friend Richard were riding across the grass, and Jerome felt better about his world when he was able to view it from this vantage point. With such beauty in his sight, it was difficult to remember the pledge he had made to himself, the cause he was to fight. Jerome had decided a direction for his life, now that he he'd left His Majesty's Service -- once he straightened out his estates and found competent managers (high on his list was bettering the living conditions of his tenants) he would take his seat in Parliament, and see what he could achieve in the way of reform. The reforms he had in his mind had to do with the poor of London, and the way they were forced to live -- surely something must be done. But where to start? That was difficult to decide, because every time he made a foray into Seven Dials or Wapping he seemed to come across yet another hideous injustice.

When he attempted to talk to Richard about his plans, his friend refused to listen. He insisted that Jerome would come to his senses, once he began to take his estates in hand -- that was what their class of people was meant to do. Richard wasn't interested in the poor or their problems -- he was simply grateful he didn't have them himself. Jerome didn't blame him for this -- he knew most of their acquaintances were of the same mind. But he wished he could find a woman who would share his vision, who could help him with the quest. He knew it was a hopeless task, if his aim was to marry this helpmate. Women of his class thought 'good works' meant giving out bibles and soup; it would never occur to them that there should be sweeping changes and reforms in the social strata. If it did occur, it would be a frightening thought to be pushed to the back of the mind -- gentlewomen in England in the first part of the nineteenth century had no time for radical thinking.

Jerome was too deeply in thought to see the high-perch phaeton coming towards them down a path. This vehicle, painted rose-pink and lavender, was unusual in more than its' design -- it was driven by a woman. The high-perch phaeton was such an unsteady, fickle equipage, designed for speed rather than safety, that it was unusual to see a woman driving one. This woman, a beautiful dark-blonde in her mid-forties, was obviously experiencing no difficulties with the management of her vehicle, even on the crowded paths of the park. Seated beside her was the girl who had so taken Jerome's fancy at the ball. Dressed in a green carriage dress and striped pelisse, with an Italian straw hat adorned by green ribbons on her head, the girl looked even more delicate and angelic in the mid-day sun than she had in the artificial light of the ballroom.

As Richard stopped his horse beside the phaeton, Jerome was jerked back to reality. The first thing he saw when he focused his eyes, was the girl, smiling over at him from beneath the broad brim of her hat. Blinking in the strong sunlight, Jerome stared at her as if he didn't believe she was sitting a few feet away from him.

The older blond woman spoke to Richard. "Richard! I didn't know you were back in London."

His friend's drawl was more pronounced than when the two of them were alone; Jerome knew it was just one of Richard's fashionable affectations. He was amused by his closest friend's frivolity, and knew it was a good foil for his own seriousness, which he was afraid would become ponderous if he wasn't careful. "The war was becoming a bore. I'd like to introduce you to my friend, Lord Jerome Kennington -- the Earl of Arden. Jerome; this is Lady Sarah Mannerly."

"I'm very pleased to meet you, Lord Kennington." Jerome

bowed to her as much as he was able from horseback. She continued, "This is my niece, Alicia."

Jerome bent further in the saddle and took Alicia's hand, raising it to his mouth. He kissed it lingeringly, and she didn't snatch it away, but smiled again. "I'm very pleased to meet you, Lady Alicia." He looked up in embarrassment and met Sarah's laughing eyes. "And you, Lady Sarah."

"Don't overwhelm me with your enthusiasm, pray," she retorted drily. Jerome could see she was attempting to keep from laughing aloud.

"I saw you at the Duchess of Rutland's ball. You were in Hussar uniform -- have you sold out?" Alicia's voice was low and soft, and reminded Jerome of piano music.

"Invalided out, dear lady. I took a musket ball in the thigh. I believe I'm well enough to go back, but the surgeon feels otherwise."

"Don't be in a hurry to leave London and deprive us of your company, Lord Kennington." Alicia smiled at him again, tilting her head so the brim of her hat shaded her eyes. Sarah turned and stared at her niece in amazement, as if unable to believe it was Alicia who had spoken.

Jerome grinned at her in turn. "Thank you, Lady Alicia. Leaving London would be very difficult while you are in it, I assure you. Will I see you at Lady Hardwick's musicale?"

It was Sarah who spoke, the humor evident in her voice. "We will be there, Sir Jerome. Though I wonder how safe it will be, with you as one of the guests. You are a rogue, sir." Jerome laughed delightedly, and bowed to Sarah in mock gallantry. "And you would know one well, my dear Lady Sarah, having broken the hearts of so many. Your reputation precedes you."

Sarah laughed also. "But you're a charming rogue. Good day, gentlemen." She started up the horses, and the phaeton moved away down the path, leaving them sitting alone.

"What a wonderful girl Lady Alicia is," Jerome said, watching the phaeton tool away at a spanking pace.

"Watch yourself," Richard cautioned. "She's got no dowry. Lady Sarah sponsored her comeout, but with a father like her's, you can be certain she's going to jump at any offer."

Jerome frowned. "Does it seem to you that I'm in any need of dowry money? And if that girl jumps at just any offer, it would be a tremendous waste." He spurred his horse so it jumped, and rode away across the grass without a backward glance.

Richard watched him for a moment, shrugged, and followed after at a more decorous pace.

Lady Hardwick's house in Mayfair was sumptuous and over decorated, and the drawing-room where she was holding her musicale was crowded and hot. The singer, a noted soprano, was a heavy woman dressed in an unfortunate shade of purple -- a dress that would have been suited to a younger, smaller lady. Her voice was indisputably fine, but somewhat overpowering in a drawing room. Sarah and Alicia were both there, seated together on a small loveseat. They made a lovely picture together -- though they were not mother and daughter they could easily have been so, and they captured the attention of every male in the room between them. Alicia was dressed as befitted a first season debutante in a simple gown of white muslin, decorated with pale-blue satin ribbons and clusters of tiny flowers. Sarah's dress was a darker shade of the same blue, whether by design or happenstance unknown, and they wore matching silk shawls of white embroidered in blue.

With them that evening was Alicia's cousin, Charles Brent. He was dressed just as unfortunately as he had been the night of the Duchess of Rutland's ball; this time in a coat of emerald green satin, and a waistcoat of tapestry that seemed to contain every color of the spectrum, and some that had been invented especially for it. He was standing behind the loveseat on which Sarah and Alicia sat, leaning over the upholstered back with his elbows resting on the satin. Alicia was sitting forward on the divan, as if she didn't want to be too near to him. Attention was focused on the doorway of the salon as Jerome and Richard entered, both attired in the same severe evening wear they wore at the ball. They were a remarkably striking pair; Jerome dark and Richard fair, like two Jacks from a deck of cards. They were by any yardstick the most elegant men in the room, and the eyes of the ladies followed them as they made their way around the back of the chairs that had been set in the middle, over to Lady Sarah's loveseat. Young women began to discuss them behind their fans, and attempted to draw their attention while remaining inconspicuous.

As the two men approached, Charles Brent's eyes narrowed in annoyance, and he moved slightly closer to Alicia. Richard bent down to kiss Sarah's hand as he arrived in front of her. The soprano had thankfully retired for a short intermission, and been replaced by a small orchestra that played at a level which allowed conversation.

"Greetings, Lady Sarah," was Richard's first sally. "I see you're holding up under the duress of the 'music'.

Lady Sarah chuckled. "Wretch! And I see that you and Lord Kennington have managed to arrive when it is nearly over."

"The only thing Lady Hardwick knows how to do well is give a supper," Jerome replied, "As evidenced by her embonpoint. We have that to look forward to, at any rate."

Charles was standing stiffly behind the sofa, regarding Jerome and Richard with disapproval and disfavor. "Do you consider it good ton to disparage your hostess while you are accepting her hospitality?" His voice was nasal, and had a whining quality to it, as if he had been too indulged as a child and now expected everyone to do the same. It also held a note of perpetual annoyance and disappointment, evidence of the fact that no one ever did so. "I assure you, I do not."

Jerome straightened from his lingering kiss on Alicia's gloved hand. He slowly lifted his quizzing glass on its' silk rope and raised it to his eye. Without a word, his gaze raked Charles up and down. This too was slow, and almost painful in its' duration. Sarah and Alicia sat on the edge of the loveseat in anticipation, and Richard was attempting not to grin and spoil the whole scene.

"Have we met?" Jerome's voice held a note of incredulity. "No,

I believe we have not. I feel certain I would have remembered that . . .waistcoat." He dropped the quizzing glass, thereby signalling that he was no longer aware of the existence of Charles.

"My dear Lady Alicia," he continued, "It is quite stifling in this room. Would you care for some refreshment? I saw the servants laying out quite a sumptuous spread as we were coming into the room; surely they won't mind if we are somewhat precipitate in our enjoyment of some lemonade.

"Thank you, yes." Alicia sounded relieved to be able to escape from the room. She rose gracefully from the loveseat, and Jerome tucked her arm through his. They strolled slowly across the back of the room, towards a double-doorway. Through the lintel they discovered they weren't the only guests to abandon the music for the refreshments.

Charles Brent was furious. He knew he couldn't compete with Jerome in any way -- the man was an Earl, for God's sake! It didn't occur to Charles that if Jerome had been nothing but Captain Jerome Kennington of the Fourth Hussar Brigade, he still would have won any contest between them with yards to spare. Charles knew it was Sarah's fault that Alicia was slipping out of his grasp; why had the damned woman insisted her niece be given a season in town, when Charles was ready to marry her upon the death of her father? Because Sarah despised him, that was why; and was hoping Alicia would attract other offers. But Charles couldn't believe Jerome had marriage in mind when he showed interest in Alicia -- wealthy earls didn't marry the penniless daughters of unlucky gamblers. He decided he should make his claim to Alicia known, just in case there was a chance Jerome was attempting to cut him out.

"Your friend should be told, Sir Richard, that Alicia and I have an understanding." Charles realized he sounded pretentious and whiny at once, but that was the best he could do. He always sounded as if he was whining.

Richard surveyed him with definite loathing. He sat beside Sarah on the loveseat and addressed her, ignoring Charles. "Lady Sarah, who is this fellow? Surely not a connection of yours."

Charles flushed angrily, but Sarah waved him back with an imperious hand. "My nephew, alas. A more addle-pated numbwit I've yet to come across. Don't talk such fustian, Charlie -- you know Alicia would sooner become an Ape-leader than leg-shackled to you."

Red-faced, Charles turned and stalked away in a fury. "Fond of him, are you?" Laughter was trembling in Richard's voice.

Sarah snorted in a remarkably unladylike manner. "Every family has its' dirty dishes, I suppose. Charlie's one of mine. Tell me all about the war, Sir Richard."

"Anything but that, Sarah. Take me at my word it's a crashing bore."

In the refreshment room, Jerome's limp was still pronounced as he traversed the table for delicacies to bring to Alicia.

Chapter 15

The front door of the house slammed, and Jerome broke off his narrative again. "Nat's home!" Charlotte exclaimed excitedly. "Wait till you meet her, Jerome!"

Natalie came into the room, carrying a large, double- handled shopping bag, filled with paints and art supplies. "Hi, everybody." She spotted Jerome and stopped, holding the shopping bag in both hands. Her eyebrows rose appreciatively. "Well, hello there, gorgeous. Which one of you bagged *this* hunk of cheesecake? If it's you, Chari, then I think it's grossly unfair! You've already got one Mr. Dreamboat."

Jerome flushed, staring at Natalie in a somewhat bemused way.

Dierdre laughed. "Take it easy on poor Jerome, Nat! He's been dead for a hundred and fifty years -- he's not ready for emancipated women."

The bag slid from Natalie's hands and landed on the carpet with a soft 'plop' as she stared at Dierdre as though she had just realized her friend was a drug casualty. "Ha, ha -- very amusing. What's the punch-line?"

"How come all of us can see you, when you've been waiting so long for just *one* person who could?" Charlotte seemed to have been thinking about that one point of the story.

"I wish I could explain it to you, dear lady," Jerome replied. "Unfortunately, I'm only a participant in this drama, not the author."

Natalie came several steps closer, nearly falling over the shopping bag, which was now attempting to spill its' contents across the carpet. "You're all on Angel Dust! I'm living in a Crack House and I never realized it." She sat gingerly on the couch near Dierdre.

"This is Lord Jerome Kennington, Nat. He's a ghost." Charlotte said this with a grin.

Natalie started to laugh. "Go ahead, Jeri," Charlotte ordered. "Do your act."

With some irritation showing on his face, Jerome dematerialized.

Natalie was staring in total disbelief at the spot where he had been sitting, only a moment ago. When he reappeared, she rubbed her hands over her eyes . . .but he was still there. She thought perhaps he was a professional magician her friends had hired as a practical joke.

"Don't freak out, Nat," Dierdre instructed her. "Jerome was just telling us the story of his life. We'll fill you in."

Chapter 16

Dierdre's bedroom looked like the fitting room of a particularly exclusive boutique. The self-embroidered white-on white satin coverlet was piled with dresses; throughout the rest of the room and piled on the white velvet slipper chair were shoes, petticoats, slips, underwear and jewelry. Dierdre was standing at the entrance to her dressing room, now converted to a walk-in closet, looking through a selection of dresses, suits and blouses. Charlotte was sitting in the only clear space on the bed, drinking soda from a glass. Natalie was seated on the carpet beside the bed, looking through a box of costume jewelry. "Didi," Charlotte admonished her, "You bought a dress just for today. Why won't you wear it?"

"It makes me look like a fat cow." Dierdre's voice came muffled from inside the closet.

"You're hallucinating again," Natalie retorted. "Speaking of hallucinating," Charlotte swallowed a mouthful of ginger-beer, "When is Jerome coming back to finish his story?"

Dierdre emerged from the wardrobe. "I don't know. I keep calling him, but he seems to be ignoring me."

"Maybe he has a day job." This from Natalie. "I never heard any of the story from him, anyway -- just you two. I think it probably suffers in translation."

Dierdre held up a black silk dress. "How about this?" Charlotte shook her head, putting her empty glass on the bedside table. "Too boring. Wear the dress you bought!"

"No! I don't wanna look fat!"

"Jesus -- talk about paranoia! Why are you so nervous about one show? You did lots of 'em in New York."

Dierdre put the dress back in the wardrobe and removed another, a strapless evening gown of cobalt blue tissue faille, very fitted with a deep flounce at the hem. She turned to them, holding it up for their perusal. "I want my first show here to be perfect. How about this?"

Natalie started to laugh. "I hope you're joking! You're not hosting the Academy Awards. You're interviewing a rock singer who has the reputation of being a Communist anarchist." Dierdre turned to put the dress back in the wardrobe.

Charlotte said, "Have you ever seen this guy, what's-his- name?"

"Robin Herald. I've only seen photos of him. He could be good-looking; it's hard to tell in pictures."

"I've seen 'im on MTV," Natalie added. "He wears a lot of makeup. Maybe he's a fag."

"Nat," Charlotte replied, "The guys in KISS wore a lot of makeup. And you can't use the word 'fag' here -- it means a cigarette to the English."

"KISS gave up wearing makeup years ago. And everybody knows what 'fag' means when an American uses it. I hate the word 'gay' -- it's an oxymoron."

"I don't think Robin Herald is gay," Dierdre attempted to end an argument that was constantly coming up between Charlotte and Natalie. "But he's supposed to be very intense."

"Can we make a decision about your dress before we have to leave for the studio?" This from Natalie, who put down the box of jewelry and stood, shaking out the folds of her long, full skirt.

"Oh, I guess I'll have to wear the dress I bought." Dierdre sounded resigned.

"Finally! A fortune in dress won't be wasted." This from Charlotte.

"I'd better go do my makeup."

"Do you wear more makeup on television than you wear on the street?" Natalie had progressed to trying on hats that were hanging on a wooden coat tree.

"In Didi's case, that would be impossible." Charlotte took one of the hats and put it on herself, making a face in the cheval mirror.

Dierdre shook her head at Charlotte as she seated herself on a small stool in front of her crowded makeup table. "No, I don't. Television techniques aren't that primitive anymore."

"Well, now that we've settled what the queen is going to wear for her first court appearance, what about us ladies- in-waiting?" Natalie removed a fuschia hat with a gauze veil and enormous gauze bow, and put it back onto the coat tree.

"Guess I'll go look in my closet," Charlotte replied. "I can never make up my mind until the last minute, anyway." She started out of the room with Natalie following, leaving Dierdre to sort through her enormous chest of cosmetics.

Later that afternoon, Charlotte and Natalie were seated in the front row of the audience section of a studio at Thames Television. While they were talking to two of the crew members from Dierdre's new show, the bustle of activity surrounding them was a good indication that the show would soon be underway. Dierdre's set was very extreme in design; done in Art Deco furnishings with a touch of 1980's high tech, the only colors used were red, black and white. Dierdre was standing a little way away from them, talking to a woman with a clipboard. She wore a long, fitted jacket of silver jacquard silk and a shimmering, metallic scarf tied around her neck in a large bow. The nearly-ankle length, gored skirt was of the same fabric as the jacket, and her silver leather pumps had very high, stiletto heels.

"Did Robin Herald's video arrive?" She asked the woman with the clipboard.

"Yes, and we watched it in the booth. This guy is a little strange onstage."

"You mean you've never seen him perform before?" Dierdre sounded surprised. Perhaps this was because the woman had improbable burgundy colored hair with black streaks, and wore a dress that closely resembled a burlap sack, dyed flat-black.

"No," she replied. Dierdre noticed that her fingernails were the same color as her hair. "I'm not into that kind of stuff. I mean, politically-oriented glitter rock? I ask you."

Dierdre laughed. "May I quote you?"

Before the woman had a chance to reply, they were diverted by a commotion at the door of the studio. Two large men with the aura of bodyguards entered, with Robin Herald behind them. He was followed by a small group of teenaged girls who were trying desperately to get his attention and into the studio. They were thwarted in this attempt by the studio guards, who blocked their entry but not their high-pitched cries of frustration.

Dierdre was astounded to see something she hadn't realized from photographs of Robin -- the singer looked exactly like their ghostly friend Jerome. It could have been a stage play or film with the same actor playing both roles. His hair was shorter, and he wore heavy makeup -- Dierdre was certain it was the latter that had made her miss the resemblance before. The facial makeup seemed superfluous; as he made his way across the studio, Dierdre couldn't spot even the hint of a blemish on his pale skin. He had black eyeliner around his eyes, and slightly tinted lip gloss on his mouth, which wasn't too large, and sensual looking. Dierdre was amazed to realize she was attracted to him -- she couldn't believe she was actually assessing the prospects of a man who wore lip gloss!

But his tight black leather pants revealed muscular thighs and shapely buttocks, and his very full, white silk shirt (despite the ruffles at the neck and cuffs) offered the glimpse of a froth of black hair at the slightly open neck. Black motorcycle boots with somewhat higher heels than most men would wear (now, he didn't need those, Dierdre thought -- he had to be six feet tall without them); a heavy black leather belt studded with rhinestones. In the neck of the shirt, just touching the black hair, was a large rhinestone and silver cross, and he wore one dangling earring in the same design.

The woman beside Dierdre said drily, "Here's Mr. Glitter himself. Hey! Who let all these kids into the studio?" This was said as a second group of Robin Herald's fans rushed past the door guards and swarmed into the audience area of the studio. "Call security!"

She rushed away in what seemed to be a futile attempt to assist the door guards and film crew subdue what was becoming a good sized crowd. Robin's two bodyguards were singularly unhelpful in this effort, and remained passive as long as none of the fans got too close to their boss. Dierdre started toward Robin, and met him in the middle of the studio. But as she came closer, she felt it had to be a joke -- they were playing a practical joke on her. But how had they done it?

"Jerome! How did you manage this one? I thought you couldn't get out of the house!"

Robin stared at her in some amazement, one black eyebrow raised. When he spoke, he had a slight Scottish accent that made his speech soft and deep, and sexier than Dierdre would have liked. "Are you, uh . . .Dierdre Hall? I'm not Jerome, I'm afraid. I'm Robin Herald. Sorry. You may keep me prisoner in your house anytime, however -- as long as you remain with me." He grinned.

"Oh!" Dierdre wished he wasn't quite so good looking -- or was it the makeup? He didn't seem in the least feminine, however -- he was certainly no Boy George. "I'm sorry, Mr. Herald! It's just that you look so much like someone I know."

"Someone you keep tied up in your closet? I'm willing to go that far, but as I said, you'll have to stay in there with me."

Dierdre didn't want to laugh, but she couldn't help herself. "No, you see . . .oh, never mind. I am Dierdre Hall, and I'm so pleased to meet you. Welcome to the show."

"Thank you. I saw your show when I was on tour in Los Angeles, and I loved it. But you've got to promise me you won't play any of your notorious practical jokes on me. Or . . .was that the opening for one?"

"That? Oh -- oh, no! The jokes were only played on air. But the show's not live here, so the effect would be lost. No, you really do look like someone I know. And the funny thing is, he never had any children."

Robin stared at her in bewilderment, thinking what a pity it would be if this beautiful, vivacious woman had burned out her brain on drugs and it was just now catching up to her. "I beg your pardon?"

Realizing he probably thought she was a lunatic, Dierdre attempted to back-pedal. "Oh, please excuse me -- I was thinking about something else. Come with me, and I'll show you the set for the show. We tape in a few minutes."

She led the way to the stage set. He was still watching her with stunned curiosity as he followed her, wondering what strange, disconnected thing she might say next. As Robin mounted the steps to the dais, Charlotte and Natalie were watching him with more astonishment than he was feeling over his conversation with Dierdre.

Most of Robin's fans had been cleared from the studio or seated in the audience section with Charlotte and Natalie. Now Charlotte said, "Nat, look at Robin Herald! He looks just like Jerome!"

"It must be a coincidence -- Jerome told you he was killed the night of his wedding."

"No, the morning after the wedding -- that was what he said."

Natalie tore her gaze from Robin Herald to blink at Charlotte's words. "Then how could he have had any children? Oh . . ."

"That's right -- in the days before the pill, once was all it took."

"But Robin Herald is Scottish."

Charlotte was becoming impatient. "Don't be stupid, girl -- Jerome died over 150 years ago. In all that time, don't you think one of his descendents could have moved to Scotland?"

"How can they look so much alike?"

"A trick of genetics, I guess. After all these years, the same combination of genes reappeared. Or . . .maybe there've been lots of Jeromes down through the years. We certainly wouldn't know, and neither would he -- he's never been outside the house."

"So what do we do, go up to him and say, 'Hey, Rob -- we know your great-great-great-great-great grandfather?"

"Even he doesn't look wierd enough to believe that. Didi seems pretty amazed by him, too; I'll bet she forgets all her questions."

Natalie shook her head. "No chance; she's been through worse than this. The time those three video producers switched the order of the tapes they were playing, and one of the guests ran off the set and stormed the control booth . . ."

Charlotte started to laugh. "Or when the punk rockers in San Francisco put their cigarette butts in the water pitcher and tipped Didi's chair over -- with her in it!"

Now they were both laughing, and Robin Herald's fans were turning to stare at them. "I saw that one -- she kicked one of 'em off the dais when he bent over to pick up the ashtray that fell on the floor." By this time the young men and women who made up the rest of the audience thought they were both crazy, and began muttering things to one another about 'mad Yanks'. This only caused Charlotte and Natalie to laugh harder, until they caught the attention of Dierdre and Robin.

"Are those your friends in the audience? They seem to think something is terrifically funny," Robin commented.

"I think it's you," Dierdre replied, arranging her skirt in the chair.

"Oh, thank you very much. I can't tell you how enthralled I am that I agreed to do this interview. Rather comparable to having oral surgery, I anticipate."

Now Dierdre started to laugh. "I didn't mean they were laughing *at* you! It's because you look so much like Jerome."

"Jerome again. I think I'd like to meet this bloke who looks just like me -- then I'll know how ugly other people think I am."

"If you're looking for a compliment, forget it.   Under all that paint, it's obvious there's a real beauty."

"I could say the same thing to you."

"Fortunately, I don't have to reply to that -- they're signalling sixty seconds until we begin taping. Now you'll have to behave if you want me to."

"All right, but this is the only time I'll make a promise like that to you."

Chapter 17

When Dierdre, Charlotte and Natalie arrived home that evening, they went dancing into the living room in search of Jerome. When Charlotte switched the lights on there was no sign of their resident ghost, but they went into the room and sat on the couches anyway.

Dierdrc said, kicking off her silver pumps so one skimmed across the room and hit the baseboard, "I can't believe I didn't realize from those photographs of Robin! Jerome, come out of your closet! We have to talk to you!"

Charlotte, laying full length on one couch with her feet over the end replied, "Who can tell with a picture -- particularly a picture of Robin Herald! The man wears more makeup than I do!"

Natalie went to the buffet against one wall of the room. It had been converted into a bar, and she bent down to open the doors and remove a bottle of cognac. "Charlotte," she said impatiently, "Children of ten wear more makeup than you do. Jerome! Where are you? We have some important news for you! Who wants brandy?"

As Natalie was engaged in removing glasses from the buffet, Jerome materialized in the chair next to Charlotte's head. He was wearing a pair of jeans and an Intarsia sweater with a black and red design. He said to Natalie, "I'll have some; thank you for asking."

"Shit!" Charlotte jumped to a sitting position and stared at Jerome. "You might warn a person before you do that, Jeri. What are you wearing?"

"After talking to you I decided it was time I updated my wardrobe. What do you think?"

"Very nice," Dierdre told him approvingly. "Especially the black jeans. I wonder if Robin would look that good in them." She accepted the glass of brandy Natalie handed her, smiling up at her.

Jerome took his with a small bow. "Who's Robin?"

Natalie turned back on her way to the bar. "Wait a minute -- where did you get that stuff? You told us you were imprisoned in the house until you discovered what happened to Alicia."

Jerome shrugged, sipping his brandy delicately. "I called Harrod's. They deliver."

Dierdre and Charlotte exchanged glances. "Where have you been?" Dierdre asked Jerome. "I've been calling you for days."

"I don't know. When I hear you, I come. Therefore, I must conclude that I don't always hear you."

Charlotte took her glass of brandy from Natalie and nearly downed it in one gulp. "Terrific. We get a ghost, and he has to be a space cadet."

Natalie came and sat on the carpet between Jerome and Charlotte, her own brandy on the coffee table. Dierdre said, "Jeri, we have some amazing news. We think we met a descendent of yours today."

Jerome seemed confused by this. "Descendent? I don't have any descendents. I never had any children."

"Are you sure? Was your marriage ever consummated?" Jerome flushed and seemed embarrassed. Charlotte snorted impatiently, finishing off her brandy. "Well, was it? Did you and Alicia make it before you were offed, or not?"

Though he appeared to understand her cryptic question, Jerome seemed disinclined to give them any information on the subject. "Surely this is not a fit subject for unmarried ladies to be discussing," he protested weakly.

"I'm divorced," Dierdre stated, "And so is Natalie. If you're thinking of Charlotte, you must be demented as well as dead. You can discuss it with us -- you have to, if we're gonna to help you. Is it possible that Alicia got pregnant before you were killed?"

He seemed much struck by this theory. "Yes . . .it is possible."

Charlotte rose from the couch and crossed to the bar for more brandy. "I'm telling you, Jeri -- Robin Herald is your descendent."

"Who is this man?"

"A rock singer," Dierdre supplied. "I interviewed him on my television show today."

"Then I can see him when your show airs?"

"Yes, of course! Tomorrow night."

"Don't you still have that photo of him somewhere, Didi?" Natalie asked.

Dierdre rose from the couch and looked around the room. "Yes; but I don't know where I put it." She threw a pile of magazines onto the carpet and found the one she wanted at the bottom. "Oh -- here it is!" She triumphantly flashed the magazine at him, and walked back to the couch, flipping through the pages. When she reached the photograph of Robin Herald, she folded the magazine back and handed it to Jerome. "This is him, Jeri. You can't deny he looks just like you."

Jerome was studying the photograph. He looked up with disgust, allowing the magazine to fall into his lap. "Why . . .he's nothing but a damned caper-merchant!"

Charlotte choked on her brandy, and started to laugh. "I realize this is a difficult request, Jeri; but could you try to speak English?"

"What?" Jerome was again looking at Robin Herald, turning the magazine in an attempt to see him more closely. "Oh, sorry. But the man wears makeup!"

"I thought men wore makeup in the 18th century, Jeri," Dierdre said.

"Maybe so, but by the 19th they had stopped. Well, I suppose if it's the fashion. But I've seen the men Charlotte and Natalie keep company with, and I never noticed them wearing any."

"Can you imagine Paul in lip gloss?" Charlotte asked, breaking into laughter again.

"Actors and singers wear makeup," Dierdre explained, glaring at Charlotte. "Especially rock singers. It's part of the . . .persona."

"Well," Jerome conceded, "I must admit that he does look a great deal like me. But the name; Herald. There was never a Herald in my family or Alicia's, that I knew of."

"I'm sorry to have to be the one to tell you this, Jeri; but Alicia's child probably grew up with the last name of Brent."

"Oh . . .of course. Charles Brent would never admit she was pregnant by me."

"We're sorry to spring this on you, but we thought you'd want to know." Dierdre smiled apologetically.

"No . . .no. It's something of a shock, but at least I know I didn't die in vain. The thought of poor little Alicia tied to that loose screw Brent for over a year; and with my baby." He put his head in his hands as if the image he was conjuring was too much for him to deal with.

"Don't cry, Jeri," Natalie said. "It was so long ago. Tell us the rest of your story. You never finished, you know." She sounded as if she was trying to coax a child out of a depression.

Jerome looked up at her with a smile, and wiped a tear out of his eye with the sleeve of his sweater. "Well, since you've brought me such good news, I guess it's the least I can do. I don't remember where I was, though."

"At the musicale," she informed him. "You and Alicia had gone to get punch, or something; and Charles Brent was really pissed off."

"Pissed off . . .interesting expression. Well, after that evening I saw Alicia frequently. You should know that during the season in

London, the upper "Ten Thousand" spent most of their time at parties and balls, and this was how men and women met suitable marriage partners . . ."

Chapter 18

In 1811, dinner parties were lavish affairs. That is, amongst the people who could afford dinner parties, and these only existed in the Upper Ten Thousand. The merchant class might have guests for dinner; they were the only ones apart from the gentry who could afford to, but they wouldn't call it a 'dinner party' and it wouldn't have five courses with upwards of fifteen dishes each. The food thrown away from an English dinner party could have fed hundreds in the slums and stews, if only they could get to it. They couldn't, of course, and there was certainly no question of it getting to them. Although the English upper classes hadn't become quite so self-satisfied or priggish as they would during the reign of Victoria, they were comfortable and certain in their privilege. Part of that privilege involved throwing food away when so many people in London went hungry -- it was their food, and they felt they had a right to throw it away if they chose to. If someone was lucky enough to get ahold of it before it joined the ranks of 'garbage', the owners (who had already discarded it) would almost certainly have branded him or her a thief.

If any of the guests at Lady Broadmoor's dinner party on April 29, 1811, gave any thought to what happened to the food that left the table uneaten, they would probably have agreed it was Lady Broadmoor's privilege to dispose of it as she pleased, after her servants had obtained their share of the leftovers. One, however, did not, and Jerome Kennington seized on the dinner party as a perfect time to attempt to draw converts to his cause. Halfway through the meal, however, he only had one, and had given up during the between-course sherbets. Now he set out to charm Alicia with what he assumed would be polite small-talk.

"How are you enjoying the season, Lady Alicia?" Jerome was thinking how delicious the black currant ice was.

"Very much, my lord." Alicia appeared to be equally appreciative of her own lemon ice, and Jerome wondered if she had chosen it to match the pale primrose silk of her gown. With her hair dressed simply and adorned by a spray of silk daisies, Alicia resembled a small sunbeam. Jerome thought her by far the most attractive woman in the room, and not simply because she was beautiful. She had an inner flame that he found irresistible -- the same flame he had noticed in her aunt. Women like Sarah and Alicia had much to give a man -- in the bedroom and beyond it. "But this is the only season I will have, so I know I should make the most of it."

Jerome was shaken out of his reverie by this remark, which didn't sound in the least self-pitying or even regretful. Perhaps Alicia didn't like being paraded in front of a group of prospective husbands like a prize cow being auctioned. "Why should it be the only season?" he asked her. Although he was certain Alicia would receive an acceptable offer of marriage before the end of the season, he couldn't imagine why she thought she wouldn't return the following year with her husband. Or had she meant that she had only the one season to find the husband? Richard had mentioned her father left her penniless. Since Alicia was always dressed in the height of fashion and taste, Jerome knew it must be Sarah who was paying the bills. Perhaps Sarah was only willing to finance the one throw of the dice.

"Why should this be the only season?" Even as he spoke, Jerome knew he was crossing a social boundary. Financial matters were never discussed outside the family unless it couldn't be avoided; if Alicia was only to have one season because there wasn't money for another one, she shouldn't say so. Everyone might know it, and even discuss it, but not in her presence.

Alicia finished her ice with a little sigh, and left the tiny silver spoon sitting in the glass. "Because at the end of it I will marry

Charles Brent, and he prefers life in the country. At least, he says he does . . .I've never known him to spend much time there."

"Humph!" Jerome finished his own ice, wishing he could have offered Alicia a taste of it, and feed it to her himself. "I'd say Brent means he intends to leave his wife in the country while he seeks the less salutary pleasures of the city." He let his spoon drop into the glass with a clink that attracted the eyes of several other people at the table. Charles Brent wasn't one of the guests, and Jerome was glad. He couldn't believe Alicia was serious. "Surely I couldn't have heard you correctly -- did you say you were going to marry Charles Brent?"

"Well, I daresay I will. You see, our parents were close friends, in addition to his being my third cousin. They would have wanted me to marry him."

"And do you always do what your parents want you to?" Jerome's voice was harsher than he intended, and Alicia gazed at him in surprise.

"They are dead, Sir Jerome, and have no more wishes to relate. Besides, it's doubtful I will receive another offer during the season -- my father left his estates in terrible disrepair, and there was little but debts remaining when he died."

Jerome smiled at her as a maid removed their empty dishes. Other servants were placing the next course on the table in covered platters and bowls. "I can't help but know that, can I? Your dear cousin Charles has made it public knowledge -- with the idea of chasing away your suitors, perhaps? A beautiful girl like you should have many, dowry or not."

"You flatter me, sir; there have indeed been a few . . .but Charles has, as you say, sent them away."

"Would you like some of this fish? It looks quite delicious. He shall not be so fortunate with me, I assure you." As Jerome placed a small portion of Sole Almandine on Alicia's plate, her blue eyes flew wide open, and she stared at him in amazement. "Sir?"

Jerome helped himself to a larger piece of fish. "Lady Alicia, will you come driving in the park with me tomorrow afternoon?"

Alicia sounded like a child who has been promised an enormous ice-cream sundae. "Yes, I should like it above all things!"

"Do your feelings always show on your face so very much, my dear? You'll never be a success in society unless you learn to prevaricate."

When Alicia blushed, turning away to spoon vegetables onto her plate, Jerome smiled down, lifting his wineglass in a toast she didn't see.

Chapter 19

London, 1811

In Hyde Park during the season, fashionable ladies and gentlemen crowded the paths and greens, walking and driving to see and be seen. This phenomenon did not occur, however, until late in the afternoon -- to be seen earlier would be unthinkable to those aspiring to fashion, though frequently trysting couples could be spotted there at early hours in order to avoid their peers.

On this sunny day in May, the park seemed even more crowded than usual with vehicles. Jerome was impatient with the poor driving skills of his fellows, and wished they would all go home and leave him alone with Alicia. Though if they were alone, it would be deemed unsuitable by Lady Sarah and they wouldn't be in the park at all. With a sigh, Jerome edged his elegant perch-phaeton in behind a ham- handed buck who looked as if the slightest disturbance would overset his equipage.

Alicia smiled up at him, and Jerome thought she looked very much like a piece of candy or a small cake. Her afternoon dress of pale pink striped muslin became her well; he realized that nearly everything she wore complimented her. She never wore enormous ruffles or layers of frills; her hair and brilliant eyes were enough decoration. Returning her smile, Jerome leaned down to whisper in her ear, causing her to laugh.

From a small grove of trees near the path, Charles Brent was watching Jerome and Alicia. Seated on a rawboned hunter, Brent watched them pass, his hands clenched into fists at his sides.

A few nights or perhaps a week later, Jerome and Richard went to White's, where they were both members. There they had dinner, and adjourned to the card room to drink brandy and play piquet with two friends. It was during the card game that Alicia's name was mentioned.

Sir Andrew Charleston said, "Saw you in the park one day with Alicia Mannerly. Lies the wind in that direction?"

The second friend shook his head derisively. "Don't be foolish. Why would Jerome be interested in her? She's no portion to speak of, and the whole family is rolled-up."

Jerome realized that his irritation with the subject was out of proportion, but he was tired of hearing how poor Alicia was. He stared hard at his friend. "What can that signify to me? I have plenty of blunt."

The other man, a Mr. Darlington, stared back with some amazement. "You mean -- you intend to offer for her?"

"Yes . . .I suppose I do, though it hadn't actually occurred to me."

Richard laughed, dealing a new hand of cards. "Looks like you enlightened our friend here as to his real motives, Peter."

Peter frowned. "Damme if I meant to. Still, pity to see such a pretty, sweet girl married to that loose-fish Brent."

"No one seems to like him," Jerome replied. "I wonder why he's tolerated."

Sir Andrew shrugged. "Plenty of money, and of course his family is good -- at least on the mother's side. The father has some trade in his background. Still, I suppose that's becoming more acceptable."

"It's not his money or his connections I object to," Richard replied scornfully. "I can't abide the man."

"No one can," Darlington added.

"That's my point, you see. Oh!" Jerome was pleased by the turn of the cards. "And this is my point, also!"

At the other end of the room, Charles Brent was hidden by a large man in a snuff-colored jacket. But he could see Jerome, and the light of hatred and rage burned in his pale eyes. Suddenly, as if he had made up his mind about something, he put his wineglass down on the sideboard and started across the room. The man in the snuff-colored coat put his hand on Charles' sleeve in an attempt to stop him, but Charles shook him off and continued to approach Jerome's table. He arrived between Richard and Andrew, who ignored him.

Clearing his throat, Charles said, "I'd like a word with you, Kennington."

Jerome looked up from his hand with supercilious surprise. "Would you? Whatever for, I wonder. I would certainly not choose to have a word with you."

"Bad ton to interrupt a game, Brent," Andrew added acidly.

Charles flushed angrily, but refused to budge. "Are you trying to insult me, sir?" This was directed at Jerome.

"I'm certain that would be beyond *my* feeble powers. Whatever do you want, Brent? As you can see, I'm busy. And you've annoyed Sir Andrew." Jerome's drawl was pronounced, and Richard had to hide his grin behind his cards.

"I would ask you to come away from the table," Charles managed through gritted teeth.

Jerome seemed to consider this for the space of several seconds, but could have been perusing his cards instead. "Would you, indeed?" He finally replied. "I don't believe I can oblige you, however. No; whatever you have to say to me, say it here."

Charles took a deep breath in an attempt to steady himself. "I want you to stay away from Lady Alicia Mannerly. She is my betrothed."

"Is she, then?" Jerome seemed surprised by this news, but not disturbed. "Does she know of this arrangement?"

Charles clenched his fists. Jerome's friends straightened visibly, and seemed to tighten themselves in readiness for an attack. "I assure you," Charles managed, "There is a long standing agreement. It was thought, however, that Alicia would enjoy having a season before she settled down to marriage."

"I would have thought any number of seasons preferable to marrying you, Brent." A snicker ran round the table, and amongst the men closest to Jerome, who had also heard the remark.

"You insult me, sir!" Charles was shaking with suppressed rage.

"Do I?" Jerome grinned. "Yes, I believe I do." He pushed back his chair and rose from the table. "Well, there's nothing for it, then; is there? You'll have to demand satisfaction." Charles seemed to deflate like a balloon losing air. There was an intake of breath around the table.

Charles stuttered, "Oh, I . . .no need for that, old man. I mean . . .sure you meant nothing by it." He ended weakly, earning glances of scorn and derision from the other members of the club who had clustered round to see the exchange.

Richard started to laugh, and put a restraining hand on Jerome's sleeve. "Jeri, stop badgering the man. Won't call you out. Be a fool if he did, you being the best shot in London."

Jerome glanced down in horror at Richard's hand. "Dear friend, you are wrinkling my coat." His limpid gaze rose to meet Charles' terrified eyes. "Get out of my sight, Brent . . .you are a dog. Lower than a dog. What is lower than a dog, gentlemen?"

Chapter 20

There was a pounding on the door of the townhouse in Hampstead, interrupting Jerome in the middle of his narrative. Natalie jumped to her feet. "Jesus! Who the hell is trying to knock our front door down? I'll go see, but don't you dare go on with the story until I get back, Jerri." Natalie left for the vestibule.

Jerome said, "I'd better go until your guest leaves."

"No," Charlotte told him, "Stay where you are! Let's find out if whoever it is can see you."

"Oh, no -- it has to be someone living in the house."

"How do you know?" Dierdre asked him.

Before he could answer, Natalie came back into the room, followed by Paul. He was carrying a large cake box from Harrod's. "Hello, ladies! The candy-man is here!"

Charlotte started to laugh, rising from her place on the couch and kissing Paul. "In America, that would mean you have drugs in your box. Somehow I don't think that's the case." She took the box from him, putting it on the table.

"Well, no. Will a raspberry whipped-cream tart do?"

"Infinitely better", Dierdre asserted. "Have a seat, Paul. I'll get us some plates and make coffee, in a minute."

Paul stood staring at Jerome, as if waiting for something. When it wasn't forthcoming, he said, "Hello, I'm Paul. Ladies, aren't you going to introduce me to your friend? Very remiss of you, even if you are American."

Charlotte punched him in the stomach, and he doubled over in mock pain. Then she realized who he was referring to, and her astonished gaze met Jerome's. The ghost stood and made a small bow. "I am Lord Jerome Kennington, sir. Pleased to make your acquaintance."

The girls watched Jerome shake hands with Paul, and the biologist seemed to sense nothing amiss with their friend. When they were both seated again Paul said, "Nice outfit. Gothic punk, right? Oh, I'm Paul Harkness -- a friend of Charlotte's." Natalie started to laugh, and the other two women joined in after a futile attempt to control themselves.

Jerome glanced at them in bewilderment. "Gothic punk? Elucidate, please."

Charlotte leaned over and whispered to Paul, "He doesn't know what a Gothic punk is, silly. He's been dead for nearly two hundred years."

Paul glanced at her suspiciously, then around at the rest of the group. "OK, I'll bite. What's the joke?"

"We'll tell you," Charlotte said, "But we're in a hurry to hear about Jerome's duel with Charles Brent, so you have to listen the first time."

Paul stared at her indignantly. "I always listen the first time!"

"You guys can fill Paul in while I make coffee and tea. To go with the tarts. Is it a big tart, or individual ones?" She opened the lid of the box and peered inside. "Oh, good -- a big one. There's enough for Jerome too, then."

"I thought you said he was dead. How can he eat?" Paul asked her nastily.

Dierdre shrugged, and clambered up from her seat. As she walked toward the kitchen she said, "You're the biologist -- you figure it out." She disappeared from view, and Paul frowned down at Charlotte.

"I'm waiting for the explanation that I know is going to amaze me. If only because I never realized you three were acid freaks."

"Paul, that drug was in style twenty years ago," Charlotte retorted with the air of a parent speaking to a retarded child. "You Norwegians are so behind the times."

Paul raised one eyebrow. "Waiting impatiently, Muffin . . ."

"Well," Natalie said, "It began in 1811."

"I suppose I should've guessed that."

"Do you want to hear this, or do you want a pie in the face?" Natalie reached over and eased open the lid of the Harrod's pie box.

"I'm listening!"

"As I said, it began in 1811 . . ."

Chapter 21

The following morning, Dierdre descended to the living room to find the clutter from the night before still strewn over the coffee table. Tightening the sash of her satin robe and wondering irritably whether it was her turn to clean-up (and whether she would leave it for Dorinda), she began to pick up cups and plates, and take them to the kitchen. "Jerome?" She called out, stifling a yawn, "Are you here?"

Jerome appeared from the kitchen, dressed in a black silk robe with a Chinese dragon embroidered across the back in a rainbow of primary colors. He crossed to the coffee table and picked up the plates Dierdre had left behind. As they passed he said, "Good morning, my dear."

She stopped in the kitchen doorway and looked back at him. "Why do I feel exactly as if I'm married?"

"Perhaps you will be, soon. I have a premonition." Dierdre laughed, and went into the kitchen. It didn't look much better than the living room, and she made a face as she went to the sink to deposit her crockery and pick up a pair of pink rubber gloves. "Just my luck. The first time I marry a bum, the second time I could marry a ghost."

Jerome arrived with his own plates, and put them down on the counter. "Not me, silly girl. I'm already married."

Dierdre started the water running in the sink, and added some dishwashing liquid from a clear bottle. "Perhaps history wouldn't agree. After all, Alicia married Charles Brent. You were dead, remember?"

Jerome went to the Krupps coffee-maker that was sitting on the counter underneath the cupboards. As he prepared the coffee, first grinding the beans in a matching grinder and then putting the ground coffee into the bin of the Krupps, he replied, "I know, in her heart, she always believed herself to be my wife. And I have always thought so. No, I meant someone else. I don't know who."

Dierdre rinsed the plates and put them into slots in the dishwasher. "Perhaps we can put an ad in a Personals column."

Jerome looked over from where he was adding water to the coffee-maker. "What's that?"

"Sort of a modern-day Almack's."

Jerome turned away from the coffee-maker, replacing the bag of beans in the cupboard. "I see you've been reading your history. Almack's was a boring place . . .weak lemonade and stale cakes."

Dierdre laughed, placing the rinsed cups in the top rack of the dishwasher. "They can't have been stale every night!"

"It wasn't open every night. They must have bought them in advance and saved them for a few days." He opened the door of refrigerator and looked inside.

Dierdre peeled off the rubber gloves and draped them over the side of the sink. "Jeri, what do you think of Vladimir filming you?"

He closed the refrigerator door without selecting anything. "I don't mind. What if I don't show up on the film, however?"

Dierdre removed a loaf of whole grain bread from a black container, and placed it on the counter. "Well, that's a possibility. We could find out. Natalie said she'll call him today, if you want her to."

"Fine. Do you suppose he'll be able to see me, also?" He was lining china mugs up on the counter, each hand- painted with replicas of birds in flight or tending to their young. "I was surprised that Paul was able to." Jars of jam and a plate of butter joined the loaf of bread.

"Maybe anyone who comes in contact with our group will be able to. We're going to have to be careful about that -- you could wind up being exploited, like some circus freak, and we'd have every tacky reporter from **The Sun** and **The Daily Mirror** all over us like cheap suits."

Jerome laughed, adding a covered bowl of fruit salad and a carton of eggs to the clutter on the counter. "Don't worry about me, little lady. I can take of myself and them, too, if need be."

Dierdre went to check on the coffee. "That reminds me - - were you really accounted the best shot in England, in 1811?"

"A slight exaggeration, I believe." He knelt down and opened a cupboard to remove an egg-poaching pan. Dierdre regarded him thoughtfully.

That evening, Vladimir came to the house to discuss filming Jerome. They were again gathered in the main reception room, which seemed to have become the unofficial 'hub' of activity for the house. Charlotte and Paul occupied their usual place on the couch, their arms around one another. Dierdre sat on the other couch, watching Vladimir and Natalie arrange some equipment on the coffee table. Vladimir was loading a mini-cam tricorder with film. In the armchair, Jerome sat as the guest of honor, wearing his evening dress from 1811.

Vladimir glanced over at Jerome, snapping shut the case of his tricorder. "This is so exciting! Disappear again, Jerome." Jerome obliged him by fading out, and then reappearing in the chair. "Can you do anything else?"

Jerome laughed self-deprecatingly. "I don't know; I've never tried."

"Well, I'm ready . . ." he levelled the camera at Jerome. "Ok, do something."

Jerome turned his gaze on a cut-glass vase of flowers, sitting a few feet away on the sideboard. After several moments the vase rose a few feet in the air. Suddenly, Jerome seemed to lose his concentration, and the vase crashed down onto the parquet floor, shattering.

"Oh, thanks Jerome," Charlotte said with disgust. "My ex-boyfriend bought me that vase."

Paul tightened his arms around her. "Then you don't want it anymore, do you?" Charlotte looked as if she was pondering this logic, which seemed somewhat skewed to her way of thinking. "No," he continued, "You don't want it. I'll get you a new one."

"Well, in that case . . ." Kissing Paul's ear, Charlotte settled back into his embrace.

Dierdre, who had been idly watching the puddle of flower water spread toward the carpet, sighed and went to pick up the pieces of the vase. Natalie glanced over at her. "Shall I get you a sponge, Didi?"

"Yes, please."

Natalie went into the kitchen as Dierdre gathered up the scattered flowers. Jerome watched her miserably. "Oh, I'm so sorry, Charlotte!"

Vladimir laughed. "No, don't be! That's a great scene! I'll buy a new vase for Chari myself, just for the opportunity to film it. Now disappear again, Jerome."

Jerome did so, and when he appeared again he was wearing different clothes; clothes for riding horseback. Vladimir surveyed him with awe. "How do you do that?"

Jerome shrugged. "I assume, since my clothes have no more substance than my body, that they were conjured out of the air."

Natalie came back into the room with a large piece of cloth. As she mopped up the water on the floor she said, "Or from Harrod's -- they deliver."

Vladimir glanced at her uncomprehendingly, but he said, "Now go on with your story, Jeri, and I'll film it."

"Should I start over at the beginning?"

Dierdre struggled to her feet, her arms full of flowers. "No! Begin with the duel -- there was a duel, wasn't there? Or did you intimidate Charles so much that he wouldn't do it?"

"Well, there was something resembling a duel . . .but won't it be out of context, to have the beginning at the end?"

"This is video-tape, Jeri -- I can cut it up into any order I want."

"Oh, I see." Though it was clear he didn't, Jerome wasn't going to betray his ignorance by asking for a further explanation. "Well, I went to duel with Charles Brent. Of course, I had no intention of killing him; but he was certainly intent on killing or maiming me."

Chapter 22

London, 1811

In 1811, Hampstead Heath was the frequent setting for duels amongst members of the aristocracy. Though duelling was outlawed late in the 18th century, it continued until the second decade of the 19th -- the law didn't intervene unless one of the parties involved was killed, and even then, the killer was allowed to flee the country if his family was influential and wealthy enough. Though duelling was done with swords or pistols (and the choice of weapon went to the challenged party), pistols became the favorite after the turn of the century.

Jerome and Richard arrived well before sunrise on the morning that Jerome was to meet Charles Brent. Jerome knew Charles had been forced into the duel against his will, and would not have been surprised if the other man reneged. When Charles' seconds arrived at the heath, accompanied by a physician, Richard approached them. "Well, where is your man? Is he going to renege?"

"Certainly not!" One of the men replied indignantly. Then he added, a little uncertainly, "Well, I don't think so." Richard snorted scornfully and turned back to join Jerome. A closed carriage pulled onto the heath, partially shrouded by the early morning mist that hung over the grassy verge. It was black, with the blinds drawn and no crest or insignia on the door. It stopped beside Jerome's carriage, and the door opened. Charles Brent emerged, looking very pale. One of his seconds rushed over to him.

"Thank god!" the man chattered nervously. "Where have you been, Charles? Very bad ton, to be late to a duel."

Charles glared at him. "Do shut your mouth, Algy -- I was unavoidably detained." He shifted his gaze to Richard and Jerome, and his eyes narrowed. "Shall we get on with this?" Jerome nodded curtly. Richard went to the carriage with the crest on the door, and removed a case from the floor inside. He carried it to where Charles was standing and opened it, showing him the inside. Lying on a bed of black satin were two ornate, carved silver and mahogany duelling pistols. Charles picked up one of the pistols and weighed it in his hand, then looked it over and checked the sight. He laid it back in the case, took the other and repeated his motions. Jerome stood watching him with ill-disguised scorn. Charles, apparently satisfied that neither of the pistols was skewed, retained the second and nodded to Richard. Jerome came up between and took the remaining pistol.

They moved to a clear space on the heath, seeming to be wraiths in the swirling mist. As they stood back to back and Richard began to count off their paces, another carriage, this time one that was obviously hired for the occasion, came careening over the grass at an alarming rate and ground to a halt beside Jerome's vehicle. This carriage also had the shades drawn, and the two men stopped to stare at it. Richard approached the door, wondering if Bow Street, just now getting up to running power, sent runners out in carriages to arrest duelists. But when he opened the door, Lady Sarah tumbled out into his arms. She was swathed in a black cloak, which entangled both her and Richard in its' folds until he managed to set her on her feet. Jerome started to chuckle, and received a black look from Charles that made him laugh even more. He stopped laughing when Alicia, clad in a cloak identical to Sarah's, emerged from the carriage behind her aunt.

"Aunt Sarah!" Charles sounded exactly like a spoiled child about to be deprived of a treat. "What the devil are you doing here?"

She fixed him with what would have been called 'the evil eye' a couple of hundred years earlier. "You always were a fool, Charles. Obviously, I'm here to stop you from a useless death you clearly deserve for your stupidity."

"You shouldn't even know about this!"

"Nothing happens in London I don't know about, nephew -- you should have realized that by now. You would have, if you weren't such a rattle-pate." The last was said smugly, as if Lady Sarah was well-pleased with herself.

Jerome, overcome, started to laugh again, and stepped forward, replacing his pistol in the still open box that Richard was holding. "While I agree with your assessment of Charles' character, Lady Sarah; he is correct in saying that you shouldn't be here. And Lady Alicia even more so."

Sarah waved a negligent hand in the direction of her niece. "Oh, the tiresome chit insisted on coming."

Alicia threw back the hood of her cloak with a dramatic gesture, and struck a heroic pose. Jerome realized she was enjoying this as much as Sarah. "I won't allow anyone to fight a duel over me!" She announced. Just so, Jerome thought, had Joan of Arc led her troops into battle . . .

"Get back in the carriage, Alicia!" Charles Brent's voice was loud and commanding. Alicia stood and glared darkly at him. With a muttered oath, he took a step towards her, still holding the pistol, but found Jerome blocking his path.

"I think not, Brent."

"I told you -- she's my betrothed!"

"I am not!" Alicia was indignant.

"Well, you will be -- at the end of the season." Charles felt his argument slipping out from under him, and wanted to put his hands around Alicia's throat and squeeze until she begged him for mercy.

Jerome cleared his own throat, as if he could read Charles' thoughts. His voice was still level; almost conversational. "I think not, old man. Lady Alicia has consented to be my wife. You see the inherent problem in her being yours, also." Everyone in the group, including Alicia, stared at Jerome in amazement. Except

Richard, who turned to put the pistol-case back into the carriage, forgetting that Charles was still holding one of the weapons.

"That's not possible!" Charles spluttered, feeling more helpless by the moment.

"Why does no one know of this, Sir Jerome?" Lady Sarah sounded annoyed, but Jerome knew it was only because she had been left out of the surprise. He wasn't about to admit he hadn't officially asked Alicia to become his wife, however - - if he was to be rid of Charles Brent, it had to be now.

"No one knows because Lady Alicia only agreed to be my wife yesterday, and I have had no opportunity since then to speak to you, Lady Sarah. You are her legal guardian, are you not?"

"Yes, I am."

"The reason for this 'spectacle', as you put it, is that Mr. Brent insisted Lady Alicia was his fiancee, and as you can see, I knew that to be impossible."

"But you never said she was yours!" Charles voice had taken on its' usual whining quality.

"Am I a piece of meat, to be argued over?" Alicia's eyes flashed as she glared at Charles and Jerome in turn. Jerome noted with admiration that she bore very little resemblance to a china-doll in her anger, and knew he'd made the right choice, impetuous as it had been. Or perhaps not so impetuous . . .he now realized he had been thinking about Alicia for weeks to the exclusion of much else, but it had taken the repulsive Charles to push him into making a stand.

His chosen lady continued. "We will adjourn to the Hampstead Inn for breakfast. If you two insist on continuing this foolishness, I will marry neither."

"But Alicia -- are you betrothed to Sir Jerome?"

Her voice softened slightly. "Yes. I never said I would marry you, Charles. It was what my father wanted, but you shouldn't have assumed -- I must marry where my heart is."

Charles threw his pistol onto the ground in a fury, and stomped off to slam himself into his carriage. A moment later that vehicle was careening across the heath, headed for Regent's Park. Richard leaned down and picked up the pistol, examining it. "A poor loser," he said contemptuously. "We're lucky the pistol didn't go off and wound someone. Watch out for him, Jerome -- he's not an honorable man."

Jerome didn't appear to be listening to his friend, as he was engaged in holding Alicia in his arms, and staring down into her blue eyes with something like amazement.

"Oh, not on an empty stomach, you two!" Sarah sounded irritable. "I was promised breakfast at The Hampstead Inn!" With a whoop, the men pulled Jerome away from Alicia. Even Charles' seconds piled into the carriage with them, but Jerome crossed to Sarah's carriage to help Alicia up the steps. Before she disappeared inside, he brought her hand to his lips and kissed the palm.

Chapter 23

Vladimir turned off his tape machine, frowning at Jerome. "Do you mean you never fought the duel with Brent? You said you did!" His tone was accusatory.

"Well, I meant I went to fight. There was no duel, thanks to Alicia."

"I like Alicia," Charlotte stated. "She's got guts".

Jerome stared at her in some confusion. "Doesn't everyone?"

Natalie shook her head, laughing. "It's an expression, Jeri! Honestly, we've got to get you more up to date. I think I'd better get some videos."

"If you'd watch television," Charlotte added, "It might help. Just don't watch BBC One -- they're about as antiquated as you are."

"Television!" Dierdre leapt up. "It's time for my show!" She switched on the television set, a large-screen, minimalistically-designed creation in black that didn't seem quite at home in the reception room of the townhouse. She switched it to channel four, where a commercial for Tetley tea was ending. Then a logo of a singer with a microphone appeared, the words *Below London* written in script beside him. This dissolved to show Dierdre and Robin Herald seated in the chairs on her studio set, just as they had been the day of taping. Dierdre smiled at the audience.

"Good evening, and welcome to the first *Below London*. For those of you who saw the few *Below Manhattan* segments broadcast here on Channel Four as part of *The Tube*, you know my format. My guest tonight is Robin Herald, lead singer of the group *Experimental Monkeys*. Interesting name, Robin. How did it come about?"

The camera switched to show a full view of Robin. Jerome leaned forward in his seat to study his descendent. "I have no idea, Dierdre. I don't remember."

Dierdre stared at him blankly. "You don't remember how your group got its' name?"

"It was just there one day, like a cancer."

"Why didn't you bring the rest of the group with you tonight?"

Now Robin stared at her. "You didn't invite them." Dierdre grinned. "Didn't I? How remiss of me. But you did bring your new video, didn't you?"

"Yes, of course."

"Well, I'm sure it would be very nice to see it; but I think maybe the audience has already seen it -- some of them, anyway. Do you suppose that's possible?"

Robin was now watching her suspiciously. "I suppose . . ."

She cut him off. "But I'll bet the one thing they've never seen is you performing live with no rehearsal."

This startled him. "No -- and they never will!"

"What do you think of that statement, boys?" As she finished the question, three more young men ran onto the dais from behind screens at the edge of the set. Robin jumped up in amazement, staring at his band-mates.

"What the hell are you guys doing here?" He didn't sound too pleased; perhaps a little worried.

One of the band members, a very thin young man with long, stringy blond hair and a sculptured face, grinned at him. "You didn't invite us, so we came anyway."

The second, a small compact Welshman in burgundy velvet

trousers and a brocade jacket reminiscent of the 60's, added, "We're gonna play on the show. Ms. Hall asked us to."

"Play? Where?" Robin started to look around hysterically, probably wondering if he could get to the exit door. "Nobody told me about this!" He fixed his gaze on Dierdre. "You promised me -- no practical jokes!"

Dierdre was still seated in her chair, smiling sweetly up at him. "Why, Robin -- this isn't a joke! You really are going to play."

A curtain to the side of the dais slid back to reveal a soundstage, set up with equipment. Robin stared at it in horror. Dierdre took his hand and led him off the dais, followed by the rest of the band members. As they watched the group play, Dierdre and her friends discussed Robin Herald. Paul started to laugh at the look on Robin's face. "Didi, you rotter! You promised Robin Herald you wouldn't play any jokes on him, and then you brought his whole band into the studio without telling him!"

Dierdre smiled; the same serene smile she had given Robin Herald just before she railroaded him into playing live. "He should've realized my technique. He's seen my shows from New York."

"You know," Charlotte put in, still watching Robin sing, "I don't think he really minded. He was all right for the rest of the show. Maybe he's just a control freak -- a lot of men don't like women taking control from them."

"Are you saying a lot of women *do* like men to do it to *them*?" Paul seemed amused by this possibility.

Natalie replied, "I'm sure they're used to it, by now. But I don't personally like it."

"You surprise me," Paul retorted drily. "I would have thought it otherwise."

Natalie made a raspberry at him, and he laughed. She said, "Robin Herald knew what to expect before he went on the show."

"If people refused to be your guests," Vladimir said, "You'd have to stop tricking them like this."

"Since no one has turned me down," Dierdre told him, "I guess they aren't bothered by it."

"Or they're so desperate to get on television they'll submit to anything," Paul told her.

"I appreciate being compared to an ax-murderer or something gruesome."

Charlotte hugged Paul. "Ignore Paul; he was born cynical." Paul looked down at her with great tenderness, as if he could argue with this judgement if he chose to. "Jerome, what do you think of your descendant?"

Jerome was watching the band perform, and didn't seem to hear her. "Hey, Jerome!" He looked over at her. "Well -- is Robin Herald worthy of you?"

"You make me sound terrifically starched-up. He has a good singing voice; I haven't heard him say anything, really." He turned back to watch the band again.

The telephone rang, and Natalie rose to answer it. "Hello. Yes, it is. Who is calling, please?" was all that could be heard in the reception room. Then she put her hand over the receiver and started to giggle. "Didi -- it's Robin Herald!"

The rest of the group seemed to think this terrifically funny, since they were still watching Robin Herald's forced performance on Below London. Dierdre glared at them all in general, and jumped up to go to the telephone, which was sitting on the sideboard. *Experimental Monkeys* had finished their performance and were back on the dais, talking to Dierdre again. "Hello? Oh, hello Robin. Yes, I'm watching it now. I think you look very handsome. I don't know why you imagine you need to wear so much makeup when you perform; it makes you look like a gargoyle. Well, sorry -- I guess Americans *are* pretty blunt. Oh, ok. Bye."

She hung up the telephone and returned to her place on the couch, where the rest of the group were split between watching the television show and listening to her conversation with Robin Herald.

Charlotte laughed, saying, "I'll bet he *loves* you, girl."

"He said he's coming over to kill me. I'm not worried; he doesn't know the address."

Jerome waved a peremptory hand at them. "Hush! He just said something about the government. He's a damned Tory, on top of everything else!"

Dierdre smiled, shaking her head. "He's a Socialist, Jerome. There are no Tories anymore."

"Oh. What does that mean?"

"I'll get you some books from the library."

"I can explain it to him later," Vladimir said. "This is just getting interesting." They turned back to the television screen as Robin Herald started into a diatribe against Margaret Thatcher and what he called her 'butchering' tactics. The three Americans didn't realize at the time that this was meant to be a pun, since Thatcher's father had been a butcher.

When the show was over, Charlotte and Paul went into the kitchen and fixed dessert for the group -- coffee, tea and a chocolate whipped-cream cake from Harrod's, provided once again by Paul. As they sat around the coffee table eating the cake, Dierdre complained about Paul's generosity as she swallowed an enormous bite of chocolate.

"I wish you'd stop bringing these desserts from Harrod's, Paul. I'm gonna blow up like a blimp and get fired from the show." As if to emphasize her point, Dierdre took another bite of cake.

"Try sex," Vladimir advised.

Dierdre choked on her cake and started to laugh. Charlotte handed her a cup of coffee, and she quickly took a sip. "No, thanks. I've tried it -- it works, but it always leads to other things that aren't worth while in the long run, like love."

"And you said *I'm* cynical," Paul remarked to Charlotte. There was a knock at the front door.

Dierdre put her empty cake plate on the table and stood, brushing down her cotton knit minidress. "There's Robin Herald, come to strangle me." When she reached the front door, however, she opened it to find herself confronted by an enormous bouquet of white and peach roses. Robin Herald's head peeked around the flowers and grinned at her.

"Why, Robin!" Dierdre was genuinely surprised, and even moreso because she was pleased he had come -- until that moment, she hadn't realized how much she wanted to see him again. And he was just the way she wanted to see him, too . . .without makeup, clad in a pair of tight black jeans and a leather motorcycle jacket. Apparently he had taken her comment about looking 'like a gargoyle' to heart. She was sorry now that she had made it, but thought it was worth it to see him like this. He was incredibly handsome; much moreso than she had realized; and far more masculine. "I thought you were coming to kill me!"

"May I come in?"

"Oh, of course! Please do." She stepped back into the foyer, and he followed her. He handed her the roses.

"This is a beautiful place. The roses emit a poison gas. And just to be certain; a box of chocolates with strychnine." He produced a large box of Belgian chocolates from behind his back.

Dierdre laughed, and took the box. "Thank you! I see your plan now. You're in league with Paul to make me too fat to do the show."

She had started across the foyer, but realized he wasn't following her.

"Who's Paul?" He seemed genuinely distressed.

"Come in the reception-room, and you can meet him." She started off again, and he was forced to walk behind her. When they entered the reception-room, Jerome was gone. Dierdre was sorry to see this, because she wanted Robin to meet his ancestor. Perhaps, she reflected, he wasn't quite ready for that yet.

Robin hung back in the doorway. "I beg your pardon, Dierdre - - I didn't realize you were having a party."

She reached out to take his hand, but both her own were filled with chocolates and flowers. She smiled at him instead. "It's not really a party. They came to see the show. You met Charlotte and Natalie at the studio."

"Yes; hello, again."

"And this is Paul Harkness and Vladimir Rochovsky."

Paul and Vladimir stood, and shook hands in turn with Robin. "Very interesting points you made about Thatcherism, Robin."

"Don't get started now, Paul. Robin just arrived. Have a seat on the couch, Robin. Would you like some coffee and cake?"

Robin glanced at the chocolate cake. "Yes, please. A small piece. It looks very rich."

Charlotte cut Robin a piece of cake, while Dierdre went to the sideboard to find a vase for his flowers. "Oh, it is," she replied, her head inside the cabinet. "Paul's nightly contribution to decadence from Harrod's bakery. Ah, here's one!" She emerged with a blown crystal vase of rainbow-hued glass. "Look, Chari -- I'm the first to use your new gift from Paul."

Robin smiled at her as he accepted his cake from Charlotte, and a cup of coffee from Natalie. Putting his cake on the table, he added cream to his coffee but no sugar. "Thank you, Natalie. And Charlotte. Thank you everyone! There, that should cover it, just in case someone else offers me anything."

"Be right back." Dierdre went into the kitchen with the vase, which now contained Robin's roses.

Paul settled back into the couch with an air of purposefulness. "Now, Herald -- about your views on the government."

Charlotte put her hand over his mouth. "No, Paul. You know Dierdre hates anyone talking about politics. And Robin is her guest." She removed her hand, but Paul was silent.

"Why should she hate anyone talking about politics?" Robin

asked, lifting a bite of cake to his mouth. "Oh, this is delicious. Thank you, Paul."

They laughed, and Charlotte said, "Well, she likes Margaret Thatcher. That makes it difficult, when everyone else our age hates her. Except Yuppies, that is -- we don't know many of those."

Robin's fork paused in midair with another bite of cake. "She likes Thatcher? That's not possible."

Dierdre came back into the room and placed the vase carefully in the center of the sideboard. "Don't ask Jerome to levitate the vase tonight, Vlad. Paul just bought it for Chari."

"Ok, mom -- I'll have him levitate the cake, instead."

"No way!" Charlotte quickly cut herself another sliver of cake, and popped it into her mouth.

Robin was frowning, momentarily distracted from the horrifying thought that Dierdre liked Margaret Thatcher. Hadn't Dierdre mentioned Jerome before? "Who's Jerome?"

"He's a friend of ours," Dierdre replied, sitting in a puffy, pale rose suede chair that was situated next to the sofa on which Robin was sitting. "He looks a lot like you, actually. Where is he?" This last question was directed at Charlotte.

"Gone. Never said why he was going; just . . .gone."

"And this Jerome can levitate objects?"

"Sort of -- only when he levitated my vase, it fell on the table and broke. So Paul bought me a new one."

Robin put his empty cake plate on the tble. "Why didn't Jerome buy one, since he broke it?"

They all laughed at this idea, though Natalie thought fleetingly of Jerome's use of the Harrod's card.

"Oh, Jerome couldn't buy anything!" Dierdre told Robin. "Unemployed, eh?" Robin asked her nastily. "As so many poor people are in Thatcher's Britain."

"He's Lord Jerome Kennington, the Earl of Arden."

"Rich and useless . . .and he can't even buy a vase?" Robin switched to the one thing about Dierdre that he couldn't abide. "Dierdre, how can you support a woman who would allow so many people to go hungry?"

Dierdre was beginning to wish Robin had never showed up at her door, that evening. She would gladly do without the flowers and chocolates. "I don't consider it to be the fault of one person that so many people are unemployed in England; and I don't discuss politics."

"You discussed them on the show; you just didn't tell us your opinion of Thatcher -- afraid we'd lynch you?"

"I didn't discuss it at all; I let you give your viewpoint. That's my role on the show -- not to give mine. And I won't give it now, because I don't discuss politics. And it's none of your business."

Robin stiffened; Dierdre realized she had offended him, but didn't care. She kept her views to herself and wished other people would, too. She was about to attempt a switch in the conversation when Robin said, "I beg your pardon. I'm sorry I interrupted your party. I'd better go now."

"Fine." Dierdre had decided she didn't want him there, anyway. "Thank you very much for the flowers and chocolates. Would you like one?"

"No, thank you." Robin stood and included the entire group in his next remark. "Very nice meeting all of you. Thank you for the cake." They murmured polite remarks, embarrassed by the quite obvious tension between Robin and Dierdre. "Dierdre, will you send me a copy of the broadcast?"

"Of course. I have your office address." She stood also, deciding she wasn't going to give him the opportunity to castigate her as being a bad hostess. "I'll walk you to the door."

Robin inclined his head slightly. At that point in time, they could all see his resemblance to Jerome very clearly. He and Dierdre walked to the doorway of the living room together and passed through into the vestibule.

When they were gone, Paul said, "I wish I'd never mentioned Margaret Thatcher."

"So do we all," Natalie retorted.

Vladimir shrugged. "If he came over here hoping to make points with Dierdre, it was a hopeless case anyway. Anyone can see they'd make a terribly mismatched couple."

Charlotte hugged Paul. "Some of those turn out for the best."

Vladimir shook his head decisively. "Not those two -- they're on opposite poles. Better he knows now than later. They're obviously physically attracted -- but that's not enough."

Chapter 24

Robin and Dierdre stood awkwardly in the foyer of the townhouse. All Robin thought he wanted to do was escape from her; all she thought she wanted him to do was get out and leave her alone. She managed to say, "Thank you very much for coming, Robin."

"Thank you for having me on the show." He turned away and put his hand on the door handle. Then he turned back, to look down into her eyes. They were remarkably green, he thought -- startlingly so, like emeralds sitting in a pool of cloudy liquid. He took hold of her hands and jerked her into his arms, bringing his lips down onto hers and kissing her with little gentleness.

She kissed him back fiercely, twining her hands in his thick, black hair. They clung together, breathing raggedly, for an untold number of kisses.

Finally Robin said, "Let's take a walk on the heath. It's a beautiful night."

Dierdre nodded wordlessly. He took one of her hands and opened the door. She passed through before him like a sleepwalker, and he closed the door behind them, making certain it wasn't locked.

They walked the length of the heath and back before they couldn't stand it anymore, and half fell onto a stone bench beneath a large chestnut tree. Their kisses resumed, becoming more passionate as they attempted to roam over one another's bodies through their clothing. Dierdre was wearing a short, loose top of white, hand-painted silk, and Robin found it a simple matter to slide his hand up underneath. He quickly found the nipple of her breast through the thin bra, and shortly thereafter realized it clipped together in the front. Fumbling with the clasp, he felt the bra fall apart in his hands even as his fingers slipped over the cool, soft skin of her breasts. He moved his mouth away from hers and down her neck toward the neckline of the top.

She was panting slightly as she said, "I think we'd better go back to the house before someone comes walking along here." Robin nodded, but felt he couldn't possibly move until his lips had felt the softness of that breast. He moved his head quickly, pushing the white silk aside with one hand, and took the nipple of the breast in his mouth. Dierdre gasped and threw her head back, clutching his black curls with both hands. He seemed to continue forever, flicking his tongue over first one and then other breast, until she thought she would melt under his touch and become nothing more than a puddle in the heath. "Robin; I've got to fasten my bra again." Reluctantly, he sat up, and she turned away from him in order to clasp the bra together. Before she could do so, however, he pulled her back against him and slid his hands up under the top, enclosing both breasts. "Oh, Robin . . ." She leaned into him, feeling his erection through his jeans. She turned her head slightly and they came together for another kiss . . .deep and passionate.

Chapter 25

It was late the following morning, and Dierdre and Robin were still asleep in her bed, his arms entwined around her. Dierdre's bedroom was difficult to classify as to style, unless 'expensive minimalism' could be considered a style. The furniture was black lacquer, and seemed to float off the rose plush carpeting, like chests and a bed in a space-ship cabin. The bedclothes, curtains, indeed everything that could be seen were of white satin, shimmering and gossamer. It was a strange combination, but one that worked and seemed to describe Dierdre's taste perfectly.

Dierdre awakened with a start, feeling that someone was watching her. She looked up, straight into Jerome's unblinking gaze. She sat up, clutching the embroidered sheet to her breasts. Robin stirred beside her but didn't awaken. "Jeri," she hissed, "What the hell are you doing? Didn't anyone ever knock in 1811?"

"I'm sorry, Didi. I wanted to see Robin." Jerome was, indeed, staring intently at his descendant.

"You could've seen him last night if you hadn't phased out."

"I didn't. I was pulled, somehow. I think if he wakes up, I'll be gone again."

"You mean he won't be able to see you?"

"I don't know how he can, if I'm not here."

Dierdre frowned. "Oh, dear. I was going to tell him about you. Now I'm not sure if I should."

Robin stirred beside her, and stretched in the bed. Jerome faded out, slowly, as Robin came awake. "Didi? Where are you?" Dierdre turned and slid down in the bed, into Robin's arms. They tightened around her, and he smiled sleepily up at her. "Oh, good. I thought I dreamt you, last night."

"Did you feel as if you were drugged?" She asked. "I did."

"Intoxicated, was more like it."

"What shall we do now?"

Pulling her down on top of him, Robin kissed her deeply. His hands went to cup her breasts as she swung her leg over his body and straddled him. "I could think of a few things."

"I can think of one in particular, and I'll bet you think I'm not ready for it." Gripping her waist with his arms, Robin lifted Dierdre from him and repositioned her over his pelvis. Dropping her slowly, he pushed himself up and into her until she was again sitting on top of him. She arched her back with a low moan, and gripped his sides with her legs.

That afternoon, Dierdre finally staggered down to the second reception room to make telephone calls. She was just finishing when Charlotte came in. All Charlotte heard was, "We film on Friday afternoon. I can meet with you next Wednesday, if you like. All right. 2 pm. Ok, see you then." Dierdre hung up the telephone and wrote some notes in an appointment book before turning to regard Charlotte with curiosity.

The other woman was carrying a basket that appeared to contain some kind of small animal, as it had a grate at the top. Dierdre stared at it. "What's that, Chari?"

Charlotte put the basket on the dining table, as the second reception room was, in reality, the dining room. "Kittens," she replied. "Paul and I liberated them from the university medical lab. He took three and I have three. That's one for each of us."

Dierdre put down her appointment book and approached the table eagerly. "Kittens! Oh, let's see."

Charlotte removed the grate from the basket; it was held on at the sides by small hooks. She lifted out one white kitten, and one black one. They were still small, probably five or six weeks old. One kitten was left in the basket; a very small, grey one. Dierdre looked in, and lifted him out. He seemed sleepy . . .or drugged, she thought with alarm.

She held him up to her face, and he curled into her neck, purring. "They're so small," she said with a catch in her voice. "How can people use tiny babies like this for experiments? It's immoral."

Charlotte nodded. "That's why we took them. Paul is always talking about how horrible that lab is -- he can't bear to go into it. Fortunately he doesn't work in there; no one knows he has a key. Didi, there are puppies, too."

Dierdre swallowed, cuddling her kitten. She gazed at Charlotte in dismay. "Puppies? Oh, god . . .Paul can't go back and take them, Chari -- he could lose his job."

Charlotte smiled conspiratorially. "But we could." Dierdre bit her lip, considering this. "Do you think we dare?"

"I'll bet Nat and Vlad would go with us. One look at these little darlings and she'll melt all over the carpet."

"Yes; and Robin! He'd love stuff like this."

"Oh, so it's Robin now, is it? Has he left yet?" Dierdre flushed. She should have known her friends had guessed at the presence of Robin in her bedroom, even though they hadn't seen him. Perhaps they had been too noisy during the night. Sometimes she heard Charlotte and Paul, though she had never told her. "About an hour ago. But's he's taking me to a party on Saturday."

They carried the kittens to the couch and sat with them, the white and black ones both cuddled in Charlotte's lap. The grey one was asleep on Dierdre's shoulder. "Funny," Charlotte said, "I could've sworn you two didn't like one another." Then she burst out laughing, and Dierdre couldn't help but join in.

"I think it must be chemical. Oh! We need cat food, and a box, and litter and stuff. I'd better go to the store. I have some errands to run, anyway."

"Ok; take my car -- it's in the drive. I would've stopped myself, but I wanted to get these guys home. I'll give them some milk."

"If Nat comes home, talk to her about the puppies. The sooner we get them out of there, the better. Who knows what those inhuman monsters might do to them. Have you seen Jerome?"

"Not today. I'll see if I can get him. With everything that's been going on, we haven't really been working on his problem. Maybe he can tell us the rest of his story tonight. You going out?"

"No, I'll be here. I have a bunch of stuff to print from that fashion shoot I did the other day. Tomorrow I think I'll go roam the streets, though. I was thinking of going down to All Saints."

Dierdre stopped, looking back at her. "You don't mean in Nottinghill, do you?"

"That's the only All Saints Way in London, I think."

"Chari, you can't! Not even the police go down there. What are you thinking of?"

"Of getting some good shots for my showing next month. Maybe I should take Paul with me, but he's constantly going- on about my being careful and such. He hampers me."

"Please *do* take him. I'd worry all day, you down there on your own. I don't think you realize how beautiful you are, or how much you'd stand out in a place like that with all your blond hair." Dierdre turned away again and soon disappeared from Charlotte's view.

She continued to stroke the kittens, somewhat dissatisfied with life in general. Perhaps, she thought, she should cut all this hair off and wear it very short. Then people (make that men, she thought ruefully, then amended it when she thought of the time she and her friend Tess had been attacked by East End teenagers on a tube-train) wouldn't harass her. She wanted to photograph the people nobody else bothered with, the ones forgotten by the media and life in general. And thus far she had made pretty good progress on her goal, but places like All Saints had remained slightly beyond her grasp, because they were so dangerous. Perhaps it **would** be better to take Paul with her, since she was absolutely determined to go. She hoped he wouldn't make too much of a fuss. She wondered how she could be in love with a man who was so stuffy sometimes; who was so much of an . . .adult. Adult was a word Charlotte avoided as much as possible, because it sounded like someone who was married and had children; someone who lived in a house in the suburbs and never did another exciting thing as long as they lived. No, 'adult' was a word Charlotte wanted as little as possible to do with. And Paul was one of those.

Well, she amended, perhaps not completely. He had surprised her when he suggested they 'liberate' the kittens from the lab; now she knew he would go along with their plan to rescue as many of the animals as possible, because he couldn't bear their suffering. No, Paul had proven he wasn't completely an 'adult'. In Charlotte's mind, adults didn't care much about animals suffering, as long as it might bring them (the adults, not the animals) something in exchange -- like a cure for AIDS or new cosmetics. Adults wore fur coats, and never bothered to inquire how much the animals had suffered to provide those, either. Charlotte had a fine contempt for people she considered to be adults. Though she had never discussed it with Dierdre or Natalie, she was certain they felt the same way.

Charlotte was unable to locate Jerome that afternoon, and had just entered her darkroom to begin processing film when Dierdre returned from the grocery store. "Chari -- I'm home! Where are the kittens?" She could hear from the vestibule, which was just above her.

She banged on the ceiling with the pole she kept for that purpose (it was really a broken broomstick) to let Dierdre know she was in the darkroom, and would be out when she had finished her film. She completed the roll she was working on, and climbed the stairs to the main floor of the house. Dierdre and Natalie were in the kitchen, where Natalie had discovered the kittens asleep in a basket Charlotte had prepared for them, filled with soft, old towels.

Natalie was stroking the white kitten softly with one finger, and it curled up, purring.

"I see you found the bed I made for the kittens," Charlotte said. She watched Dierdre unpacking cat food, vitamins, cat litter and a litter-box. "Did you buy enough stuff?" She picked up one of the boxes. "Wow -- I didn't even know they made dry food especially for kittens. I gave them some milk, but they seemed worn out, poor little things."

"Have you two already chosen your kittens?" Natalie asked. She was obviously much taken with the white one.

"The grey one's mine," Dierdre replied. "His name is Cloud."

"Her name," Charlotte corrected. "And you can have either the black or the white, Nat. I love them both."

"Well, so do I . . .all of them, actually. But the white one . . ." Natalie had obviously made her choice.

"He's yours," Charlotte replied. "Now we just have to find homes for the puppies."

"Puppies?" Natalie looked around eagerly. "Where are they?"

"We haven't rescued them yet," Charlotte told her. "I'll tell you the plan . . ."

"Wait a minute," Dierdre cut in. "Did you find Jerome?"

"No; I called him, but I guess he couldn't hear me. Why?"

"I want to try to impress on him a gentleman doesn't walk into a lady's boudoir when she's entertaining a lover."

Charlotte stared at her. "You mean . . .my god, he's incorrigible!"

Dierdre nodded emphatically. "Now, you can tell Nat the animal rescue plan while I feed the refugees we've already got."

Robin was late getting to rehearsal that afternoon, and he couldn't seem to carry even one song on cue, much less remember all the words. Finally, worn out and irritable with himself for wasting everyone's time, he called a break and wandered into the small kitchen of the studio to find a soft drink. The small refrigerator was kept stocked with a good selection as well as an assortment of beer and ale. Robin chose a can of Ribena and popped the top, allowing the cold black currant soda to flow down his throat.

"So," came a voice from behind him, "What's got your knickers in a twist?" It was Jock, the band's engineer. Jock was an enormous Scotsman, well over six feet tall and about 250 pounds. He had naturally flaming red hair and a large beard to match, and lacked only a kilt to complete the picture. He was grinning at Robin as if he already knew what ailed the singer.

Robin shrugged. "I didn't get much sleep last night."

Jock pulled a bottle of Whitbread's from the refrigerator and knocked the cap off against the battered plastic sideboard. "New bird, eh? They're always hell at first -- course that's the best part, right?"

"I'd say everything about this woman is the best part. I just don't think she's the one for me."

"That's a confused statement, me old mate. Sure you got those knickers untwisted when you put 'em back on?"

Robin gave Jock a withering look, which the large man laughed away. Then he walked outside with his drink, gazing up and down the unprepossessing main street of Finsbury Park. A dismal neighborhood, he thought. Not as bad as where he had lived before Nottinghill, but nothing came close to as dismal as Brixton. Still, there was something so repressive about lower middle-class working neighborhoods in London. He gave himself a mental shake. That was certainly no way for a dedicated Utopian Socialist to behave. But his thoughts kept going back to that beautiful townhouse in Hampstead, and its' even more beautiful occupant. For the first time in his life, Robin Herald understood why men made fools of themselves over certain women, and gave those women everything they had.

Chapter 26

That evening, the party in the second reception room was enlivened by the antics of the kittens, rested and well fed after their rescue. The usual group was assembled eating take-out Chinese food, and their cartons were spread over the dining table. Dierdre wished Robin was a part of that group, but thought it might be pushy to invite him for dinner when she'd be seeing him in a couple of days. Their conversation that night centered on the rescue of the still captive puppies. That changed her mind.

"Do you think you can really get a mini-cam into the lab, Vlad?" Dierdre removed one of the kittens from the table, where it was wandering towards a carton of asparagus- beef.

"Why not?" Vladimir helped himself to shrimp fried rice. "I can easily conceal one underneath my coat. If Paul gives us the right keys, we can get into the building and the lab without tripping the alarm. We can take the puppies, and I can film the rest of the poor creatures in the lab. We can deliver the film to your TV station, and you can play it on your program. No one will be able to stop us, because no one will know you're going to run it film until it's too late."

"Where will I say it came from?"

"Say it was delivered by an anonymous messenger," Natalie offered, as if she was participating in a spy ring.

"Paul," Charlotte interjected, "You can't go with us."

He stared at her, and swallowed a mouthful of sesame noodles.

"I have to! You won't be able to find your way to the lab without me." He sounded like a child who has been told he cannot go to the circus.

"Draw us a map," Dierdre told him. "You can't risk being seen there."

Charlotte sipped green tea from a small china cup. "Too bad Jeri can't go; he could walk through the walls until he found the lab, and the security guards would never see him."

Jerome's voice came from behind her. "I'll go if you want me to."

Charlotte's arm jerked violently, and her tea splashed over the table. Paul laughed as Jerome materialized at Charlotte's side, and quickly put his napkin over the spilled tea. "Jeri! You nearly gave me a heart attack! Where have you been?"

"Are you feeling all right, old man?" Paul asked him, as Jerome sat in the empty chair between Paul and Vladimir. "Don't have a ghostly hangover, or something? You can't leave this house." He deposited his now sodden napkin on his plate, and pushed both away from him.

"I can now." Jerome looked smug. He took a small cup for himself, poured two cups of tea and handed one to Charlotte. "I went to the market with Didi today. Amazing, these 'supermarkets'; don't you think?"

"What!" Dierdre was staring at him with disbelief. "You didn't, Jerome -- I didn't see you."

"I seem to be invisible outside the house," he explained. "But I followed you, and the barrier that used to keep me here is gone. I can't leave on my own -- I tried that; but since I went with Didi, I assume I could go with any of you."

"This is incredible," Vladimir enthused. "I wish I could film it; but the footage I shot of you before is blank. All that the viewer can see is a vase lifting itself into the air and falling onto a table."

"That could be good." This from Paul, who was still eating. "I suppose people would think it was just special effects, though."

"I'm going to the lab with you," Jerome stated emphatically.

"You can't, Jeri," Dierdre replied. "I'm going to ask Robin to go."

"Why? I can be of more use to you than he can."

"He has a point, love." Charlotte had pushed back her chair and was gathering empty cartons and rubbish from the table, and putting it onto an oversized black lacquer tray. "We understand that you want to include Robin, but I think we should take Jerome."

Dierdre was entering her stubborn mode. She had the feeling she would eventually give in, but she didn't want to . . .she wanted Robin included. "But I've already telephoned Robin and asked him to come over."

"What did you tell him?" Charlotte upended a carton of prawns and vegetables onto Paul's plate, and added the empty box to her pile. He glanced at her indignantly, but she just grinned, and kissed him.

"Just that I had something important to talk to him about."

"Tell him you couldn't wait until Saturday night," Natalie advised her. "It would be the truth." She also stood, and began to pick up the little china cups, piling them one on top of the other. No one at the table was eating by this point, Paul having abandoned his plate with the prawns and vegetables still in a mound in the center.

Dierdre shot Natalie a withering look, just as the front doorbell rang. Natalie looked up from her cup gathering. "Here already, from Nottinghill Gate? A record, I'd say."

"Must've had the car running and waiting outside the house," Charlotte added, heading for the kitchen with her laden tray.

"Very amusing, minds in the gutter." Dierdre attempted to make a dignified exit into the foyer. Once there, however, she rushed to the door and jerked it open. Robin was standing there grinning, dressed in a faded, very tight pair of blue jeans, and a black tee-shirt. Without a word he stepped into the foyer, took Dierdre in his arms and kissed her passionately. Eventually he said, "I was hoping you'd call me! I couldn't stand not to see you until Saturday."

Dierdre giggled nervously. "Then why didn't you call me?"

"I didn't want you to think I was only interested in sex. Had dinner?"

"Now I understand you have two interests; sex and food. The whole gang's here. Come in and have some Chinese food, if the scavengers have left any."

They trailed into the reception room, arms entwined around one another's waists. Charlotte returned from the kitchen, without the tray, as they entered. "Hi, Robin," she said. "I see you and Didi are on better terms than you were the other night."

A flush ran up Robin's neck above the tee-shirt, staining his normally pale skin strawberry-pink. "Oh, we came to an understanding about our differences," he managed awkwardly. The group laughed as if they thought this remark hilarious.

Paul gestured conspicuously to a chair. "Have a seat, Robin. Want something to eat?"

Robin started towards the table, surveying the cartons still left, and now clustered neatly in a group. "Anything left?"

"Oh, sure." Vladimir handed him a clean plate from the sideboard behind him. "Nat always buys enough food for 12 people."

Robin took the plate and circled the table to the chair Paul had offered him. Dierdre began to pass him cartons, after inspecting them to make certain they still contained enough food to be presentable. Robin sat as she spooned a serving of prawns onto his plate.

Jerome's voice came from the chair, beneath Robin. "I wish you wouldn't sit on top of me, great-great- great-great-grandson. At my age, I *must* be fragile."

Robin looked around warily, as Dierdre stopped in the act of serving him chicken and mushrooms. Her serving spoon paused in mid-air, she was staring in horror at the chair. Robin seemed to think Paul or Vladimir had a tape-recorder hidden somewhere; he even resorted to checking underneath the chair. As he straightened again, Jerome materialized beneath him. He screamed and scrambled out of the chair, falling to the carpet in amazement.

Dierdre began to laugh, and dropped the serving spoon onto the black wood of the table, where it sat in a blob of sauce. Charlotte, attempting to keep her laughter to a minimum, managed to say, "Robin, this is your great-great- great-great-great grandfather. At least, we think that's right."

Robin was staring up at Jerome disbelievingly. "I . . .beg your pardon?"

Dierdre leaned down and took Robin's hand. He rose from the carpet quite gracefully, but staggered slightly as he made his way to another chair. This one was placed against the wall as an extra, and he moved it to the table, setting it beside the one holding Jerome, and falling gratefully into it. He took his plate from Dierdre, who had filled it with food. "Here," she said, "Have something to eat, and I'll get you a glass of wine. Red or white?"

He transferred his blank gaze to her. "What? Oh . . .white, please. Uh . . .who did you say you are? And how did you do that?"

Dierdre put a glass of wine in front of him, and one for Jerome. Only Robin received a napkin. "Yes, Jeri -- how *did* you do it? I thought you dematerialized to some limbo when Robin came into the same room."

Jerome sipped his wine complacently. "I've managed to compensate. I'm not sure how. Concentration, I suppose." Robin started to eat the food on his plate without noticing what it was. He was watching Jerome warily, as if he expected him to disappear or do something bizarre.

Dierdre sat in her own chair again, after refilling her wine glass. She sipped a little and said, "Jerome will tell you his story, Robin. We haven't heard the end of it ourselves."

"Oh, Jerome," Robin retorted. "The man you keep in the closet."

Jerome raised one supercilious eyebrow, his handsome face taking on a mask of indignation. Dierdre could imagine him, in 1811, intimidating Charles Brent enough so the other man wet his pants. But Robin was Jerome's descendent, and she could see the same steel in him. She wondered exactly what she was letting herself in for. "I assure you, child -- no one keeps me prisoner. I am a prisoner of my own fate, merely. Perhaps now . . .well, we shall see."

"Go on, Jeri," Charlotte urged, moving her chair closer to Paul's so he could put one arm around her. "And hurry up about the first part. You were up to the duel that never happened."

"OK." Jerome beamed. "You see, I have managed to pick up some American cant expressions from my girlfriends, here." Robin stared at him blankly. "Cant? What does that mean?"

"It's slang," Charlotte replied, as if she was addressing a particularly slow child who wouldn't learn to tie his shoes. "Now stop interrupting, so we can get the rest of the story."

"Sorry," Robin responded icily, and addressed himself to his wine. "Please continue, whoever the hell you are."

"Well, Robin; I was born in 1783 in the village of Hampstead, where we are now."

Robin sat with his wineglass poised in mid-air, staring at Jerome in stunned disbelief.

Chapter 27

London, 1811

Just outside of London, the town of Richmond was a favorite with the ton, who journeyed out there for garden parties and picnics at Kew Gardens. On this beautiful day in May, Lady Sarah and Alicia attended a garden party on the grounds of the Earl of Carr's country estate. Edging the Thames, the sumptuous lawns of the manor house reached down to the water and offered a view of Kew across the river. This day a number of brightly colored pavilions had been erected on the grass, holding tables full of food, tables for eating that food, and chairs for those who shunned the sun.

Jerome and Richard (who had been in pursuit of a dashing widow these past few weeks) were to meet them at the party, but Sarah and Alicia arrived first, and wandered around the grounds together, shielded by their silk parasols. Alicia was happy with her robins-egg blue muslin dress, trimmed with Alencon lace at the hem and sleeves, and showing slightly more of her bosom than Sarah had previously allowed. Sarah herself was more than satisfied with the way Alicia's season had turned-out. She knew her ward was a beautiful girl, but she felt that the feeling between Alicia and Jerome went beyond the merely physical; it was as if they had a bond, that both felt on that first meeting and which had strengthened as they came to know one another better.

"Has Jerome mentioned a date for the wedding, Ali? He hasn't spoken to me about it."

"He asked me when I would like it to be. I would love June, but I suppose that doesn't leave long for an engagement."

"And does he desire a long engagement?"

"No; he said the sooner the better. I think he feels somewhat . . .frustrated."

Sarah glanced sharply at Alicia, peering beneath the rim of her parasol. "Ali, you and Jerome have been circumspect, haven't you? You aren't allowing him too many liberties?"

Alicia sighed, as if the frustration wasn't entirely on Jerome's side. "Oh, no. But it is very difficult, Aunt Sarah. He makes me feel so strange, so . . .tingly, all over. I can't explain it satisfactorily."

"Never mind, dear -- I understand. How fortunate you are, to have achieved such a success in your first season and a love match into the bargain. Charles is still very angry, you know. It would be better if we attempted to avoid him until after the wedding."

"I certainly have no objection to that plan."

"And I don't see why we cannot be ready by June, if that's what you want. Shall you be married at St. George's?"

"I suppose so. I would really rather choose the chapel in Hampstead, but Jerome is so very important, and everyone is married out of St. George's. Why, I cannot imagine -- it is quite the ugliest church in London."

"We could probably locate an uglier, if we looked." Sarah started to laugh. "But you're right . . .it is an eyesore, but too tonnish to pass over. St. George's in June. We are fortunate Jerome is so very important -- otherwise we would never be able to book the church on such short notice."

"Look -- there are Jerome and Richard!"

Sarah managed to restrain Alicia, who was on the verge of dashing across the lawn and throwing herself into Jerome's arms. As they moved decorously past the other guests, Richard was obviously looking around in an attempt to spot his widow. Jerome bowed over Alicia's hand.

"Can I possibly endure luncheon, knowing you are but a few feet away?" He asked her.

"You'll have to, won't you?" Sarah told him. "Besides, never make love on an empty stomach. Ruins the digestion." Before Jerome was able to reply to this outrageous sally, Sarah slid her arm through Richard's. "Come with me, Richard darling -- I've seen your quarry on the other side of the yellow pavilion."

She led him away, and Jerome heard Richard protesting that he had been looking for no one but her. He gazed down at Alicia fondly, and a little hungrily. "You look so beautiful today, my dear."

"So do you, Jerome." He laughed, and drew her arm through his the way Sarah had done with Richard's.

"No, little one! I must look handsome -- you must look beautiful. Only exquisites are willing to be beautiful men -- you wouldn't have me be one of those, would you?"

Alicia thought about this. "I don't believe so. The high-heels they wear on their shoes always look so uncomfortable. Still, to me you are beautiful. The most beautiful man in the world."

"And you're the most refreshing lady. Didn't your aunt ever tell you that being a member of 'society' includes the art of dissembling?"

"Oh, yes -- she told me. I wouldn't have let you know how perfect I think you are, if you hadn't asked to marry me."

"Do you mean you had already decided, before I asked you? By the way, I don't recall that I ever did ask you."

Alicia stopped short, jerking Jerome back with her. Her large, blue eyes were troubled as she raised them to his. "What do you mean? Don't you want to marry me?"

"Of course I do, silly goose! All I meant was that I never asked you -- your wonderful cousin Charles forced my hand, and I had to announce our engagement before I ever had the opportunity to ask.

I don't think Sarah was too pleased about that."

"Oh, she understood the situation. And to answer your question; yes, I had already decided you were perfect. I never thought you'd fall in love with me, however. A man like you should be with a high-flyer, I assumed."

Jerome grinned down at her. "Now where did you hear that expression, I wonder? Dear Charles?"

"Well, he never said it to me, of course . . .oh, dear. Sarah and Richard are attempting to get our attention. I suppose they're ready to eat luncheon; everyone else seems to have gone into the pavilions. Shall we?"

"Something tells me we aren't being given a choice. Perhaps after luncheon I can get you alone somewhere. Your lips are screaming to be kissed."

"Are they? How strange that I can't hear them myself."

"They scream for me, only."

Two hours later, Jerome couldn't wait any longer to get Alicia alone. He knew his feelings were about to overwhelm him, and he couldn't allow himself to get carried away by them -- it wouldn't be fair to Alicia. But he was losing the battle, day-by-day, to his libido. They were seated on a cloth that had been spread out on the lawn; Jerome and Alicia, Richard and his lady-friend Emily; Sarah and her court of middle-aged admirers. Jerome stood and straightened his coat, turning to address Alicia in what he hoped was a nonchalant manner.

"Lady Alicia, would you care for a stroll around the grounds?"

Taking his cue and his outstretched hand, Alicia rose gracefully to her feet. "Yes, thank you. I've heard the gardens here are spectacular." Her eyes were sparkling like sapphires as they met his. "We'll be back shortly, Aunt Sarah. Jerome is going to show me the gardens."

"I'm trusting your decorum, Jerome," was the only reply Sarah made.

Jerome bowed to her, knowing that neither of them was fooling the other. "Of course, Lady Sarah." He led Alicia away down a path that wound down to the formal gardens, holding her hand in his.

He managed to restrain himself to one kiss while they were walking, but this was a strain on his self-control. Her innocent passion and obvious liking of the activity made his blood boil until he wanted to throw her down on the manicured lawn and leap on top of her. Finally they reached a small summerhouse of open-lattice-work, with ornamental couches inside. They sat on one of the smaller ones, and Alicia allowed Jerome to put his arm around her, leaning back into his embrace. "Perhaps we should be getting back," she said, sighing. "We've been gone a long time."

"Sarah won't worry," he replied. "She knows you're with me."

Alicia giggled. "I expect that's why she *will* worry."

"Well, we're betrothed now. We can be allowed a little more freedom."

She turned and looked up into his face. "To do what, Jerome?"

He leaned down and kissed her, which was what she obviously expected. She put her arms around his neck and wriggled closer to him, and he picked her up and deposited her in his lap. A few minutes of this, and Jerome felt as if he was about to expire. Tentatively he moved his hands down her back, caressing her beneath the thin muslin dress. When she didn't object to this treatment he became bolder, and slid one hand up her side, tracing his fingers over the outline of her breast. This also didn't elicit any feminine indignity; instead Alicia sighed and nuzzled his neck. The hand closed over the breast and kneaded it gently, softly, while he fingered her nipple through the cloth. Her breathing was quickening, as was his, and she put her mouth up again for another, more passionate, kiss. Telling himself to stop . . .that he must stop or suffer the consequences . . .Jerome slid his hand into the top of Alicia's dress and over her bare breast. With a little moan, she pushed the top of the dress down, the tiny puffed sleeves sliding down her arms, until both breasts were free. They were small and rounded, and the nipples were so pink; they stood up so proudly . . .Jerome fastened his mouth over one and slid his tongue over the skin, in little circles.

It wasn't until Alicia was lying naked in his arms that Jerome realized what he had done. She was drowsy and half- asleep, and her hair had come out of its' loose arrangement to fall down her back in blond waves.

"Alicia? Oh, God . . .I'm so sorry!"

She sat up, those adorable breasts bouncing against him, and looked down into his face. "Why, Jeri -- don't you want to marry me, now?"

"Of course I do! But we shouldn't have . . .*I* shouldn't have . . .until after the wedding."

"Well, I don't see what difference it makes. We'll just have to be married rather quickly. In the event . . ." she blushed. "Well, you know."

"You're the most wonderful girl in the world, Ali. I do love you."

She hugged him enthusiastically. "And I you, Jerome! So much."

"No," he cautioned her, "Don't do that!" He put her forcibly away from him, and looked down at the little couch with some dismay. "Oh, Lord! We got blood on the Earl's sofa! What are we to do?"

"Pile some cushions over it and hope nobody sees for a long time, until they can no longer guess who might have done it!" Alicia started to laugh, and Jerome couldn't help but join in. Jerome and Alicia were too wrapped up in one another to notice Charles Brent; indeed, they had nearly forgotten his existence. In this they were making a mistake, for Brent had certainly not forgotten them. One night in the late spring, approximately a month before the ton would begin to desert London for their country estates, they attended a ball at Almack's, the famous subscription ballroom. At Almack's, young ladies were only allowed to waltz by permission of the hostesses -- an intimidating group of social matrons who held the strings to which the debutantes danced. As annoyed as nearly all the matrons were, that spring, to see a penniless chit like Alicia snatch up a matrimonial prize like Jerome, Alicia was allowed to waltz. Jerome wouldn't have listened if anyone had told him she couldn't; they were betrothed, he was the Earl of Arden, and that was the end of it, as far as he was concerned. And where nearly everyone else was, also. They might resent Jerome marrying Alicia, but the matrons and their daughters knew there was nothing they could do about it, and to show resentment or envy would only bring on a blistering set- down.

But Charles Brent was too obsessed with Alicia to care if he made a fool of himself; indeed, he knew he already had and reasoned, therefore, that he had little left to lose. He stood in the shadows at Almack's and swore revenge on Jerome Kennington for stealing his bride, and on Alicia for falling in love with someone else. He was biding his time, until he could find a way to take his vengeance on them.

Jerome finally managed to get Alicia out of the ballroom and into one of the small withdrawing rooms that had been set-aside for young ladies to retire and repair their gowns. There had been no repeat of the incident at the garden party, and Jerome was even more frustrated now he had discovered the delights of Alicia's body. He dreamed about her every night, and woke up with sheets soaking wet from his perspiration and emissions.

Alicia was putting up a token resistance as he tugged her into the room. "Jerome, we can't! Someone will see us."

"They won't think anything of it; we're engaged, remember?"

"That's what you said at the garden party, and look what happened then!" As his face fell, she rushed to reassure him. "Don't think I didn't like every minute of it, beloved -- I believe I liked it far too much."

"How is that possible?" Jerome raised one quizzical eyebrow.

"I was under the impression that the sexual side of marriage was a joy to the man, but a duty to the wife."

"Surely Lady Sarah never told you that?"

"No, and I realize she enjoyed marital relations with her first husband. But Jerome, it seems so shockingly wanton to actually desire you to do those things to me."

Jerome drew her into his arms, his eyes lighting with glee and desire. He kissed her passionately, and she responded heartily, despite her protests. Taking her hand, he led her to a little satin loveseat and they sat together, arms about one another. Their kisses were long, and neither one was aware of the passage of time. Again Jerome's hands wandered over Alicia's body, and one came to rest on her breast. The thin silk of her ballgown was easily pushed aside, and he began to trail his kisses down her neck.

Alicia clutched his black curls, dragging them out of their careful arrangement. Her breathing was ragged. "Oh, God, Jerome -- I never thought I could feel like this! Like I'm on fire! And we won't be married for another six weeks -- I already shouldn't be wearing my white wedding gown as it is."

Distracted momentarily from his attempt to cover every inch of her flesh with his kisses, Jerome looked up with a grin. This offered Alicia the opportunity to drag the bodice of her gown back up to its' intended position. "I wouldn't worry about it, little one. No one knows but me, and I'm not likely to tell, am I?" As if his hand was working without his brain knowing about it, it absently slid up again to caress the other breast through her dress. "This is nothing, compared with what we have in store for us. I knew I wasn't wrong about you. I could see the fire in those cornflower-blue eyes."

"But I feel immoral."

"As long as you are my wife, you may be anything you please . . .so long as you always love me."

"I might just agree to that." She turned her face up, inviting his kiss.

Chapter 28

In the living room of the townhouse in Hampstead, Robin had maneuvered his chair close to Dierdre's. She was now sitting in his arms, while he stroked every place his hand could conveniently reach.

Vladimir was laughing as he drained his glass of wine. "So you and Alicia didn't wait until your wedding night, you old dog!"

Jerome flushed. "Well, we waited until six weeks before! We tried, but we just couldn't."

"It didn't sound like you tried very hard," Charlotte retorted acidly. "No wonder you were embarrassed when we asked you if Alicia could have been pregnant after your wedding night! She was probably knocked-up before!"

Jerome stared at her blankly. "Knocked-up?"

"Pregnant -- she was probably already carrying your child," Dierdre explained. "I see your descendants haven't changed in a hundred and fifty years. They still can't wait."

Robin grinned and nuzzled her hair. "If I'd lived then, I'd have gone nuts."

"Well," Charlotte said, "At least men had their 'other' women they could go to or keep. You know -- I think they called them 'lightskirts'."

"Yes," Jerome conceded. "But it wasn't the same, I can tell

you."

"I'll bet it was harder on the women though," Natalie commented, absently stroking Vladimir's leg.

"I confess, I'd rather be alive now."

"I can hardly believe you're not," Robin said incredulously. "I'm really glad you asked me to come over tonight, Didi. I wouldn't have missed meeting Jerome for anything. I've never bothered to find out about my ancestors. I can see I'm going to have to do some research into them, now."

"Oh, that's not why we asked you to come over, Rob."

He looked down at Dierdre in surprise, then grinned hopefully. "It's not?"

"Not that, either. We're going to break into the lab at the University and liberate the puppies . . .and bunnies."

"Wait a minute!" Vladimir paused in the act of pouring wine for everyone at the table, and peered at her suspiciously. "No one said anything about rabbits."

Paul shrugged, accepting his glass of wine. "Face it, Vlad. Once you get the girls into that lab, you won't be able to get them out until they've taken every animal in there." Robin frowned. "You do realize you could be arrested for this. It's breaking and entering."

Natalie stared at him in surprise. "We never thought *you'd* be squeamish, Rob."

"I'm not; I just want you to realize the inherent dangers. I'm all for it -- I detest animal experimentation."

"Besides," Paul retorted, "It won't be breaking and entering. I have the keys."

Robin laughed. "Just theft, then."

"Vlad is going to film the lab and the animals, and I'm going to run it on my show," Dierdre told him proudly.

Robin seemed stunned by this. He gazed down at her adoringly.

"Didi, I'm proud of you. Will the station let you do it?"

"The producer will; by the time it's on the air, it'll be too late to do anything to stop it. Besides, I'm on channel four; remember?"

"That's true, the station that will do anything."

"Do you want to come with us, Rob?"

"You mean *all* of you are going? Don't you think you should leave this to the men?"

Enraged, Dierdre jerked away from him, and punched him in the stomach. "Ouch! Didi, I'm trying to protect you!"

"Forget it, man," Jerome advised him. "These ladies today can more than protect themselves."

Charlotte choked on her wine and started to laugh and cough at the same time. *"Forget it, man*? Jerome, have you been watching TV?"

"You told me I should," he retorted in an injured voice. "Didn't you?"

"I suggest you come up with some different clothes before we hit the lab," Natalie advised. "Call Harrod's."

"Wait a minute . . ." Robin shook his head as if to clear it. "Are you telling me you're taking a ghost with you to liberate animals from a lab? What am I saying? I don't even believe in ghosts."

"Now you do." Dierdre grinned up at him.

"It seems there's a lot I believe in today that wasn't part of my life a couple of days ago." He hugged Dierdre, and kissed her neck. "However, why would you take a ghost with you?"

"Because he insisted on going," Vladimir told him.

"Hey," Jerome protested, "I can be a lot of help! If a security guard comes along, I can distract him while you guys make a get-away. And he won't see me, because I can't be seen by anyone outside this house."

Charlotte regarded him with admiration. "Wow, you really

picked up the language fast."

"I watched TV all last night. I don't sleep, remember?"

Robin shook his head, laughing. "I can just see this thing is going to turn into the funniest comedy of errors since The Three Stooges hit Washington."

"And one stayed, in The White House," Natalie added.

"Two stayed. You're forgetting Quayle." This from Dierdre.

"Three. Ollie North." Paul concluded.

"How can you feel that way about *them* and still like Thatcher?" Robin asked in confusion.

"Don't start on me, Robin," Dierdre replied testily. "We agreed we wouldn't discuss it."

"I just asked a question," Robin retorted in a wounded voice.

"Well, *don't*," Paul advised him. "You two will argue all night, and we won't get this thing planned out."

"The last thing I want to do is argue all night," Robin agreed. "When are you going to do this dastardly deed?"

"Next Thursday night," Charlotte told him. "Paul is certain no one is working late that evening."

"Do you have a plan of the building?"

Paul pushed back his chair and crossed to where his battered leather briefcase was leaning against the wall. Picking it up, he returned to the table with it and sat in his chair again, propping the briefcase up on the table. He opened it and shuffled through the papers inside.

"If you haven't decided what to buy Paul for his birthday, Chari, I can give you an idea," Dierdre said, regarding the briefcase with something like loathing.

Paul looked up from his search. "I hope you don't mean a briefcase, Didi. I'd never part with this one -- it has too many memories."

"I can see that, and each and every one left its' mark on the leather."

"That's why I like it. I got the building plan from the administration office today, and they didn't even ask why I wanted it."

"Why should they?" Vladimir shrugged and drank the rest of his wine. "You're considered one of the most promising young biologists in England."

"Stop telling him that!" Charlotte admonished Vladimir. "He's becoming horribly conceited."

Ignoring her, Paul crossed to the table and spread the plans to the university building out in front of them, pushing glasses out of the way. "That has nothing to do with my talent as a scientist," he told Charlotte severely. It's the things you keep saying to me in the night that are making me vain." A scarlet blush started up Charlotte's neck, and they all laughed as it crept up her cheeks to her pale hairline. Paul continued, "Come and look at this, everyone. We don't want one of you getting lost, do we?"

They all rose from their respective places at the table and gathered around Paul. All except Jerome, who remained where he was, drinking his wine. Paul looked up at him in surprise. "Jeri, don't you want to see this?"

Jerome dismissed him with a wave of his wine glass. "I don't need to. If I get lost, I'll just float through the walls until I locate you again, or find my way outside."

"That should be convenient if one of us is following you," Vladimir retorted drily. Putting his glass down on the table, he careened around the room, pretending to smack himself into walls as he went. Finally, he fell down on the carpet as if he had knocked himself out. By this time they were all laughing, Charlotte and Robin almost uncontrollably.

"What were we saying about the Three Stooges, earlier?" Natalie asked no one in particular. One of the kittens scampered across the carpet and came to rest on Vladimir's chest, purring.

Chapter 29

It was later that night when Charlotte finally got up enough courage to ask Paul about going with her to All Saints' Way. It wasn't that she wanted him to, particularly; she was certain he would attempt to stop her from her purpose. She wasn't going to let anyone stop her, and that would start a fight. She didn't want to lose Paul, either.

They were lying in bed together. Paul was at his most mellow after sex, which he pursued with an almost frightening abandon. Charlotte had never known anyone like him, and had never known such satisfying lovemaking, either. But she realized there were aspects of her life Paul didn't approve of, and she wasn't willing to give them up -- what she was doing was too important to her, and she had never been much afraid of physical danger.

She knew he was trying to protect her, but didn't want him to. And she wasn't willing to become just another fashion photographer, taking pictures of beautiful men and women that would become obsolete after a few years. Well, she amended, to be fair there were some photographs that had become lasting fixtures in the art world, but Charlotte knew she was no Man Ray or Francesco Scavullo; her real talent lay in the streets and the underworld of London. She had to have photographs from All Saints to complete her showing at The Submarine Gallery, and she was determined to get them. "Paul . . .are you asleep?"

"No, love. Just thinking about our plans for next Thursday. A little worried, you know?"

"Didn't you tell me you were off work tomorrow afternoon?"

He pulled her more closely into his arms, and she lay with her head on his broad chest. "Yes, love. They're having some kind of a state inspection. Not," he ended bitterly, "that it will make any difference to those animals."

"Don't think about that now -- soon, we can do something ourselves. But will you be with me tomorrow, then?"

"Would you like me to be? What are your plans?"

"I'll be out taking photographs. I'd love you to come with me."

"Ok, sure. Doing a fashion shoot?"

This was it, Charlotte thought. She hugged him closely, as if she was afraid he would slip away into nothingness once she told him her plans, as Jerome might have. "No, some photos for my showing. I've only got a few more weeks."

Paul's body tensed, as if he knew what was coming. "And where will you be?"

"All Saints' Way."

He moved away from her and looked down, to see if she was serious or playing one of her numerous jokes on him. "No, you won't. Think of somewhere else. God knows there are plenty of street people in London; surely you haven't covered them all."

"No, that's true. I haven't been to All Saints'. I'm going tomorrow."

Paul sighed. He knew that tone of voice, and realized it was better for him to be with her, than if she went alone. "All right, Chari -- I'll come with you." He turned his back to her and put his head down on the pillow, as if he wanted to go to sleep.

But Charlotte could tell by the tense set of his shoulders and back that sleep wasn't what was on his mind -- she was, and how much trouble she was, how stubborn and independent. She couldn't let him drift into sleep thinking those things . . .

She put her arms around him, and snuggled against him. Though he pulled away, it was only a tentative movement. She ran one hand lightly up his leg and over his buttocks in a slow caress. This was repeated until she felt his muscles start to relax, and she pulled him down until he was lying flat on the bed. Sliding over him until she was half- covering his body, she continued stroking him until his arms came around her and began their own caresses of her body.

She moved down and cupped her breasts around his penis, which was rapidly becoming hard, and enlarged. Sliding up and down, she ran her tongue over the tip. He groaned and gripped her shoulders, then pulled her towards him so she was sliding up and over his body.

Putting her hand around him, she guided him inside of her, moving slowly. But he put both arms around her and pulled her down, fiercely, thrusting up inside her and imprisoning her in his embrace. His kiss was equally demanding, rough and unloverlike. His tongue moved quickly down her neck and flicked over her breasts, back and forth between them, until she felt she would explode. And he grew inside her until she thought she would burst. If this was her punishment for dragging him into the slums, she thought, she'd have to do it more often.

Vladimir lay watching Natalie sleep beside him. Their affair had progressed so quickly, he couldn't remember having spent any time thinking about it. At least, not much, and Vladimir was used to thinking a lot about things before he did them. Perhaps it was a reaction against his Russian upbringing amidst a noisy crowd of brothers, sisters, aunts, uncles and people he never did figure out the relationship for, in the city of Smolensk. Perhaps it was because, during his school years, he didn't have a lot of friends and came to rely on books and learning for companionship. He'd had relationships before, though he suspected that even though he was older than both Paul and Robin, his affairs had been far fewer than those two gentlemen.

That last wasn't difficult to explain, he thought with a self-deprecating chuckle. Paul and Robin could easily have moved into the spheres of international modeling or acting, even films, with no problem (perhaps they couldn't act, he amended, but that was hardly a problem with the first or the last) -- they were both incredibly good-looking. He knew himself to be only passable; there had been women who liked his face -- they usually referred to it as 'aesthetic' or 'pleasing'; even 'intelligent'. But Vladimir knew those qualities didn't usually win a girl like Natalie. He considered her the prettiest of the three women. She had a marvelous sturdiness (which appealed to his Russian nature) and a fragility of movement and persona that made him feel big and strong. This in itself was remarkable, given her height. He smiled down at her, wondering how he could have been so lucky -- and how long the luck would be with him.

"Have you finished staring at me, or do I have an enormous zit I missed?" Natalie's hazel eyes opened and gazed up at him questioningly. Then she smiled, and Vladimir's heart jumped up and down with delight.

He laughed. "Any blemish you had would be a beautiful one. It's a rather unromantic thought, though -- completely ruined my mood."

"Ah, romance . . .come down here and tell me all about it." She pulled him into her arms and snuggled against him invitingly.

Chapter 30

The following day, Natalie planned to spend most of the morning and all the afternoon painting. She was neglecting her work shamefully, she knew -- the attractions of London and Vladimir combined had been her undoing. But the money she'd gotten from her court settlement wouldn't last forever, and while she was willing to do whatever she had to in order to survive, she was hoping that didn't mean serving drinks in a pub.

One painting was finished for her first show, and three others were in progress. Those, with the ones she'd shipped from the states, would make a respectable presentation. But if she sold some, or received orders for custom paintings, she would definitely need to increase her working hours.

Vladimir arrived at the house after lunch, to announce that he was flying to Berlin the day after the day they were to liberate the animals from the lab. He'd be gone a week, and would have to miss Dierdre's broadcast of the film he was planning to shoot of the 'liberation'. Since he wouldn't be able to announce himself as the filmmaker anyway it wasn't important that he be around for the broadcast, but Natalie had planned on them being in the studio audience together.

He sat in the sunshine pouring through her French windows and looked out over the green expanse of the communal lawn that the townhouse shared with the other houses on their block. Sipping coffee, he explained the need for the trip to Berlin. "I've been asked to do a documentary on all the East Berliners who are flooding into the West. The problem, of course, is that the social services in West Berlin and the rest of Germany are overloaded to the max, and they haven't been able to find jobs for all these people."

"No, I guess they should've expected that. But surely they'll disperse; they won't all stay in Berlin, will they?"

"At this point, who can say? I wonder if the entire country will be able to absorb them. Anyway, I'll be gone about a week."

"I'm sorry you won't be here for the broadcast of the 'liberation' film -- I'll video-tape it for you, of course."

"You'll be in the audience that night?"

"Oh, sure -- with Charlotte. Robin will be on the show, along with *Experimental Monkeys*. They'll be endorsing the liberation of the animals."

"Didi could lose her job over this, you know."

"Oh, I know. So does she. But I think she's found her cause, and she's gonna stand behind it. And it's not as if she needs the money -- if she loses the job, then she'll go on to become a celebrity in the animal rights field. She was born to be a star of one kind or another."

"What do you mean, she doesn't need the money?"

"Please don't tell Robin I told you this; not even Paul knows. Didi's very wealthy -- she comes from one of the richest families in the U.S."

"Then why is she living here with you?"

"She just wants to. She's paying all the rent -- she won't let Chari or me pay anything, even though that was the arrangement we made when we first came."

"I did think this house was a little lavish for three artists; but I know Charlotte does well at fashion photography, and Didi probably gets a good salary from the show. I figured you were squandering your court settlement on your part."

"Well, I'm not! So hah! Shows how much you know -- I'm not as dumb as I look."

Vladimir fixed her with a smoldering look, that made him resemble nothing so much as a villain from a silent movie. "You don't look dumb at all. Sexy, desirable and almost irresistible . . ."

Natalie waved her brush at him. "Don't you even think about it! Stay in your corner."

"I'm not in a corner." Vladimir grinned.

"I'm warning you; don't move from that chair."

"A challenge!" Vladimir leaped up, depositing his coffee mug on a small table. "You should know that Russians can't resist a challenge . . ."

"No!" Natalie brandished her paint brush like a sword, waving it in front of her. "I told you I have to paint this afternoon."

"You can go back to it -- you'll be better, then." Laughing, Vladimir picked up another brush and daubed it in Natalie's palette, picking up a coating of turquoise paint. He held it in front of him and jousted with Natalie's brush, which had black paint on it. With his longer reach he was able to daub a streak of paint across her already splattered sweatshirt. "A hit! You must yield to me, varlet!"

"Oh!" Natalie lunged at him and painted a black streak down his face. Then she started to laugh, dropping the brush into a glass of clear liquid. "Now you look like Adam Ant!"

Vladimir deposited his brush next to hers and snatched her into his arms. "You are my prisoner!" He kissed her, smearing the black paint over the two of them.

"Now we'll have to take a shower."

"Not a bad idea! Let's do it now."

"I give up -- as long as you promise to let me paint, later."

"I'll even bring you food; you'll never have to leave this room again."

"Except now, to take the shower."

"A short respite, merely."

"Not too short, I hope."

Chapter 31

The following evening, Paul told the assembled group the story of his trip to All Saints Way with Charlotte. He was the story-teller because they knew Charlotte would gloss over the troublesome bits, and they wanted to hear everything. Jerome was present, but seemed preoccupied, and Dierdre realized that they had been neglecting their ghostly friend and his mystery while they were occupied with their own problems and those of the animals trapped in the university lab.

"So, were you attacked by any street people or skinheads?" Vladimir asked him.

"Well, I had the feeling it was a little close there for awhile, but once they understood why we had come, they were pretty cooperative. Especially the skinheads -- what a bunch of poseurs they turned out to be!" Paul laughed, sipping his ale. He was more relieved that the episode was over than he was willing to reveal -- he'd really thought, for a few minutes there, that he'd be defending Charlotte's camera equipment and virtue against a group of the meanest characters he'd ever seen. "The punks were a little more difficult -- they wanted to be paid for having the photos taken."

"And did you pay them?" This from Natalie.

"No; Chari has a policy of not paying people -- she thinks it makes her artistic statement less pure, or something." When Charlotte opened her mouth to explain, Paul said to her, "No, you don't get to clarify the point at this time. My turn to talk." Then he waggled his finger at her.

"You're really enjoying this, aren't you?"

"Of course I am! How often do I actually get to talk without you interrupting me?"

Charlotte lapsed into wounded silence, drinking her own ale.

"The street people were ok -- I feel sorry for them. Most of them seem so lost, so frightened. Frightened of everything, as if all they want is for the world to go away and leave them alone."

"That pretty much sums it up," Robin put in. "If you'd been treated the way they have, you'd feel the same."

"But why would they choose to live that way?" Vladimir seemed genuinely puzzled. "Do they choose it, do you think; or is it just a series of events that draws them lower and lower until they're in a pit they can't dig their way out of?"

"Probably the latter." Robin swirled the remains of his ale around the glass. "People prefer to think it's the former, because they want to believe it could never happen to them. But we all live so close to disaster, it could descend on us any day. Anyone could end up that way, given the uncertainty of circumstances in life."

The people in the room nodded their agreement but Vladimir thought, watching Dierdre, that she was the one person in their group this could never happen to. He wondered what it felt like to know there was always that cushion of security, holding you up. She never behaved any differently than the rest of them, however, and he admired her for that.

"The important thing is," Paul concluded, "That Chari got some good photos for her show. It's gonna be a big success, don't you think?"

They all agreed that the show should impress even the jaded 'in' crowd of London, whoever they happened to be that month. Or perhaps that definition should be 'that week', considering the alarming rate at which trends and people passed in and out of the limelight in the mecca of the strange and wonderful. Now Dierdre said, "You know, we never finished Jerome's story. Perhaps now would be a good time, before we become too involved with the lab animals."

Natalie nodded. "Yes, I'd love to know the end, even though we already know the outcome. But Jeri, now we know Charles Brent was the killer, how come you're still with us? Wasn't that the curse, that you had to discover who your murderer was?"

"There's no such thing as curses, Nat," Jerome answered drily. "It was a self-imposed quest, you see. And I'm not fully satisfied as to the outcome -- at least, I think Charles Brent did it, but I'm not sure. I guess that's why I'm still here."

Robin frowned. "Are you sure you want to go, Granddad? Maybe you just like it here, with all these pretty girls."

They all laughed, but Jerome replied, "No doubt about that, descendent mine. But I do want to be with Alicia -- she was the only girl for me. When the time is right, I'll know. And it's coming soon -- perhaps I'm staying to rescue the animals, and when that's accomplished, then I'll be ready. I was never able to do all the things I wanted to do in life; this way, at least I can do one good thing in death."

Even though they had been living in a house with a ghost for several months, mortality was something the three women hadn't contemplated. At least, not their own mortality. Still in their late 20's and early 30's, it wasn't something they were ready for; not yet. But this casual remark on the part of their dead friend made them re-evaluate their roles in life and their accomplishments thusfar. Natalie made a mental note to finish her painting the following day.

"Enough of that, Jerome -- don't be so morbid. Perhaps the next time, you'll be allowed to do all those things. What about the story?" Dierdre wanted to get away from the subject of death.

But Vladimir had heard her comment, and thought something about it was rather strange. "What did you mean, Didi -- about 'next time'? Are you talking about reincarnation?"

"Of course. Surely you realized Jerome will be coming back as someone else?"

"Actually no, I didn't realize it. How do you know?"

"Because he told me so." Dierdre seemed perplexed by his bewilderment.

The other two women took his explanation as fact, so they had obviously been involved in Dierdre's discussion with Jerome about the subject of his 'coming back'. But the three men seemed intrigued by this idea -- Vladimir was the only one it seemed to distress, however.

"I don't understand," he said. "Do you mean it's true - - that we'll all be coming back as another person? That we live more than one life?"

"Of course," Jerome replied. "I thought everyone knew that, now."

"How could they?" Paul asked. "So many of them are Christians."

The way he said it made Vladimir sit up straighter. "Wait a minute -- I'm a Christian. Am I the only one in this room?" The rest of them stared at him as if he had confessed to being a crack dealer. The silence told him. "Oh, I guess I am. Natalie, I just assumed . . ."

"Sorry, love. I was brought up Russian Orthodox, but I gave it up years ago."

"I don't suppose you'd consider . . ."

"Afraid not. I don't mind if you believe in it, though. I'm pretty open-minded about these things."

Vladimir frowned, as if he couldn't really believe the things that were being said. Robin interrupted, impatiently. "Can we leave Vlad's problems with traditional myth-systems until later? I want to know about reincarnation. I mean, this isn't just another one of the pseudo-intellectual discussions about the after life. We've got a real representative right here before us. Tell us about it, Jeri."

"Not much to tell, I'm afraid. I mean, I didn't see an awful lot.

But when I died, I went to a hospital trauma center. You see, they have different places for the different categories of people -- those who know they're going to die are more prepared than people like me, who were taken by surprise. Mostly murder victims, where I was. I spent some time there, being counseled about my death -- they told me I was in shock. I was, of course. I was an unusual case, even for a murder victim -- most people aren't killed on their wedding night.

"From there, I went to a reprocessing station. That's where people are assigned -- most rest for fifty or a hundred years before being recycled. At the station, I had some tests -- they called them 'psychological evaluations' - - and it was discovered that I wasn't satisfied with the way my life had ended. Not surprising, since I had been murdered. Then I was given the choice of resting, or returning here until I solved the murder. They have a wicked sense of humor, though -- they wouldn't let me out of the house once I arrived. Until you three moved in. I guess you were the catalysts - - but it took a hell of a long time for you to get here."

Robin frowned. "Do you mean they were using terms like 'psychological evaluation' in 1811?"

"Oh, yes. And the information was stored in those machines you call computers. At least, I know what they're called now. When I asked about them then, I was told to forget about them -- that they hadn't been invented yet and wouldn't be for another 150 years."

They stared at him in stunned silence. Finally, Vladimir burst out, in a voice filled with angst, "I don't believe it! It's a joke -- he's putting us out."

"That's 'putting us on', Vlad. And I don't think he is," Natalie retorted, trying not to laugh.

Jerome looked puzzled. "What's wrong, Vlad? Does it bother you, the thought of coming back?"

"Well, I've always believed what they told me in church."

Paul seemed disbelieving. "How can such a hip guy be so

credulous? Surely you realized the universe couldn't be that simplistic."

"I never thought about it. I'm going to go home, and think about it now. How many times do we have to come back, Jeri?"

"As many times as is necessary. Some people need a lot more training than others."

"That means we'll be stuck with Hitler's soul for eternity."

"Who's Hitler?"

"Never mind, Jeri. All I meant was that people who commit murders and torture people -- they have to come back a lot more times, right?"

"Of course. Particularly the ones who persecute others in the name of religion. They don't like that, on the other side. Gives them a bad name, you see?"

"Them?" Vladimir was like a man who didn't want to know anymore about a nasty subject, but couldn't help from asking. "What do you mean, 'Them'? Isn't there a God?"

"Not in the way you think of a God. There's no one entity -- in a way, we're all God. But the souls who have passed over, who have finished their training, so to speak - - they are the representatives of the Universe. So will we be, when we finish here."

"Are you finished, Jeri? Will this be your last life?" Dierdre poured wine for everyone at the table with the exception of Vladimir, who held his hand over his glass.

"Oh, I doubt that. I can hardly say I know enough to be finished. Of course, it's not my choice. I'll have to pass through evaluation first. I've avoided that for all these years, because I chose to come back and solve the murder."

"And Alicia? What of her? Has she come back, by now?"

"Probably. I was hoping she might wait for me . . .but it's been such a long time. She undoubtedly became restless."

"Perhaps you can find her again," Charlotte offered.

"That's only allowed in very special cases, and the applicant has to apply for a dispensation of the rules."

"I'd say you're a special case."

Vladimir stood abruptly. "If you'll excuse me, I think I should go home, now. All this has been something of a shock -- I'd like some time to contemplate it." He put his wine glass down on the table. When Natalie rose to accompany him to the door, he waved her back. "I can see myself out. You'll call me, about the raid on the lab?"

"Of course." She looked crestfallen.

"Goodnight, everyone." He turned and left the room, and soon they heard the front door closing.

"Did that seem like he meant 'goodbye', instead of 'good night'?" Paul sounded amazed.

"Yes, it did. I'm sorry, Nat." Dierdre put one of her hands over the other woman's, and clasped it.

"That's ok. Better to know now, rather than later. I don't have time to deal with him, what with everything that's going on. He could have chosen a better time, with Chari and I both having our shows next month."

"That's a man for you -- they all have bad timing," Dierdre told her.

"Thank you so much," Robin muttered into his wine. Dierdre gave him a blinding smile, and he stuck his tongue out at her. "Well, let's see . . .this discussion could take all night."

"But what about finishing Jeri's story?" Chari protested. "How about tomorrow night?" Dierdre asked.

"I can't be here," Robin said. "Not until the night of the break-in. We're going into the studio, and it's hard to get time off. Sorry, love."

"Then you'll have to miss it. We'll fill you in -- we've neglected

Jeri too long -- he has to have a chance to finish his story and get the hell out of this house."

They nodded in agreement, even Robin. But Jerome looked despondent at the thought. Their discussion did continue until three in the morning . . .

Natalie never bothered to go to bed, that night. She thought about it, but instead turned on all the lights in her studio and painted until the sun made its' watery appearance over the rose garden. Then she went down to the kitchen, cleaned everything up from last night (her mother had been right when she claimed housework was cathartic) and made some coffee. Carrying a large mug of it and a plate of dark-chocolate digestive biscuits, she returned to the studio. She sat on the little wicker couch and munched the cookies, looking at the canvas she had been painting.

She frowned. It certainly wasn't anything she'd done before. Or even thought about doing. The colors were dark, and murky -- she usually favored bright colors that announced themselves boldly. And it had been a long time since she'd painted in oils -- for the last few years she'd preferred watercolors and acrylics. But it was interesting; perhaps it would even be good. And there were certainly some bright colors in it, but only reds and oranges, and these would be flames and blood. Not, in all, a cheerful painting . . .but if it was finished in time for her show, it would become the focal point. Now there was nothing to distract her (a man named Vladimir, to be exact) she could get the painting done and participate in the raid on the lab. The decision she'd made after Brice left had been the right one -- men were definitely not worth the bother.

Chapter 32

The following night, their group was diminished by two. By the time Dierdre arrived home from taping her second show (a deadly boring new group called THE BIG SOUTH, who were good musicians but had nothing to say for themselves) Paul and Charlotte were in the kitchen fixing dinner. Natalie was painting, as she had been the entire day -- it was Paul's claim that she was substituting her brush for Vladimir. Dierdre thought this was a good thing; she could have chosen a bottle of gin. Charlotte had made a trip to the library that day, and was ready to present the remainder of the information about Jerome and the Earls of Arden. This wasn't a great deal, but they were hoping they would be able to piece together the remainder of the story and convict Charles Brent almost 200 years after the crime.

Jerome didn't make an appearance until after dinner, and then he seemed depressed. By the time they were all settled in the main reception room and Charlotte had produced her notes, Dierdre was wondering what was wrong with their friend. "Jeri, don't you want to do this? You do need to know the outcome, don't you?"

"I know the outcome," he replied caustically. "I was murdered."

"If you have that attitude, then why are you here?" Paul asked.

"I've only developed it lately. It doesn't seem fair to have to leave just as I've found a purpose in life. Well, in death. I could help you -- all these years and I've never been able to help anyone before. I just found you; I don't want to go, now."

"I think you should, Jeri. After all, by staying here with us you're denying yourself the opportunity of being born again. How do you know what you might be in your next life? Your soul is obviously very evolved -- maybe you'll save the earth from our wastefulness and profligacy."

Jerome looked over at Paul, and sighed resignedly. "You're right. After the raid on the lab, I'll go."

"How will you do that?" Charlotte asked. "I mean, what would the procedure be?"

Jerome looked startled for a moment, then laughed. "Do you know, I don't have the slightest idea! I guess, when the time comes, I'll just start asking the air -- perhaps I'll get an answer. If I don't, I guess I'll have to stay."

Dierdre frowned. "Doesn't sound like a very good system. Didn't they give you any instructions?"

Jerome shook his head. "I'll bet they didn't think I'd be here this long. Maybe they just waited, thinking I'd start yelling for someone to get me out of here. When I never did, they forgot about me. Or, they're still waiting."

Now Charlotte laughed. "OK. It's time to finish that story, so you'll be ready to go when the time comes. I've been to the library today, and I got all the rest of the information available on your family. It wasn't much, since Didi and Nat got most of it on their trip. I do have one surprise, though . . .I'll let you know what it is when you get to that point in the story."

"I don't know how much more I can tell," Jerome replied. "As I told you before, we were married in June of that year. At St. George's in Hanover Square . . .one of the ugliest churches in London, and the one quite incongruously chosen by the ton for their nuptials. If people of my class were married in London, they were married out of St. George's. It was a clear day, I remember . . .a miracle itself, in London."

Chapter 33

London, 1811

It was a clear, warm day in June, 1811. St. George's in Hanover Square was surrounded by a crowd of onlookers, waiting for the guests to arrive at a fashionable wedding. A perch-phaeton, decorated with multi-colored ribbons, signalled the arrival of the groom and his men; a few minutes later a closed carriage pulled up to the curb, and the bride emerged, her train held by a maid.

Alicia Mannerly was everything that could be asked for in a bride. Blond, young and beautiful, with sparkling blue eyes and a curvaceous figure that filled her ivory gown to the admiration of the crowd. Her face was aglow with the serenity that only love can bring. Lady Sarah, dressed in dusty rose, followed her from the carriage, holding her picture hat with one hand.

It fell to Sarah's brother Vermont to give Alicia to Jerome, a circumstance she felt was singularly unfortunate, since Sarah didn't like her brother and the feeling was reciprocated. A country vicar, Vermont had always tormented Sarah with his boring life and a catalogue of her inadequacies. She had, since she was old enough to talk, responded with a scathing critique of everything about Vermont, from his lack of stature to his bulbous nose. The beauty in the Mannerly family had been confined to the female side.

But the wedding that day was everything a bride could have wanted; ten bridesmaids in varying shades of rose, a church filled with hothouse flowers, and a wedding breakfast (served all afternoon) at Jerome's townhouse. Then the bride and groom left for his estate in Hampstead, where they would spend the first week of their honeymoon before journeying on to the continent, newly made safe for English visitors by the exile of Napoleon.

Unlike most wedding nights in the 19th century, there was no fear on the part of Alicia. She had already become the lover of her bridegroom; they could only learn to know one another better, now. It was late when they fell asleep, wrapped together. Even later, Jerome was awakened by a noise he couldn't place or recognize -- it was too early for the servants to be awake, and the sound was strange . . .furtive. So he slid out from where Alicia was slumbering beside him, and something made him lean down to kiss her forehead before he picked up the fireplace poker and went slowly into the hall, peering down the darkness.

He saw the men as they jumped onto him; at least, he saw their faces. He had never seen them before, of course -- they were bully-boys, and he recognized them as such. He caught one a good blow to the head with the poker before the other stuck the blade into his back, just where it would pierce the heart. Alicia Mannerly Kennington disappeared from London the night her husband was killed, and wasn't seen in polite society for nearly a year, when she resurfaced as the widow of her cousin, Charles Brent. What she endured that year was more than a less heroic woman could have survived; but survive Alicia did, and what kept her going through all the abuse and isolation was the knowledge that she carried Jerome's child inside her. She knew it was his, because Charles Brent didn't come near her, after the night his men took her to the house he had rented in Upper Wykham. And he didn't come near her because she told him she was already pregnant. Although he didn't believe her, he kept her prisoner in the house for two months, until he was certain she told the truth. Then he hated her for the child she carried -- his hatred as obsessive as the love he had once felt, the love that gave him the courage to hire men to kill the Earl of Arden. He would gladly have killed her, too, but was afraid of Lady Sarah -- afraid that she would go to her influential friends in the government, and he would hang for the death of a peer. So he kept Alicia guarded until her child was born, but he forced her to marry him three months before that date. When she produced a son, Charles claimed the child as his own, and the Earldom passed on to the next surviving heir; a distant cousin. Shortly after the birth of George Brent in 1812 (he who should have been the sixth Earl of Arden), Charles Brent left Alicia at his country estate in Sussex and journeyed into Scotland. A collector of antique snuff boxes, Brent was going to visit another collector, who had obtained a particularly valuable box that had belonged to Charles II. In his absence, Alicia managed to escape from the estate with the help of two chambermaids, who accompanied her and baby George to Lady Sarah's townhouse in London. Sarah had believed Alicia dead (though only Jerome's body was found in the house in Hampstead, it was believed that Alicia must be dead also) and hadn't wanted to think about what could have happened to her niece before she died. No one could imagine who would break into the house of the Earl of Arden, manage to sneak past his servants and kill him -- then kidnap his wife. Sarah knew it was Charles, but had been unable to prove it -- and she thought he had killed Alicia, too.

It was fortunate that Sarah hadn't yet left for the opera when her butler came to inform her that Alicia was waiting in the drawing room, accompanied by two maids and a baby. Her silver powder brush fell from her suddenly lifeless fingers into the bowl of Chinese rice powder, scattering the white concoction over the cherrywood of her dressing-table. She lurched to her feet, caught her slippers in the train of her blue satin dress, and would have fallen to the carpet if Smallwood, her butler, hadn't caught her in his arms.

"Thank you, Smallwood." Sarah released herself from the constriction of her train, and straightened the front of her dress. "I'll come with you now." She barely made it down the steps, clutching the bannister to keep herself upright until she achieved the marble of the foyer. She knew that Colonel Robert Johnstone, her newest cicisbeo, would be arriving any minute to escort her to the Covent Garden production of Tosca; before he did so she should be composed.

That newly-shored composure vanished when she saw Alicia, clad in what appeared to be one of the maid's gowns and thinner than her aunt had ever seen her before, standing before the fire in the yellow parlor, shivering and clutching a small baby in her arms.

"Ali!" Sarah launched herself at the younger woman, gathering her and the baby into her embrace and careless of her evening gown. "Where have you been all this time? I was convinced you had died with Jerome."

"I wish I had! Charles Brent kidnapped me, and I've been kept a prisoner on his estate all this time. This is Baby George -- he's Jerome's. I can't prove it, of course. And Charles will say the baby is his, even though he was born three months after he forced me to marry him."

Stunned, Sarah stared at her niece in silence for a moment. Then she took her hand and led her over to a sofa. They sat side-by-side, Baby George lying between them. The two maids had been taken to the kitchen by the housekeeper for their own refreshment. "Let us take this a bit more slowly, shall we? What happened the night Jerome was murdered? His body was discovered by the servants, in the morning, but you were gone."

"Two men gained access to the house -- I don't know how. They struck Jerome down when he went to investigate -- at least, I think that was what happened -- I saw his body lying in the hall, with the fireplace poker beside it. They caught me while I was still asleep, and one of them shoved a cloth into my mouth before I had the chance to scream. I kicked the other one, but they managed to carry me out into the hallway -- that was when I saw Jerome. The sight of his dear body lying there, and I didn't even know if he was dead or alive . . ." Her voice broke on a sob, but she choked it back and continued. "I realized later, of course, that Charles had hired the men to kill Jerome. But at the time, I wasn't certain -- that gave me renewed strength, and I began to fight them again. But they shoved a rag soaked in chloroform under my nose, and I lost consciousness. The next thing I remember, I was lying in a bed in a house somewhere; I never discovered where it was.

"The following day I was taken to Charles' estate in Sussex, and I've been there ever since."

For a moment, Sarah was too stunned to reply. "Do you mean he's been keeping you a prisoner all this time? The baby is Jerome's?"

"Just look at him."

Sarah took the baby and gazed down at him. He had the same black curls, the white skin, even the firm jaw. And piercing blue eyes, that stared up at Sarah with unblinking gravity. She blinked her own, trying to keep herself from crying. "Oh, lord. It's Jerome."

"He's the only thing that's kept me going. I think Charles wanted to kill him, but he was afraid, after Jerome's murder. I guess he worried someone would come after him. I kept wishing it would happen, but I finally realized no one had a reason to suspect him, with me presumed dead."

"I wondered why I never saw him in town, but I suppose I was too grateful for his absence to actually think deeply on it, and I was consumed with grief, for so long afterwards -- I thought the two people I loved most in the world were both dead on one night. Damnation! If only I had known, I could have saved you so much pain and humiliation. Since he forced you to marry him, I suppose you've been constrained to share his bed as well."

Alicia shrugged. "At least I haven't conceived by him. I certainly wouldn't call what he does making love, after Jerome . . .it's over. Nothing will make me go back to him, even if I am legally his wife."

Sarah was indignant. "I should certainly hope not! Why on earth do you think I would want you to? I'll summon Robert -- he will know what to do."

"Who -- who's Robert?"

Sarah laughed. "My latest amour, child. But also a Colonel on the staff of the Regent. If anyone knows how to handle this situation, it will be Robert Johnstone. Now, I'm sure you are hungry and tired. Let's take care of those two problems immediately, and leave the rest until later." She put her arm around Alicia, who leaned on her shoulder and closed her eyes.

Chapter 34

"No! Please stop -- I can't listen to anymore!" Jerome sobbed heartbrokenly, putting his face down into his hands. Charlotte stared over at him in consternation.

"I know it's horrible, Jeri, but the best part is still to come."

"What best part -- I was murdered and my wife was kidnapped and forced into marriage by the man who arranged to have me killed! No more, ladies -- I cannot bear it, this night. I thank you for your research on my behalf. Somehow, I believed that knowing who had put an end to my life would make it easier; but it hasn't. It's worse, because I can never be revenged on the low dog."

He started to fade, and Charlotte reached out to restrain him, the book falling to the carpet. "No, Jeri -- don't go yet! Let me finish the story! Damn -- he's gone!"

"Can you blame him?" Paul shook his head in sympathy. "I'd feel the same way, in his place. What good is knowing the truth if there's nothing that can done about it?"

"That's just it, Paul -- if he'd waited then he would've known that Sarah and Alicia had enough revenge on Charles Brent to satisfy even Jerome. Jeri! Come back!"

But Jerome didn't reappear. "Where did you learn all that stuff, Chari?" Dierdre asked her. "We never found the end of the story, or even more than a brief mention."

"It was all in this book." Charlotte handed Dierdre the volume from which she had been reading.

"Strange Stories of 18th and 19th Century England. Well, I guess this qualifies as a strange story, though I doubt the people who wrote the book know just how strange."

"You don't even know the ending yet -- that's what makes it really wierd. Look -- read from that point, there." Charlotte opened the book and pointed to the middle of the page. Dierdre started to read to herself. "Not to yourself -- Paul and Natalie want to know the ending, too!"

"Oh, sorry. Let's see . . .'A week after Alicia Mannerly Kennington showed up at Lady Sarah's house, Charles Brent arrived and attempted to claim his bride. But they were ready for him . . .'"

Chapter 35

London, 1811

"Now, are you certain you understand the plan, Ali?" Lady Sarah sat on the striped satin sofa, sipping her ratafia. "Of course I do. But how will we know when Charles arrives? I mean, it could be hours or days or weeks. Surely Robert can't be available all the time."

Robert bowed from his place at the mantle, where he was leaning against the white stone and drinking his brandy. "It would give me the greatest pleasure in the world to be constantly in this house -- particularly during the night hours . . ." at this he winked roguishly at Sarah, who smiled at him seductively. "However, it will unfortunately not be required of me. You see, I have two of my men trailing Brent. He is at present still in the country, but now you have begun to appear in society again, I wager he'll attempt to snatch you back. Strange man," he ended, "Imagine wanting someone so much you'd murder to get them, and hold them prisoner for a year. Rather takes the fun out of it, I would have thought."

Alicia choked slightly on her own ratafia. "You have the most wonderful way of understating everything, Colonel Johnstone."

"Please, dear girl -- call me Robert. After all, we are planning to avenge your husband's murder here . . .with another murder."

"Do you think it's wrong?"

Alicia sounded worried. "Certainly not. If the man wasn't a coward I'd call him out, but I recall Sarah telling me Sir Jerome already tried that, and it didn't work."

"Only because I wouldn't let them do it. I wish I had, now -- Jerome was a crack shot. Charles would have been dead, and Jerome would still be alive . . ." She trailed off, wistfully. "You know Jerome wouldn't have killed him, Ali. He was too honorable. The problem with honorable men is that they expect everyone to behave the same way."

It was another two weeks before Robert received a message from his men that Charles Brent had arrived in London. He was staying at a fashionable hotel called Limmer's -- Alicia wondered why he wasn't staying at his own townhouse, but Sarah knew it was in the hope they wouldn't learn of his arrival. Robert came to the house prepared to stay until Charles showed, occupying one of the guest bedrooms. The two men who had been assigned to follow Charles were still on his trail, but he wasted little time in confronting Sarah regarding Alicia's whereabouts.

When he presented himself at Sarah's house, Charles was shown into a sitting room and left alone for half-an-hour. There was no offer of refreshments. When Sarah came in, he was in a foul mood. "Well, Aunt Sarah -- is this the way you greet your guests? I've been left here with no fire and no refreshments for over 30 minutes."

Sarah regarded him coldly. "Why no, Charles -- this is not how I greet my guests, and well you know it. You, however, are not my guest. You're a murderer, and I'm going to see you hang for it."

Charles rose slowly. Now he knew Alicia had come to Sarah, but he hadn't realized she would have the courage to accuse him of murdering her husband. "Nonsense. I can prove my whereabouts on the night Kennington was killed."

Sarah sat in a chair, smiling. "I never mentioned Jerome Kennington, Charles. But you wouldn't have done it yourself, would you? No, you're too much of a coward for that. You hired men to do it, and then you kidnapped Alicia. You kept her prisoner for nearly a year and then forced her to marry you. Her baby is Jerome's son, and you have attempted to name him your own. You are the most despicable worm alive today, and it's my misfortune to be related to you. Get out of my house, and wait for Justice to find you. I promise you, it will -- but not until everyone in society knows what you did."

Charles jumped, and was across the room in two strides. He jerked Sarah out of her chair by the arm. "Do you really think I'd let you do that to me, after all I went through to get Alicia? I'll kill you, too -- and if Alicia is in this house, I'll drag her back to the country and keep her there forever."

Sarah fought with him, wondering where the hell Robert was and why he hadn't entered with his men. "Let go of me, you crazy man! This house is full of my servants -- all I have to do is scream and they'll overpower you. And Alicia isn't here -- we knew you'd come looking for her. You're too much of a fool to think of the consequences of your actions."

"Then I guess I can't let you scream, can I?" Charles put his hand over Sarah's mouth and stared around the room, wondering what the best means of escape would be.

"Remove your hand from my aunt's mouth, Charles." Alicia's voice came from the doorway. Charles released Sarah in his surprise, and turned with a fury, only to be confronted by one of Jerome's pearl-handled duelling pistols. He remembered them well, as he had nearly looked down the barrel of one before. "Step away from her. Now! This pistol has a hair-trigger." Sarah gaped at Alicia in amazement. What was she doing there instead of Robert? Surely she wouldn't be able to shoot Charles . . .or would she? Her niece had proven to be singularly resilient.

Charles stepped away from Sarah, but smiled in a conciliatory way at Alicia. "Now, Ali, don't be foolish. Surely it's not worth hanging, just to kill me."

Alicia blinked her enormous blue eyes at him. "Hanging? Why, I have no intention of doing that. I found you attacking my aunt, and after everything that had happened, well, I guess I just had to protect her from you." At this, she discharged the pistol. She wasn't the best shot, and only hit Charles in the shoulder.

He laughed even as he clapped one hand over his coat to staunch the bleeding. "Stupid little fool! You can't do anything right, can you? I'm not even disabled. I can still drag you back home and lock you away forever."

Sarah rushed to the embroidered bell-pull and gave it a savage tug. Alicia had recovered from the considerable kick of the pistol and staggered forward again, dropping the pistol on the carpet. Charles turned to snarl at Sarah.

"Your damned servants can't do anything, Auntie -- Alicia is legally my wife!"

Reaching calmly into the pocket of her gown, Alicia drew forth the companion to the pistol. "If you recall, Charles," she said as she leveled the second pistol at him, "Dueling pistols come in pairs. Surely one more shot will do the job."

Charles stared at her in disbelief. "Haven't I suffered enough at your hands? I'm damned well not going to let you kill me after everything else -- none of this would have happened if you had just loved me instead of that damned Kennington!" He lurched forward in what he probably hoped was a lunge, but looked remarkably like a drunk attempting to climb stairs. Just as he reached out to grab Alicia's arm the pistol went off at point-blank range, sending the two of them shooting apart like bumper-cars at a carnival. Charles stared down at his chest in horror as an enormous crimson stain spread across his blue coat of superfine. Since the pistol had been discharged directly against his chest, the stain was surrounded by a ring of powder.

Sarah stared down as he slumped to the floor. "Well, Ali, you've certainly proved yourself a heroine. But where in the name of Hades is Robert?"

"He left a message with Smallwood -- he was called to an emergency meeting at Headquarters. That's when I decided to handle the matter myself. Actually," she said, dropping wearily into one of the velvet chairs, "I wanted to. And I thoroughly enjoyed it, even if I am a lousy shot."

Sarah started to laugh and cry at once. "You killed him; that's good enough for me. "You're free at last -- you and little George."

"I don't believe I'll ever be free until I'm reunited with Jerome."

Chapter 36

They were unable to summon Jerome for the next two days, and on Saturday Robin arrived to take Dierdre to the Virgin Records benefit. She agonized over her choice of outfit fully as long as she had done for her first broadcast, and finally settled on a strapless, fitted gown of hot-pink suede; suede so soft it draped across the front and down into an asymmetrical hem. Plain black velvet pumps and an enormous ruffled cape of black velvet completed her outfit.

When Robin arrived, he looked stunning in a black velvet tuxedo with a white, ruffled silk shirt. Dierdre thought that at this moment he resembled Jerome to an uncanny degree, now that he was dressed in clothes similar to those his ancestor had worn. She wished Jerome would put in an appearance, to see just how handsome his great-grandson to the 'nth' power could be. Robin whistled when he saw Dierdre. She managed to descend the stairs just as Charlotte let him into the entry- way, like a debutante from a Regency novel. Just like they did in Jerome's day . . .

"You look gorgeous," he said. "Everyone at the party will be jealous of me."

Dierdre laughed. "I'll bet the *women* will be jealous of me. Not only are you the handsomest man in London, but a rock star into the bargain. What more could a girl ask for?" Robin held Dierdre's black velvet cape for her to fasten the silk frogging in the front. Charlotte closed the door behind them, grinning as they went.

"He's not the most beautiful man in London, though," she said to herself. "Paul is. Maybe the second most . . ."

The Virgin Records party was being held at Stringfellows, one of the most exclusive and boring of the London clubs. The downstairs was frequently used for private parties, which meant the upstairs was always filled with people hoping to somehow infiltrate the elite. This night was no different, since Richard Branson, the youthful and energetic president of Virgin Ltd. counted a large number of rock and film stars amongst his friends.

What Dierdre didn't realize was that someone from her past would also be attending the party; someone who had harbored a grudge against her for five years and would be only too thrilled for the opportunity to cash in her chips.

When they arrived, Robin took Dierdre's cape and his own topcoat to the cloak-room near the entrance to the club. Dierdre stood waiting for him, watching the people move between the restaurant and the bar, and linger near the staircase that led down, to the Virgin Records party. It was then that she saw Sherry Reed, or thought she did. Sherry had been her assistant for several months when she was doing her television show in New York, but proved herself so inept (Dierdre suspected her use of Cocaine somewhat hampered her abilities) that Dierdre fired her. She wasn't certain if this was the same woman; if it was, she had put on weight (a change for the better) and dyed her hair platinum blond. And of course Dierdre never had occasion to see her assistant clad in a very tight leather minidress and stiletto-heeled patent leather pumps.

She watched the woman move from the bar, accompanied by a man who looked like an Arab, toward the staircase. As they descended the stairs Dierdre decided she must have been mistaken -- what would Sherry be doing in London, with an Arab?

Robin returned, and they themselves went down to the party. It was some time before Dierdre had a chance to look for the-woman-who-might-be-Sherry, since they were surrounded by people who wanted Robin to introduce them to Dierdre, and some who wanted Dierdre to do the same for them with Robin -- between the two of them, they seemed to know nearly everyone at the event. But finally, when everyone had greeted everyone else and drifted off to dance or drink, Dierdre spotted the woman on the dance floor with her Arab friend.

"Robin, do you see that woman in the black minidress?"

"Hmmm? Oh . . .hard to miss, I guess. How come you never wear clothes like that?"

"Because I don't want to be taken for a hooker."

"Good point. If I buy you that dress, will you wear it at home -- yours or mine?"

"What are you planning on doing, going up and asking the woman if you can buy the dress off her back?"

"Nah -- she's taller than you, and that would ruin the whole thing. Don't worry, I'll find one."

"I believe you. Do you know who she is?"

"Never seen her before -- but I'd say you've got her pegged right. The man she's with is Assore Rumani, the Iranian businessman."

"What kind of a name is Assore?"

"Arab, I guess. I always remember it because it sounds like his ass is sore, which, being an Arab, is probably accurate. Why did you ask me about the woman?"

"She looks like someone I used to work with in New York."

"You'd better hope she's not. I wouldn't wish old ass- sore on a friend of mine; I've heard some nasty stories about him."

"She's not exactly a friend. As a matter of fact . . .oh, never mind. Let's dance, shall we?"

"If we can find a square-inch that's free on the dance floor."

As she and Robin danced, Dierdre could feel Sherry's eyes on her. She was certain it was Sherry, and wondered if the woman would approach her. Was she bitter about losing her job and sinking so low in her career, if Robin's conjecture was right? And did she blame Dierdre for the sinking?

The music ended and they drifted off the dance floor to stand together and watch the next set of dancers. Dierdre had stopped watching Sherry, and was startled when she heard the woman's voice behind her. "Didi? Didi ??? It is you, isn't it?"

Dierdre turned reluctantly, and smiled at Sherry. "Hello, Sherry. I thought it might be you when I first saw you, but I wasn't sure. The hair is a big change."

Sherry tossed her hair away from her face as if immensely pleased with herself. "I'm surprised to see you here. Who's your handsome friend?"

"Robin Herald. Robin, this is Sherry Reed. We used to work together in New York."

Robin shook Sherry's hand. "Pleased to meet you. Are you still in television work?"

"Well, I'm sort of between jobs right now. Your face is very familiar -- you in television?"

"No, rock music. I'm with the band *Experimental Monkeys*."

"Oh, sure! I've seen you in videos. Nice music, but it's hard to recognize you without your makeup."

"

That's the idea. Where is your escort? I noticed you're here with Ass-sore."

Sherry frowned. "That's pronounced 'Azore'."

"Believe me, it's more accurate the other way."

"Have personal knowledge of that, do you?" Sherry asked him nastily.

"No, but I'm certain you do."

"I read an interview you did once. Aren't you part of that political group called 'Red Wedge'?"

"Yes, I am."

"And have you convinced Didi to give up her fortune, yet? Or do your views only pertain to Englishmen?"

"Fortune? What are you talking about? She took a reduction in pay to come to London -- the television here doesn't pay nearly as well as it does in the states."

"She hardly needs to worry about salary, does she? If she never earned another dime in her entire life, she could still support most of the people in this room. Surely you know, don't you?"

Dierdre could see that Robin was becoming annoyed with Sherry, and she wished she had told him about her money when she'd had the chance. She'd been afraid of losing him, and now the opportunity was being taken away from her. With Sherry being the informant, it was sure to look bad. "Sherry, I see your friend beckoning to you from the dance floor. Perhaps he wants you to dance with him."

Sherry turned and waved to Assore, and signalled to him that she would come in a moment. Dierdre sighed. She should have realized it wasn't going to be that easy, when Sherry had the prey in her sights.

"Do I know what?" Robin was starting to raise his voice.

"Why, that Didi comes from one of the wealthiest families in New York. She's a millionaire. Or I suppose that should be 'millionairess'."

Robin's face was stony. "I don't believe you."

Sherry had a tinkling, irritating laugh. Dierdre wanted to slap her so hard she'd fly over to Assore without taking a step. "If you think I'm lying, you should check on it. I don't know how many million, of course, but once you get past a couple, I figure it's not so important. Excuse me now -- I don't want my friend to start wandering around, looking for another lady."

"If her friend ever found himself in the presence of a lady, he wouldn't know what to do," Robin muttered.

"Can we go home, honey? This place has given me a headache."

"All right, but I'd like to know the truth. Was she lying?"

"No. Can we discuss this later?"

"I don't think we need to discuss it at all. I'll just take you home."

And so Charlotte, the first of the three friends to have a lover in London, was the only one to keep him. As the date for the raid on the lab neared, Natalie and Dierdre wondered if they would hear from their male friends, or if they had deserted not only them, but the suffering animals they pledged to rescue.

"Let's get drunk." Dressed in a pair of faded black jeans and an oversized white tee-shirt, Didi sat on one of the satin couches, her legs over one end. She was thinking, for the thirtieth time, how incredibly boring British television was and how nice it would be when they finally got cable. Knowing the British sense of timing, however, they'd use most of the stations to run more incredibly boring documentaries. "I can't stand this stupid show -- I can't even understand what the people are saying."

Natalie, wearing her own paint-splattered jeans and a sweatshirt with the arms cut off, switched off the television. "They manage to have remotes here, but nothing to watch once you turn the television off. Do we have any scotch in the bar? A serious drunk needs scotch."

Didi shuddered. "I'm not *that* depressed. I'll take Vodka -- I'll get drunk and I won't barf all over the furniture. Better yet, let's go down to a pub in the village."

"Are you nuts? All the yobboes will try and pick us up."

"No they won't -- we'll go just the way we are, and we won't even wear any makeup. The last thing I need right now are men -- I'm liable to brain one of 'em with a beer bottle." Didi and Natalie staggered out of The Blue Owl just after the last call, grateful they had taken a minicab rather than driving themselves. They were trailed by their 'court' of men, ranging in age from twenty to forty. Didi was wrong about her assessment of their clothing -- when they arrived at the pub, the nicest they could find, all the women were dressed similarly. This being the case, Didi and Natalie immediately became standouts. They attracted the attention of the men and the dislike of the women. They were fortunate the pub was in Hampstead rather than Mile End or Elephant and Castle, where the women might have physically attacked their competition.

Riding home in the cab, Natalie started to laugh drunkenly. "So much for that plan -- obviously those men like all women."

"At least the ones who can play darts and billiards. Between us, we kept them busy for hours. I even managed to forget they were men."

"How many asked for your number?"

"None -- I announced at the beginning of the first game that I was feeling no love for men, and if any of them were looking for women they could go elsewhere. You would've thought that would reassure their female friends, but they seemed to resent it a lot more than the men. How many asked you for the number?"

"Ten, I think. I said I'd give it to whoever could beat me at darts -- the only one who could was in his sixties and had his wife with 'im!" They both started to laugh.

"Vlad and Rob should see us now -- we'll show 'em we can do without men!"

"Sure, what do we need 'em for? We've got the cats -- and soon we'll have dogs, too!"

Chapter 37

It was Vladimir who came to his senses first, probably because it was much easier for him to accept that Natalie had no religious conviction than it was for Robin to accept Didi lying to him. Vlad telephoned the day before the 'animal rescue' was set to begin, but Natalie refused to talk to him. The three girls were in a particularly gruesome mood, occasioned by the loss of two male friends and Jerome, who hadn't been around since the revelation of Alicia's suffering after his death. But Vlad wasn't one to give up easily, and he showed up on the doorstep of the house approximately two hours later, carrying a strangely-shaped box wrapped in gold paper. Charlotte answered the door, and in this Vlad was fortunate, because she was the only one of the three who had no personal gripes with the male half of the universe. Just to be safe (in case Natalie had answered the door and been in favor of violence) he was holding the box in front of his face when it opened.

"Why hello, box. So glad you could come -- I haven't seen you in some time. You've got a new wrapping, I see. Very becoming."

Vladimir lowered the box slowly, grinning at Charlotte from above it. "Hello, Chari. I came to see Natalie."

"Gee, I never would've guessed. She's in her studio -- she's been there ever since you walked out, except for her nightly forays down to the pub to get drunk with Didi and their crowd of admirers. Done some great stuff for her show. Here, come in."

She stepped back, and Vladimir came into the entry-way. "I feel really bad about that -- I know I over-reacted. I think it was such a shock, you know?"

"How come? It made a lot of sense to me."

They walked together, through the entryway and into the second reception room.

"Well," Vladimir replied, "I have to admit that once I thought about it, I realized it actually does make sense. That took me a couple of hours. The rest of the time I've been trying to get my courage up to come back."

"If you'd come or called the next day, or even the next, Natalie wouldn't have been angry. But you waited five days . . .tomorrow is the rescue."

"I know, but do you think she'll talk to me anyway? I've brought her something special."

"You know where her studio is. Go take your chances. If it's any consolation, she wouldn't have been upset if she didn't really like you."

Vladimir grinned. "Now, that's true, isn't it?" He started off in the direction of Natalie's studio-room.

"Would you like to stay for dinner? We're having a planning session for the 'rescue' tomorrow."

"Perhaps I'd better wait and see what Natalie says."

But Natalie was perfectly willing to accept Vladimir's explanation of his absence, and put it down to the inability of men to accept new concepts. While he wasn't too pleased with this explanation (who wants to be lumped in with half the population of the planet), he wasn't about to take exception to it. Perhaps later, when he and Natalie were on a more solid foundation, he could mention that he preferred to be judged as a person rather than a man, thank you very much. And he made a mental note to express his own disdain of something women were unable to do -- just as soon as he came up with something. Robin, however, made no appearance right up until the hour before they were set to leave for the university on Thursday night. They had pretty much decided he was going to be a no-show, and Didi was angry that he would allow their personal differences to interfere with his intention to be part of the rescue team. Exactly one hour before they planned to leave, he arrived at the front door with a set of professional lock-picks (just in case all of Paul's keys didn't work) and a length of rope, attached to what appeared to be a link-and-pulley. The latter, he explained to Natalie when she let him in, would enable them to escape from an upstairs window if necessary. While she assured Robin that while she found his fore-thought to be admirable, she had no intention of escaping anywhere by means of a rope. If he wanted to play James Bond or Indiana Jones, then he was welcome to do so -- she was certain Vladimir would want to film the entire thing.

"Particularly the part where you fall on your head on the pavement."

"Oh, is Vlad here? And was tonight his first appearance?"

"You mean the way it is with you? No, he came back yesterday, bearing a box full of expensive acrylic paints and an apology. How about you?"

"No, I don't have any paints."

She stood in front of him as he started into the reception room, where he could see the rest of the group assembled and studying Paul's plan of the building. "Robin."

"Don't, Natalie. I'm not the one who should be apologizing, here. I didn't lie to Dierdre, and deceive her about who I am."

"She didn't do that, either! Did you ever ask her if she was a millionaire?"

"Oh, come on!"

"Well, did you? You may have noticed that she isn't in the habit of flaunting her wealth -- she thinks it's ill- bred and crass. Why should she just come out and tell you - - what business is it of yours, anyway?"

While this took Robin aback, he realized it was true. He and Dierdre hadn't known one another long enough to have made any kind of a commitment. Still, it seemed like a betrayal of sorts. "Well, it's not. But somehow, I feel as if she should have told me. Because she knows how I feel about wealth."

Natalie snorted. "All the more reason *not* to tell you. Besides, you knew after the television show that the two of you didn't agree on a lot of issues. But you came over here anyway, and it was obvious to all of us that you only came for one reason."

Robin seemed stunned by this revelation. "It was? But I didn't even know myself."

"Men are usually the last to know," was her cryptic comment, as she ushered him into the reception-room.

Chapter 38

Charlotte was anxious to finish telling Jerome his story, and made him promise not to disappear again until she had a chance to do so. He was amazed that there really was more of the story to come -- he had thought she was simply trying to make him feel better. They made a date to meet the following day.

The University of London was far more intimidating in the middle of the night than it had been during the day. The three girls had made the trip with Paul, who introduced them to his colleagues and earned their everlasting envy. But Jerome wasn't daunted by whatever might be lurking either outside or in -- and there was certainly no reason for him to be. They reached the third floor laboratory without any opposition, thanks to Paul's pass keys and his schedule of the security guards' rounds.

Dierdre carried a small lantern, which made a pool of light on the floor in front of them. Robin had his equipment hung over his shoulder; the small box of lock-picks in the pocket of his light-weight jacket. They were all dressed in black, including Jerome, even though he couldn't be seen by anyone but them. Vladimir had a mini-cam outfitted with what appeared to be a special attachment and custom lens, and a bag over his shoulder to carry the equipment when he completed his filming of the lab. Robin and Dierdre were careful to make certain they stayed at opposite ends of the group, which often entailed them jockeying between the other members.

"The lab is just down there," Paul told them. "The guard should have just made his rounds, which gives us about 30 minutes. We have to be gone by then."

"With the animals," Charlotte replied. They crept slowly down the corridor, wondering if one of the guards would choose to make a detour on his rounds and catch them entering the lab.

"With some of the animals, *Chari*." Paul sounded weary, as if they had been through the same argument a number of times. "You have to understand that some of them are too damaged to be able to survive without the drugs or equipment."

"Then we'll have to take them to The Humane Society tomorrow," Dierdre retorted. "We can't leave them here to suffer."

They reached the door to the lab. "Don't remove anything until I've filmed it," Vladimir instructed them. "And don't get in the way of the camera -- none of you must appear on the film."

"We know what to do, love," Natalie replied, smiling. Vladimir had given them the same instructions four times during the evening.

"I know. Just worried, a little. I wouldn't want you arrested."

Their smiles for one another were sickening, Robin thought irritably. The way Dierdre was glaring at him, he wished he hadn't come.

"This is it," Paul told them. "Let me open the door." He leaned over and unlocked it, aided by the light from Charlotte's lantern. As he swung the door open, they all craned their heads to see inside. They filed into the large room after him, leaving Jerome in the hallway on-guard. The only light to be seen was from the special attachment on Vladimir's mini-cam. Jerome was wondering if they had used up their thirty minutes when the door to the lab opened again, and Charlotte emerged, carrying a cage filled with small puppies. As Jerome peered into the cage he realized the puppies were very lethargic -- they must have been drugged, he concluded. She was followed into the corridor by Natalie, who carried a cage of rabbits, Dierdre was last, with what appeared to be a large cat asleep in a basket. The men didn't follow them.

Charlotte said, "Jeri, are you here? Is everything clear?"

Jerome materialized beside her. "No sign of any guards, but you've been in there an awfully long time. Charlotte, are you crying?"

There were tears running down Charlotte's face unheeded. "Some of the animals -- they were so ill we couldn't take them, not even to The Humane Society. The men are having to destroy them as humanely as possible."

Jerome glanced from Charlotte to Dierdre and Natalie, and realized Natalie was as pale as he was himself, and Dierdre's hands were shaking. "How disgusting," he replied. "What a world my descendants have made."

Charlotte wiped her face on the sleeve of her jacket, holding the cage precariously with one hand. "Was yours so much better?"

"Indeed not. I was hoping it would improve, however. Where are those damned men of yours?" As if on cue, the door to the lab opened and Robin came out into the corridor. He looked as if he was about to throw up.

"Have you . . .finished?" Dierdre asked him, their differences forgotten for the moment.

"Yes; Paul is cleaning up. I wish I hadn't eaten dinner; I feel like I might lose it." He turned his head sharply at the sound of someone walking down the corridor and heading for their wing.

"Someone's coming!" Natalie hissed.

"I knew you were too long," Jerome moaned. "Get back in the lab; I'll take care of them."

Robin took the cage of animals from Dierdre and ran into the lab, followed by the three women. Jerome faded as they closed the door behind him, and turned to wait for whoever was approaching. This turned out to be two security guards, carrying large lanterns.

"I know I heard noise in this area," the first guard said. "Someone's in the building."

"Of course someone is -- we are!" the second guard retorted contemptuously. "You've been drinkin' too many pints before work, mate."

Jerome crept forward to intercept them. Now he caught hold of one of the lanterns and jerked it out of the guard's hand, smashing it on the tile floor. The guards jumped back and stared down at the lantern in amazement.

"Did you see that?" demanded the guard whose lantern had been broken.

"I saw you drop your torch," the other replied. "It's like I said, too many pints."

"I didn't drop it! It was jerked outta me bloody hand!" As he screamed this at his companion, the other lantern was snatched out of the man's hand and smashed beside the first.

Jerome was giggling with glee, grateful they weren't able to hear or see him. "Now tell me that was *you* dropping *your* torch!"

"Joe, there's something in here besides us." Jerome stuck out his foot and tripped the guard named Joe, who fell sprawling to the floor.

"Joe! Are you all right?" the other guard asked, frantically trying to find his friend in the darkness.

Joe scrambled up again. "You're right, Ben -- get the hell outta here! We're gonna hafta call the police! Something just knocked me down."

"Do you suppose something escaped from that blasted lab? Sometimes I hear strange sounds coming from that room," Ben replied, peering through the gloom at the lab door.

"I'm not waiting around to find out -- come on!" They ran down the corridor and disappeared around the corner.

Jerome ran back to the lab-door, laughing and hugging himself in his glee. "All's clear!" He shouted in the door. "Come out, squad of monster chasers!" The three women came back into the corridor, this time followed by the men. Paul looked disgusted, and Vladimir grim. Robin was still pale.

"The only monsters in there are the doctors who work on those poor animals," Charlotte told Jerome indignantly.

"The guards don't know that," Jerome replied smugly. "They think I'm something that escaped from there and is after them!"

"And who would blame you, if you were, for going after every human in sight?" Vladimir asked, his lips a tight line of disapproval.

"Let's go," Paul urged them. "They'll call the police. We'll go out the back door, same way we came in. The stairs are this way."

"We know, sweetheart," Charlotte reassured him. "We came up them." They followed him down the hallway. In addition to the cages the woman were carrying, Paul and Robin had closed cases with breathing holes in the sides.

"I'm sorry," Paul replied. "This whole thing has me really upset."

"You're not the only one," Jerome told him. "Robin almost lost his dinner."

"Probably lives on fish, chips and beans, like all bachelors," Dierdre retorted.

Robin sneered at her, but didn't reply. They reached the door to the stairs and Paul put his case down in order to hold it open so the rest of them could pass through. Jerome picked up the case and carried it, attempting to peer into the breathing holes to see what it was he had appropriated. Paul took one last look down the corridor before closing the door behind himself.

Chapter 39

Amongst the animals rescued from the lab was a tiny monkey, surely only a baby, though the girls didn't know what species it was. They managed to feed it some milk and mashed-up bananas, and the day after the rescue Charlotte telephoned a friend of hers who was a nurse to a veterinarian. When the friend came to the house in Hampstead she examined the little monkey, who only seemed content when Dierdre carried him on her shoulder. She frowned at the wound in the back of his head, which the women had dressed with antiseptic ointment and a bandage. This made him look like a tiny drunk who had hit his head on something and tied a cloth around it.

Charlotte's friend Jayne gazed down at the little monkey, who was clinging to her finger like a baby. "How did this happen? Did he fall off something?" The tone of her voice said that she didn't believe a monkey could have done that.

"Jayne, if we tell you, you have to promise you won't tell your boss."

"Why? I know *you* wouldn't have done it -- but I can tell it was deliberately inflicted. Surely one of your male friends didn't do it, did they?" Her tone implied what she thought should be done to and with anyone who would do such a thing to a helpless animal.

"Of course not!" Natalie was indignant. "We liberated him -- from the experimental laboratory at The University of London."

"Ohhhh . . ." Jayne let out her breath in a rush. "Now I understand. The wound was caused by some kind of an electrode attached to his head. This is totally gross -- to do that to a baby animal. How ever did you manage it?"

"Paul did it," Charlotte told her. "Promise you won't tell anyone. Natalie's friend Vladimir is a film-maker, and on her show tomorrow night Dierdre's gonna run his film of the animals in the lab. It was horrible, Jayne. Some of them had to be destroyed -- we couldn't save them, and we weren't about to leave them there to be tortured until they died anyway."

"Show? What show?" Jayne looked at Dierdre in some confusion. "Have we met before?"

"No, but you probably recognize her," Charlotte replied for Dierdre. "She's the host of the new show on channel four, Below London. She's done three segments so far -- maybe you saw one of them."

"No, I haven't. But you used to do a show called *Below Manhattan*, right? I saw a couple of those when they were run as part of *The Tube*. Pretty funny. Isn't this a little out of your line?"

"Yes, but I'm running it anyway. All they can do is fire me, and by the time that happens, the segment will already have aired." Dierdre smiled contentedly.

"I don't think I'd be willing to risk my job, even though it's a great cause."

Dierdre shrugged. "I'm lucky in that I don't need the money. And I can always find another one. If they blackball me because I chose to make a statement through the show, then I don't need 'em -- there are lots of other things I can do."

"Like become an animal-rights activist," Natalie said, attempting to round up the kittens so Jayne could check them. "After all, you'll already have made a start."

"Do you think my little monkey will be all right?" Dierdre watched Jayne as she gave the monkey an injection.

"I don't know yet. I'm going to give you some medicine to give him, but since I have no idea what they were giving him in the lab --

and you can be certain it wasn't anything that was doing him any good -- I won't be able to tell for about a week. If he gets any worse, please call me. I'll come over any time. I really admire what you did. When will the show air?"

"Next Friday."

"This is one segment I'm not gonna miss."

"Thanks so much for coming, Jayne," Charlotte said, as Jayne gathered up her equipment and put it into her black bag.

"How much do we owe you?"

"Nothing. Call this my contribution to the effort. Oh, but before I go I'd better have a look at the kittens. How are they doing? You didn't tell me you'd gotten them from the lab, when I came before."

"We weren't sure we should," Charlotte replied. "But with the monkey, there was no way of keeping it from you without your thinking we'd been torturing it. Nat, do you have the kittens?"

"Two of them -- Cloud seems to think we're playing hide and seek."

Robin and *Experimental Monkeys* were back in the studio to film the television show on which Dierdre played Vladimir's lab-footage. But he didn't speak to Dierdre except when they were filming, and he didn't telephone the house. He had taken one of the puppies from the lab, as had Vladimir -- Paul couldn't because he was afraid one of his colleagues might see it. Negotiations were in process to have Paul move into the house -- at least on the girls' part. Dierdre had decided she was going to buy the house, and the protestations of the owner that he had no idea of selling hadn't put her off. She was a little worried that it might not be big enough for all of them, but decided they would find a way to cope, if Paul decided to come. Some remodelling would surely help -- once they were sure the animals were going to be all right, she decided to put her mind to it. But she was angry about Robin, and couldn't figure out what she should do.   She understood that he felt betrayed because she hadn't told him about her fortune, but since she never told anyone about it she couldn't understand why it was something she should have told him.

The day before the animal-rights show was to air she decided to go to his house and confront him. She telephoned first, and when he answered she hung up, got in the car and drove to Nottinghill Gate.

Robin's flat was the entire basement of a building at 15 Stanley Crescent, and while he had obviously put some money into the decoration of the flat and the garden, Dierdre didn't like it because she   hated   basement   apartments.   But,   she   told   herself philosophically, she wasn't the one who had to live there, and perhaps he deserved to.

She rang the doorbell, and could hear his steps making their way through the reception room to the door. This had insets of leaded glass, and though her image was somewhat skewed he could clearly recognize her. He hesitated for a moment before opening the door, and then stood gazing at her, as if he wasn't certain what to do. Dierdre hoped he didn't have a girl in the flat. "Why, hello, Didi -- I didn't expect to see you today."

"Surely you didn't expect to see me ever, since you made it clear that was your preference. May I come in?"

"Of course. I didn't mean to be rude, I was just surprised." He stood back, and Dierdre came into the reception room. She had seen it before, and thought it needed some kind of organization. It was just like a single man to buy all sorts of mis-matched objects and pieces of furniture just because he happened to like each one individually.

"As surprised as I was the night you showed up at my house. It should   have   been   obvious   to   us   even   then   that   we   were incompatible."

Robin looked as if he would take exception to this, then changed his mind. "I suppose so," he replied. "May I get you a drink? Or tea -- a soda?"

"Soda would be fine. Whatever you have. It's very hot today, for September. Don't you think so?"

"It happens sometimes, even in London. I'll be right back." He disappeared into the kitchen.

Dierdre removed her shirt and laid it over the back of a chair. Then she did the same with her skirt, and placed her flat sandals beside the chair. She sat on the couch, wearing only a fuschia lace bra and very short, matching tap-pants. When Robin came back, holding two glass of soda and ice, he stopped in place at the sight of Dierdre, legs crossed, sitting and leaning against the back of his leather couch. "Don't just stand there letting the ice melt," she told him. "Bring me my drink. As I said before, it's very hot today."

Robin seemed mesmerized by the sight of Dierdre's lingerie. He handed her the glass of soda numbly, and sat beside her, drinking his own in huge gulps. She sipped hers'. "You shouldn't drink so fast. You'll get hiccups."

"What?" He gasped.

"I said you're drinking it too fast -- you'll get hiccups. See, you've drunk the whole glass already." She took another ladylike sip of her own soda.

"Didi -- you've taken your clothes off!"

"I was so hot -- I didn't think you'd mind."

"Mind?" He sounded hysterical. "No, of course I don't mind. You have on spectacular underwear, today. And your body is so beautiful . . ."

"People as rich as I am can afford lots of plastic surgery."

"Huh?"

He swallowed an ice-cube whole, and started to choke. This seemed to give Dierdre great satisfaction. "You're joking!"

"Yes, I am. I thought you'd believe me because you hate rich people."

He frowned at her. "I don't, exactly. But I don't believe anyone should be rich, either. Not when so many others are suffering."

"I agree with you. But I'm not willing to give away all my money, either. I know it's hypocritical, and I do give a pretty hefty amount to a number of causes -- but I have the feeling you're against millionaires in general."

"I am. On principal, I mean. That doesn't mean I don't know any -- I have friends who are wealthy. Why didn't you tell me?"

"I didn't think you'd want to see me anymore. I love you, Robin."

He put his glass down on the coffee table. "Did I really seem that closed-minded to you? I suppose I might have, after that thing about Margaret Thatcher. You'll come to agree with me; just wait and see."

"I hope you plan to be around for my change of viewpoint."

Robin removed Dierdre's glass from her hand and put it on the table beside his. Then he moved so he was right beside her, and put his arms around her, pulling her tightly against him. "I was afraid you wouldn't want me to be."

"What, after I spent hours finding this lingerie to send your senses whirling into oblivion? Be real."

"It's done that, all right." He picked her up and sat her on top of him, so she was straddling him. "So soft," he murmured into her neck.

"I should hope so -- it's silk."

"Not that -- you!"

"And you're hard . . ." She slid her hand in between them to assure herself of this fact. "We make a good pair."

They were asleep in Didi's bed. It was the night before what they thought of as 'the' television show, and Didi had been nervous all night. She'd had difficulty falling asleep, and had lain listening to Robin's even breathing beside her. She wondered what it was about him that made her so determined to have him -- with most men, she would've forced herself to forget them after an incident like the one at the party. But there was something about Robin . . .

It was the whimpering of Sir Galahad, the little monkey, that woke her. She glanced at the clock -- it read 5 a.m. She sighed -- she had only been asleep about two hours. She leaned over the bed and lifted the little basket up onto the sheet. Gala was crying in his sleep, reaching out for someone. His mother, probably. Didi settled the basket beside her and put her hand in so he could curl around it. He quieted immediately and rested his head against her fingers.

She didn't realize she was crying until Robin stirred beside her, and put his arms around her. "What's wrong, angel?" He asked her sleepily. "Are you crying?"

"It's Galahad -- he's so very sweet. But I don't think he'll make it -- sometimes he seems to be in pain. I hate that, Rob -- Jayne told us she thinks he has terrible headaches, and we're hoping they'll pass. But -- would it be better to have him put to sleep? He's suffered enough, hasn't he?"

Robin was silent for a moment. Galahad was indeed a most endearing little fellow. The kittens and puppies (Robin's and Vladimir's were living mostly at the house, and the rest had gone to friends and neighbors in Hampstead) accepted him as one of them, and after watching the kittens use their litter box for a day, he followed suit. Now the kittens disdained the box, having discovered the outdoors and particularly the heath, where the women sometimes took them while walking the puppies, but Galahad remained true to his first toilet. He wouldn't go outside, either, but watched wistfully as the rest of the animals played on the communal lawn between the townhouses. When one of them attempted to carry him out, he would shriek and run away, hiding until he thought it was safe to come out.

"Give him a few more days. After all, it hasn't been very long for him to recover. He's not being subjected to torture anymore -- remember that." He hugged her against him.

"I have to do more, Rob. I have to give some money."

"Surely you already give money to charities, don't you?"

"My accountant in the states does it for me. I designated a hundred thousand a year when I came into my inheritance, and gave her a list to distribute it amongst. There are about ten animal charities, but none in England."

A hundred thousand dollars . . .for charity. Robin swallowed. "When did your parents die, Didi?"

She seemed surprised by this. "They're not dead. My mother lives in New York, but I hardly ever see her. She was a real pain when I was young, and wanted to arrange a marriage for me -- enlarge their dynasty, so to speak. My dad's somewhere in the middle east -- I think -- I hear from him every now and then. He's an archeologist. Why did you think they were dead? Because I don't mention them?"

"No, because of the inheritance."

"Oh, that. It's because my grandfather's will was a little strange. He couldn't stand my mother, or my uncle. He made out his will so that they received some of his money, and the rest was held in trust for their children. I was the only child my parents ever had, so when I was twenty I received all the money he'd designated for her children. My cousins weren't so lucky -- my uncle had six children, and they've been fighting over the money ever since."

"Would you have fought with your brothers and sisters, if you'd had to share your inheritance with them?"

"I don't think so. I would've been happy just to have siblings. Do you have any?"

"A sister -- she and my mom live in Australia. I go and visit them whenever I'm on tour."

"Galahad's settled down now. I think I have to go back to sleep, sweetheart." Her voice trailed off as she settled back into his embrace.

He kissed her hair. "You do that, poor little rich girl."

"Hmmm?"

"Nothing, love. I love you, Didi." But she was already asleep.

Chapter 40

The night of Dierdre's television show, their entire group was gathered in the reception room of the house in Hampstead. On the rolling cart was a half-empty pitcher of what appeared to be white sangria; on the coffee table, an enormous pottery bowl of tortilla chips and smaller bowls of guacamole and salsa. As they watched the news, waiting for the show to start, Robin leaned over from his place on the couch and selected a chip, dipping out a large portion of guacamole and popping the entire thing into his mouth, munching with obvious satisfaction.

"Where did you ever find these Mexican chips in London?" Charlotte grinned, taking a handful of the chips and settling back in her place beside Paul.

"Harrod's, where else?"

One of the kittens leapt from the arm-rest of the couch into the middle of her lap, batting the tortilla chip out of her hand. It sailed through the air and Paul caught it deftly, popping it into his mouth. "Thank you, little one. You have a future as a waiter."

They all laughed, watching the second kitten leap into the air and attack the first. They both fell off the couch, landing on the carpet and rolling about in a mock battle. Robin said, a little wistfully, "Look at them; the most precious creatures I've ever seen. How could anyone torture them, I wonder?"

Natalie was stroking the grey kitten, asleep in her lap. "At least these few are safe. How's your puppy?"

"Chewed up all my shoes except my boots, thank God. Adorable as anything; jumps all over me everytime I come home. Didi, where's the little monkey?"

Dierdre, in the process of drinking her Sangria, put the glass down with a clunk. Her face contorted, as if she was trying not to cry. "He . . .died during the night. I woke up this morning, and he was gone. I thought he was better, but he had lost the will to hang on. Poor little thing." The tears poured from beneath her eyelids and down her cheeks. Robin put his arms around her, and she turned her face into his shoulder, sobbing. "I'm sorry I asked, love. Think about the animals that are all right . . ."

"Oh!" Natalie exclaimed. "The show's starting! Where's Jeri?"

Jerome appeared beside her on the couch, making her scream. "Right here, Viking Princess."

"Jesus, Jeri -- don't do that! Look -- the show's starting."

"I heard you -- what are those?" He pointed to the bowl of chips."

"Tortilla chips. Help yourself."

Jerome levitated a chip from the bowl as the logo for Dierdre's show appeared on the screen. It floated to his mouth and he chewed it slowly, as if evaluating it. Nodding with satisfaction, he levitated another chip, dunked it into the bowl of guacamole, and floated it to his mouth, also. The others watched him in amusement until Dierdre appeared on the screen. She was seated on the dais with Robin and several other people; Robin was in the chair beside her's.

"Good evening," Dierdre began, "And welcome to *Below London*. What we are going to show you this evening will be shocking in the extreme, and we want to warn you, before the show begins, that it is not only graphic but more than a little disgusting. With me are Robin Herald, lead singer of the group *Experimental Monkeys*, and two members of The Animal Liberation Front. Several days ago, Robin delivered to the studio a film taken in the experimental laboratory at the University of London. As you probably recall, last week the lab was broken into and most of the animals removed. This film, which was apparently made the same night, was mailed to Robin, who then brought it to me and asked me to play it on this program. We then contacted The Animal Liberation Front, who have denied responsibility for the break-in or the making of the film. However, they are with us this evening to assist in answering the telephone calls I am certain we will receive, once this film is aired. We will go directly to the tape, and accept telephone calls as soon as it has finished running; it runs approximately 15 minutes in length."

The picture on the screen changed, to show Vladimir's film of the laboratory at the university. Dierdre jumped up and switched off the television before anything but one monkey could be seen; the same small monkey she had attempted to save -- in a cage, attached to some kind of electrodes in the brain. When the film began, it was with a closeup of this monkey.

"I'm sorry," she said to the group at large. "I can't watch it again."

"Never mind, honey." Robin patted the couch beside him. "We don't need to see it again. Have some wine, or whatever this is."

"Sangria, Robin," Charlotte said. "We've told you that three times."

"Sangria is red," he retorted. Dierdre sat beside him, holding one of the kittens in her lap and crooning over it like a mother with a baby. Robin put his arms around her and cuddled her as if she was his baby.

"So this is white Sangria. A new taste experience for you."

"Let's have a new *subject*. We're going to tell Jerome the rest of his story."

Jerome snorted, levitating another chip. "As if I didn't know it already. And it's as depressing as Vlad's film."

"Not the ending," Natalie told him. "Alicia shot Charles Brent."

Jerome's chip, doused in salsa, landed on the pale carpet with a plop. He stared down at it in chagrin. "Oh! I'm so sorry -- it was such a shock, I lost my concentration." Dierdre smiled at him. "Don't worry about it, Jeri. While they tell you the whole delicious story, I'll go into the kitchen and get something to clean it up. The carpet's been stain-treated, so it's really not a problem."

"What a marvelous place," Jerome said, as Dierdre walked toward the kitchen and Charlotte placed his discarded chip in an empty ashtray. "Even the carpets don't stain."

Robin had followed Dierdre into the kitchen. "Oh, yes," she said bitterly, dragging open the doors underneath the sink. "An absolutely marvelous place. The carpets don't stain, but we can't stop maniacs from torturing small animals."

"I think Jerome would tell you it was even worse in his day. Cheer up, sweetheart. Think of all the calls you got at the station, all the people who supported the raid on the lab."

"I know. You don't think they might find out at the university that it was Paul, do you?"

"Of course not. There are hundreds of people who work there; any one of whom could have had access to the key. They'll suspect the student assistants, and when they can't find anyone, they'll drop it. By the way, I forgot to tell you -- the band has been asked to play a benefit for The Animal Liberation Front. Next month; we've agreed to do it."

"Rob, you're quite a perfect human being, you know." Grimacing, Robin said, "I don't think I can live up to that, sweetheart. I'll try, but don't say I didn't warn you."

Dierdre smiled and hugged him, whispering in his ear. "Ah. I see someone else is going to be cleaning the carpet." He picked Dierdre up in his arms, carrying her back into the living room. "Somebody clean the carpet, right?" Robin said to the group as he passed through the room to the stairs. Dierdre just waved at them as they went by.

"Hey," Paul yelled after them, "You said *you* were going to clean it!"

"Too late, love." Charlotte stood. "I'll do it."

Paul caught her around the waist and lifted her, heaving her over his shoulder. "I liked Robin's idea. Let somebody else clean it up."

"Hey," Charlotte protested, "You aren't taking exactly the same tack. The way Robin did it was very romantic; the way you're doing it is more like a Neanderthal hauling away his kill."

He carried her to the staircase. "We Norwegians are very primitive."

Natalie and Jerome exchanged glances. "Like a scene out of a movie." She sighed, and rose from her chair. "Since Vlad has deserted me for the fascinating events in Berlin, I guess I've been elected as carpet-cleaner."

Jerome watched her go to the kitchen, glanced down at the stain on the carpet, and faded into the wall with a sigh.

The following afternoon, Natalie came down the stairs ready for painting, and discovered Dierdre on the telephone. It wasn't an unusual occurrence, but there obviously was something strange about this particular conversation. Dierdre was waving her arm frantically and gesticulating in an attempt to get Natalie to come to the phone. Finally she put her hand over the receiver and hissed, "Nat! Over here!"

Dressed in jeans, a t-shirt and an apron that were liberally splashed with paint, and carrying a jar of clear liquid containing an assortment of paint brushes, Natalie crossed the room to Dierdre's side, regarding her curiously. "What's wrong?"

"Are Charlotte and Paul here?"

"No -- Paul's at the university. Charlotte's out shooting that group of artists who live under Paddington tube station."

"Paul can't appear anywhere near this house today." Into the telephone receiver she said, "Yes, I'm here. What now? Well, all right, I guess so . . .I don't see what this has to do with me. I mean, I can't tell you anything. The tape was given to me by someone else. All right . . .this afternoon? Yes, I suppose so. Goodbye."

She hung up the telephone, scowling down at it.

"What was that all about?"

"The university is sending two investigators over here today to talk to me. I'm going to telephone Robin and tell him not to come over or phone until I call him. Where's Vlad?"

"Still in Berlin. He won't be around this week at all."

"OK. Boy, I'm really looking forward to giving these guys my opinion on what they're doing down there in that lab."

"In order to get that, all they had to do was watch your show last night. Do you think they have any clues as to our involvement?"

"No -- if they did, they would've done something by now. Want to see them with me?"

"Oh, I wouldn't miss this performance. I'll change before they get here." She and Dierdre smiled grimly at one another. Natalie went into the kitchen with her brushes.

"Now all I have to do," Dierdre said to the air, "Is keep the kittens out of the way. Maybe Charlotte will be back by then."

Later that afternoon, Dierdre was dressed in what Charlotte termed her 'intimidation jumpsuit'. Designed by Bill Blass, it was of pin-striped grey wool suiting, the type used for men's business suits. It had wide lapels and buttons to the waist, pleated trousers that were full, like the ones worn during the 1930's. With high black pumps and a wide black leather belt, it was very impressive. Natalie was also dressed in grey; a soft grey heather-wool dress, very long, with high black boots.

They both sat in the second reception room with two men in badly fitting suits; one navy blue, one camel. They were both 'generic' English in appearance -- dark blond hair, receding in the front; pale, watery blue eyes, slender build. Not much chin to speak of . . .

Dierdre said, "I really don't know how I can help you. I've told you everything I know. Robin Herald gave me the tape, which was mailed to him. I played it; that's all."

The first man glared at her, loosening his neck-tie. "Why did you play it?"

"Because I think animal torture is disgusting."

"Surely you must have realized this tape was made illegally."

"What makes you think I give a fuck?" The second man's eyes opened a little wider at Dierdre's choice of words. Natalie thought it was wonderful that Dierdre could maintain such a haughty attitude and use such nasty language. "I didn't do anything illegal by playing a tape that was given to me. I think I'll play it again."

This sent the second man into what appeared to be a coughing or choking fit. The two women watched him impassively; his colleague jumped up and thumped him on the back. "Miss Hall," he managed to gasp, "We must insist you give the tape to us."

"No."

He waved the first man back to his seat in an over- stuffed armchair. "Can't you understand that this could cost us millions in research grants and donations?"

"Then stop torturing animals, and perhaps people will give you money again," Natalie snapped.

The first man was becoming clearly agitated. "It's not as simple as that. The research we're doing there is vital."

"According to the people from The Animal Liberation Front, that research could be done by computer. You won't do that, because you're greedy, insensitive fascists." Dierdre smiled widely, as if she had just complimented him.

"You're taking a very biased viewpoint." Natalie admired the man's perseverance, if not his stupidity. "You've been influenced by The Animal Liberation Front, and they're extremely radical in their viewpoint."

"So am I," Dierdre told him proudly. "I've joined. And I have buckets of money, so I can help them liberate lots of helpless animals from the clasps of greedy fascists." Natalie expected her friend to stick her tongue out at the man and make a raspberry.

"I suppose Robin Herald convinced you to do that," he retorted bitterly. "He's an anarchist."

Natalie stared at him in disbelief. "Do you even know what that word means?" She sounded as if she was talking to a six-year old who had used the 'F' word.

This angered him even more. "Of course I know what it means! Robin Herald would like to overthrow the existing government of this country."

"Robin Herald is a rock singer," Dierdre told him, in a tone of voice that plainly said she thought she was talking to a moron. "I interviewed him on my show a few weeks ago, so he thought of me when he received the tape. He brought it to me, I played it, and that's it. I have nothing more to tell you. I think you're members of a sub-human species of giant cockroaches caused by the erosion of the ozone layer, and I want you to leave my house."

The second man looked as if he wanted to say something. "Now!" She added, very loudly.

They looked at one another and rose from their seats. "I assure you, you'll hear from us again," the second man said. "And so will the studio. Perhaps they can be made to listen to reason."

Dierdre and Natalie stood also. "On my next show, I think I'll tell my viewers about your harassment. I'll give out your names."

"That's blackmail!" the first man sputtered.

Dierdre didn't reply, just swept past them to the doorway. There she made an elaborate gesture for the two men to precede her into the entryway. As they passed her, she turned and winked at Natalie.

Chapter 41

That night, Robin took Dierdre out for dinner at a little restaurant in Hampstead. They had learned to avoid the larger, better known places, unless they were in the mood to be harangued throughout the meal by people who were fans of one or both of them. That night they just wanted to be alone. Dierdre told Robin the story of the investigators from the University, knowing which would be his favorite part.

He started to laugh in the middle of his prawn cocktail, with the result that he choked on a prawn. "I can't believe you said that to them! Giant cockroaches, caused by the erosion of the ozone layer!" He started to laugh again, and then to choke. "Stop, Robin," Dierdre admonished him. "You'll choke to death on prawns."

Robin swallowed a mouthful of wine. "No chance; what would happen to Mudslide?"

She stared at him uncomprehendingly. "Who?"

"That's the name of my puppy; Mudslide."

"I see. Interesting choice of name."

"You won't think so the next time you see him in the garden."

"I'm looking forward to the party tonight, Rob."

"I'm glad you feel better. I was worried about you last night."

Dierdre sipped her wine slowly. "I have nightmares about that poor, little monkey. It's not so bad when you're with me, though."

"I guess I'll just have to spend every night with you. Come to my place tonight? Mudslide gets lonely, too."

"God, are we a couple of saps where animals are concerned. I'd hate to see us with children."

"I was thinking it would be rather nice, actually . . ." He fixed her eyes with his, meaningfully. She flushed and lowered her head to eat a prawn.

He frowned down at his own empty glass. "Of course, the situation we're in right now wouldn't be too plausible, would it? My place is hardly large enough for the two of us without your wardrobe, and yours is a little crowded."

She nodded, eating her last prawn. "Now that you've brought it up, there's something I wanted to discuss with you. I'll probably have a lot more room, soon. Not that I'm talking about having children -- don't get that idea into your stubborn head!"

"Who, me?" He looked wounded, and Dierdre thought how classic his face was, how beautiful. "Still, you do want some one day, don't you?"

"Maybe -- when we're too old to do anything else."

Robin laughed. "If we're too old to do anything, how are we supposed to have them?"

"I'm relatively certain you'll never get too old to do that."

"What did you want to tell me? Now that you've flattered me enormously. It must be bad news."

"No, it's great! I've bought the three townhouses that once made up the west wing of Jerome's estate. Now there's one house for Paul and Charlotte, one for Natalie and Vladimir and one for us. Or, if Natalie and Vladimir don't stay together she can get roommates; and if we don't stay together I'll have one house to myself."

"That should give you enough closet space, anyway. But what makes you think we won't stay together?"

"Well, you never know. We broke up once before."

"And if I moved in with you, how much would my rent be? I was thinking of trying to buy a place myself."

Dierdre stared at him blankly. "Rent? What are you talking about?"

"Did you think I'd be willing to live in your house without paying any rent? What do you think I am, a free-loader?"

"Of course not! But that's ridiculous; I don't want your silly old rent. Why not buy a place like you'd planned on doing? You don't actually have to live there; you could rent it out to some unfortunate who doesn't have a rich girlfriend."

He shook his head, watching as the waiter rolled a cart to the table and began to prepare their entrees. "Aren't you going to charge Charlotte and Natalie rent, either?"

"You're the one who said rich people should help others. I'm just trying to follow your advice."

"How are they going to feel about this?"

"Oh, they'll argue. We'll see what happens. Oooh, there's my salmon -- looks delicious."

"I can see I'll get no more sensible conversation out of you, tonight -- you're too fixated on food."

The following day, they arrived back in Hampstead in the late afternoon. Jerome was sitting in the second reception room, watching television and looking at a pile of magazines. Robin was amused by the way his ancestor was attempting to absorb modern culture. Cloud, the silver kitten, and Ebony, the black, were asleep on the couch together. When they came into the room from the entryway the silver kitten heard them, and launched himself off the couch. Running to meet Dierdre, he complained as loudly as possible in his tiny voice. The black kitten lifted his head and regarded this scene for a moment, decided it wasn't of much interest, and went back to sleep. Dierdre bent down and picked up the silver kitten, who snuggled against her, purring. "I told you Cloud would be upset if I stayed away last night. Hi, Jeri." She threw herself down on the couch with the kitten in her lap. Robin sat beside her and gathered up the black kitten, who snuggled happily into his sweater.

"We can introduce Cloud to Mudslide and they can keep one another company."

"Hi, Guys," Jerome responded to Dierdre's greeting. "Mudslide?"

"The incredibly elegant name Robin chose for his puppy," Dierdre informed him.

"It fits," Robin insisted. "Oh, Jeri -- I meant to tell you, but in all the excitement and trauma, I forgot. I checked through some papers my mother left me, things I never bothered to look at before. And I went to one of those genealogical bureaus; the ones that trace people's ancestry for them. My grandmother's maiden name was Brent! What do you think of that?"

Jerome smiled. "It doesn't surprise me; you are so obviously my descendant. I've been waiting for you, Robin. I wanted to talk to you before I left."

Robin frowned. "Left? I don't understand -- where are you going?"

"I'm going over -- to the other side."

"Other side? Oh, no -- Jeri!" Dierdre was stricken, and obviously surprised. "You mean you're going to die?"

Jerome smiled sadly at her. "Sweet girl, I'm already dead. I've been waiting all these years to finally be freed. You and your friends have done it. You discovered my murderer and you brought me my descendant. There's nothing to hold me here, now."

"Please don't leave -- we love you! You're a part of our family."

"Thank you. I feel the same about you; all of you. But I have to go -- Alicia is calling me, and the pull gets stronger all the time. I must go, tonight."

"You can't! You'll miss Charlotte's photography show next week, and then a couple of weeks later is Natalie's gallery showing of her paintings . . ." she trailed off as Jerome shook his head. "But you won't go until the others have had a chance to say goodbye, will you?"

"If they're here this evening; I can't hold out any longer. I don't want to, Didi. I want to be with Alicia."

"We were never able to tell you about how Alicia shot Charles Brent."

"With the help of Lady Sarah and her cicisbeo, I'm certain. And I want Alicia to tell me that story. I want to be with her."

"We understand, Jeri." Dierdre was about to object, and Robin squeezed her hand. "We'll get the gang together tonight, to see you off."

Dierdre nodded, taking his cue. "We'll have a celebration, and drink champagne -- to your reunion with Alicia, after all this time of waiting."

"I never had better friends than you when I was alive." Jerome tried to keep the tears from his voice. "Robin, I want you to know how proud I am to have you as my descendant. I hope you'll continue your work with The Animal Liberation Front."

"Thank you, Jeri. I will; and so will Didi. I'm sorry you'll miss our benefit."

Dierdre frowned. "What benefit?"

"I haven't had a chance to tell you about it. My bass player and drummer are organizing it. They're getting together some bands to play a benefit for The Animal Liberation Front. Boy, the straights are really mad -- we've gotten some threatening phone calls."

Jerome seemed shocked by this. "What! Do you mean people actually condone that kind of torture?"

Robin shrugged. "Sure. They think it's the only way to find cures for diseases."

"Well," Jerome replied, "Your doctors have certainly done well in that department. But didn't Paul tell us it could be done by computer?"

"Most of it -- the odds of a certain treatment working, that kind of thing. What I can't understand is why they don't use human volunteers. If I had AIDS or cancer, I'd volunteer to be used for research. What would I have to lose?"

"I guess most people don't feel that way. You didn't tell me about the benefit," Dierdre chided him.

"I wanted to be certain it was going to work out. I'm just sorry Jerome won't be there."

Jerome grinned. "Don't be so certain about that."

Chapter 42

They were all there for Jerome's leave-taking that night, in the first reception room. They drank champagne and ate hors d'oeuvres from Harrod's. Jerome was with them, attired in 19th century evening dress. Dierdre thought he looked splendid in his velvet jacket and satin knee- breeches, and wondered if she should have a masquerade party. Robin could come as his ancestor.

As if he could read her thoughts, Robin lifted his champagne flute. "Here's to Jerome -- if it hadn't been for him, we never would've gotten out of that lab -- and Paul probably would be out of a job right now."

"I've quit," Paul replied matter of factly. The entire group, with the exception of Charlotte, stared at him in amazement.

"Paul," Natalie asked him slowly, "Did you say you quit the university?"

"Yes. I couldn't bear it there after the raid. I've been offered another job, though."

Robin sneered. "Must be tough, being so in demand."

"How would you know, rock star? Have you ever looked for a job?"

"Have you?" Robin shot back.

"Hey, what is this?" Charlotte regarded both of them as if they were aliens who had just invaded and offered to eat her children. What's wrong with you guys, fighting at Jeri's going-way party?"

"Besides," Dierdre added, "You'll have to get along if you're going to live next door to one another."

Everyone but Robin seemed confused by this. "Why would we do that? I'm not moving to Nottinghill Gate." Paul's voice was firm.

"From what I've heard about your place, *anything* would be an improvement," Robin retorted. "And that's not what she means. We're both going to be moving. In fact, everyone except Didi is moving."

Charlotte and Natalie didn't like the sound of that. "I suppose you're moving in here and throwing us out," Charlotte said.

"I wouldn't let him do that!" Dierdre objected. "You don't understand -- I've bought all three of the townhouses."

Vladimir choked on his wine, and Natalie thumped him on the back. "Sorry," he coughed, "I just can't used to all the money you have at your disposal."

"What are you planning to do with them all?" Natalie still seemed confused.

"Very thick, Nat," Robin told her, chuckling. "There are three of *you*, and three townhouses. What does that tell you?"

"You mean . . .that we get one each?" For a moment, Natalie seemed thrilled. Then she shook her head. "Forget it -- I couldn't afford the rent."

"What rent? I told you I bought them -- there is no rent."

"Not for you, but we couldn't live in them without paying rent. No, Dierdre -- don't argue. I don't want charity from anyone."

"It's not charity -- you're my friends, and I worked hard to get those houses."

"I have an idea." Paul glanced around the circle. "Am I being invited to live with Charlotte in her townhouse?" This was directed at the circle, which Charlotte found amusing.

"Shouldn't you be asking *me* that question, lover?"

"I am."

"Then why are you looking at Jerome? He's hardly going to give you permission, since he's deserting us for his two- hundred year-old girlfriend."

"Lord," Jerome said caustically, "I hope she doesn't look it!"

"I doubt it," Paul told him, "Since you don't. Well, Chari? Do you want me to come and live with you or not?"

"Why don't you get married?" Vladimir offered.

"Why don't *you*?" Paul retorted.

"OK. Hey, Nat, wanna get married?"

"What a lovely proposal. Besides, you only want me for my townhouse."

"Can we discuss this later?" Robin asked impatiently. "It's something you four need to talk about in private, anyway. This is hardly a group decision. Besides, I want to know how Paul and I could possibly be working together. My knowledge of science is nonexistent."

"He's the new director of The Animal Liberation Front. The old director left to go to the states and work there," Charlotte told him proudly. She was trying to keep Paul's obvious reluctance to marry her from becoming depressing -- perhaps he would explain himself later.

"Paul!" Dierdre leaned over and kissed his cheek. "We're so proud of you! And we'll all be working with you. Any way we can."

Vladimir nodded enthusiastically. "You know it, comrade. You have my services for nothing; filming any atrocities you come up with."

"That's an appetizing way to put it, Vlad." Natalie hugged him, thrilled that he wanted to marry her even if the proposal had been somewhat off-hand. She wasn't sure she wanted to marry again, but it was wonderful to be wanted.

Robin shook his head, grinning. "Sorry, Paul. I shouldn't've snapped at you; you know I'm behind you all the way. I think I'm just upset to see Jerome go."

"We all are," Dierdre agreed. "Who will remember to feed the cats?"

They all laughed. Jerome rose from his chair and lifted his champagne glass. "Another toast -- to my friends from America, Scotland, Norway and Russia. Who saved me and freed me from my exile, only to make me sad to leave them."

They all drank from their glasses. The three girls clustered around Jerome and hugged and kissed him. The three men watched sadly. "I never thought I'd be jealous of a ghost," Robin complained. "Nobody ever does that to me. At least not three at a time."

"And they'd better not," Dierdre warned him.

"I think I have to go, now," Jerome told them. "Alicia may become tired of calling me."

"And go find Charles Brent, you mean?" Charlotte teased him. "That seems doubtful."

Jerome made a face. "He was probably reincarnated as a giant cockroach."

Dierdre and Natalie exchanged looks, and Robin started to laugh. "Caused by the erosion of the ozone layer, no doubt," Dierdre said, giggling. The rest of the group stared at them in some confusion.

"What, I wonder?" Vladimir was staring at Natalie, who was laughing hysterically and about to spit out her wine.

"Sorry, love," she managed to sputter, "You had to be there."

Jerome rose from his chair and walked slowly in the direction of the far wall of the room. They all watched him as he moved like a sleepwalker toward the wall, which was now shimmering with a pinkish light. Dierdre blinked as if she thought it was some kind of an optical illusion, and Paul rubbed his hand over his eyes. As Jerome neared the wall it dissolved to show a field of wildflowers, with a woman standing in it. She looked up and started to walk toward Jerome. As she neared, she was revealed as Alicia, dressed in a high-waisted long dress of white muslin, tied with a blue sash. "There's Alicia, Jeri," Charlotte called to him excitedly.

He turned to look back at her, beaming and grinning. "Can you see her?"

Dierdre nodded. "Yes, love -- we can all see her. You can go to her, now."

Jerome blew them a kiss and walked straight through the wall, until he reached Alicia, who put her arms around him and kissed his lips. As the wall reappeared, they faded until they were gone from sight.

Chapter 43

Late that night, discussions were going on in three of the bedrooms of the townhouse. Robin and Dierdre were the first couple to sleep, undoubtedly because they had the least to discuss -- they had already made their decisions. Dierdre had only been asleep a few minutes, cradled in Robin's arm with her head resting on his chest, when Jerome and Alicia stepped through the wall of the bedroom and stood looking down at the sleeping couple. On Alicia's shoulder rode a small monkey, which held on to her hair with its' front paws. "He is you, my love," Alicia told Jerome. "In every detail."

Jerome smiled. "He is ours, dearest. A good man; and she is a wonderful woman. I didn't live in vain, after all."

"I never thought you had."

Dierdre stirred in her sleep and opened her eyes. She looked up at Jerome and Alicia, thinking they must be part of a dream she was having. "Jeri?" She asked tentatively. "Are you back?"

"I wanted you to meet Alicia. Alicia, this is Dierdre, the dear lady who helped me get back to you. With the assistance of her friends, of course."

"Hello, Alicia," Dierdre said, yawning. "I feel as if I already know you." She sat up in the bed with a jerk as she spotted the monkey. "Oh! Sir Galahad!" Her cry awakened Robin, who yawned and stretched.

He reached for Dierdre, attempting to take her into his arms.

"Hush, sweetheart. It's just a nightmare," he said soothingly, not opening his eyes.

Dierdre shook him awake. "Wake up, Robin! Jerome and Alicia are here, and they've brought my little monkey."

Robin's eyes opened and he stared first at Dierdre and then over at Jerome and Alicia, propping himself up on one elbow. "Oh, hello. You came back."

"Alicia thought Dierdre would like to know how happy Sir Galahad is with us."

"We have to go now," Alicia added. "They gave us a special dispensation; we're not usually allowed to come down here. A little confusing for the living, having the dead dropping in on them at all hours."

Dierdre smiled. "We're pretty accustomed to Jerome -- we already miss him."

"We'll be back," he told her. "But not as ourselves."

"Reincarnation again? I always wondered about that, but we never finished our discussion." Robin sounded as if he wished they had.

"What's it like there?" Dierdre asked.

Alicia shook her head. "You'll find out, when it's your time. That won't be for a long while yet, though. You and Robin have a lot to do down here, first."

"Goodbye, then. Thank you so much for coming. I won't have the nightmares anymore, now. I'm so glad you brought Sir Galahad."

"Try to stop them from killing anymore little creatures in such a terrible fashion, Dierdre. They have a right to life, too."

"We will," Robin said. "We promise."

Alicia and Jerome stepped back and faded into the wall, Jerome waving to them as they went. Dierdre snuggled down into Robin's arms. "Were they really here, do you think?" Robin asked Dierdre.

"How can you ask, after knowing Jeri? He wanted me to see Sir Galahad; I know that was it." She hugged Robin fiercely, kissing his chest.

"Didi," he asked tentatively, "Are you tired?" She smiled up at him. Turning in his arms, she put her face up for his kiss.

Paul and Charlotte were lying in bed, but they weren't tired, either. They should have been, for their lovemaking was particularly passionate and loving that night, but they were both thinking about Dierdre's extraordinary announcement that she had bought the row of townhouses, and her plans for them. While Charlotte felt she was ready to commit herself to someone again, and Paul was the one she wanted, she couldn't forget his reluctance and hesitation when Vladimir suggested they wed. Perhaps he didn't want to marry or have children; she wasn't much concerned about the latter -- it wasn't something she'd ever really thought about. Her career was one which demanded most of her time, and since Paul was also passionately involved in what he did, perhaps they wouldn't make the best parents. It wasn't even marriage that mattered to her; it was being asked. She wanted Paul to want to marry her -- whether the event ever occurred after the proposal didn't mean so much to her. Then again, she was a liberated woman . . ."Paul," she said, hugging his chest closely, "Would you like to marry me?"

He stared down at her golden head with some amusement. "Why yes, little flower, I would. Isn't it customary for the man to do the asking, however?"

"I figured if I waited till then, I'd make a ludicrously old bride. You didn't seem too enthused with the subject when Vladimir brought it up."

"It's not that, it's just that I hate it when someone else brings up an idea I've been thinking over. Almost as if they could read my mind, and were trying to push me into something."

Charlotte sat up in the bed and looked down at Paul, her hair brushing his face. "Do you really want to get married? Maybe we should live together for awhile."

"Psychologists say that's a good thing. But there's no reason why we couldn't be engaged while we were doing it. I'd love to buy you a ring. Everytime I go by a jewelry shop I think about which one you'd like."

"I can't believe I never knew you were thinking about it."

"And were *you*?"

"No, not until Vlad mentioned it tonight. I was so happy with you it didn't occur to me that we might move on. We haven't solved the problem of the house, however. And there's no way I'm living in your place. It's like a dungeon."

"That's how bachelor 'pads' are supposed to look."

"Psychologists say so, huh? What about the house, Paul? You said you had an idea."

"Didi doesn't want us to pay her rent to live in the house, but maybe she'd let us buy it."

"She just bought it herself! Besides, do you have the kind of money we'd need to even make a down-payment? I don't." She frowned. "I should have more saved than I do, but being in business for myself I have high overhead."

"And a brand new car. No, don't jump all over me! I understand perfectly. I've been thinking about trading my junker in, but I'm waiting to see how my new job works out."

"Are you making as much money as you did at the university?"

"More. Research Biologists are notoriously underpaid. But it means I'll be doing a lot of traveling around the country. I thought maybe you'd go with me, on some of the trips. You can have the position of staff photographer."

Charlotte seemed to be considering this. "But I already have a job. And I know you couldn't pay me as much as they do."

"I thought you wanted to get out of fashion photography.

You'll have to choose between money and making a legitimate contribution, Chari. You've known that for a long time -- why do you think you're so dedicated to the photos you take of street people?"

"Why do *you* think I am?"

"Because you know they'll last a lot longer than those stupid fashion shots. When they've been consigned to the fashion bonfire, people will still look at your street shots and find some understanding of our culture."

Charlotte grinned. "The fashion bonfire? Have I told you lately how much I love you? You're the silliest man I know, and I still love you to pieces." As if to emphasize this, she hugged him.

"Silly? Me? How can you say that? I'm a completely rational human being."

"Oh, sure -- Mr. Spock of London. Have we made a decision about the house?"

"Let's wait till the morning. I'm too tired, now."

Natalie and Vladimir had made a trip down to the kitchen for hot chocolate, and were now drinking it in bed with a plate of chocolate biscuits. "Do you think Paul and Chari will move into one of the houses?" Natalie asked Vladimir.

He swallowed part of a biscuit. "I don't know -- it depends on how heavy his conscience would be over the matter. I wouldn't do it without paying rent, myself."

"Do you want to do it?"

"Tell me what *you* want -- are we ready for this step? Paul and Charlotte have known one another a lot longer."

"But Dierdre and Robin haven't. It's obvious *they're* planning to live in this house together."

"You're not Dierdre and I'm not Robin. What do you want to do, Nat?"

"I wish I knew. Shall we wait awhile? I know Didi wants us to make a decision now so she and Robin can have this house to themselves, but I could take one of the houses -- if we want to live together, we could always do it later."

"I see; you just want that big house to yourself -- let me live in squalor. Don't let it disturb you any." Natalie started to laugh at the look on his face. Soon they were both laughing hysterically, and Vladimir leaned over her to tickle her. She started to scream and laugh at the same time, attempting to get hold of one of the bed pillows so she could hit him with it. The plate of chocolate biscuits fell to the rug and scattered.

"Charlotte, will you marry me? Chari, let's get married soon -- like we talked about. How about getting married, Chari -- I brought you my grandmother's ring." Paul stopped pacing back and forth across his narrow reception room, and glanced over at the table where the ring sat in it's velvet box. Was it even considered appropriate any longer to give your fiancee a family heirloom? His mother wore another ring that had been his grandmothers -- the old lady had been very acquisitive were jewelry was concerned -- and it was one of her favorite pieces. But Charlotte was a very modern, and Paul knew that modern women liked to choose their own rings. He frowned. He couldn't even decide how to ask her -- should he casual, or formal? They'd been lovers a long time, now, and he didn't see why they needed to live together before marrying. Surely they already knew they were compatible in most things. Paul grinned. Some more than others. He picked up the ring box. It was an unusual ring, comprised of many small diamonds and emeralds, shaped like a white rose. The diamonds comprised the rose, and the emeralds the leaves around it. Surely it was prettier than anything new he might find. Still . . .

"Well, I'll give her this one, and then ask if she'd like to pick out something of her own." She could have two rings -- a million, if he'd been able to afford them. As it was, he'd have to make payments on whatever she chose, but it was worth it. They still hadn't worked out the arrangements for the townhouse with Didi, who was proving to be quite elusive and stubborn over the whole subject of rent. Well, once their wedding plans were made, there would have to be a serious discussion on the subject. Didi could be even more stubborn than Charlotte, and that was going some.

He snapped the ring box closed. He still hadn't decided how to word his proposal, but hoped the correct words would come when the occasion presented itself.

Chapter 44

It was fortunate that the sale of the townhouses wouldn't be completed for another sixty days, because none of the three girls would have had time to move, anyway. It started with Natalie's showing at The Camden Arts Centre, followed two weeks later by Charlotte's photography show at The Submarine Gallery. These two shows were as different as they could be, and both be considered artistic endeavors. The only similarity in them was that all three women were at both shows, and they wore evening dresses. Even this fact wasn't exactly accurate, in that each of them had a different idea of evening dress. From Dierdre's micro-mini of beaded sequins to Natalie's floor-length midnight-blue satin fishtail gown and Charlotte's gold lame catsuit, they were a striking sight at The Camden Arts Centre the night of Natalie's show.

They had pooled their resources to draw in a crowd guaranteed to make the show a success. The resulting guests were a mixture of television and film people, fashion designers, painters and rock stars. All of Natalie's paintings sold, and they pronounced the night a total success.

The three women thought their escorts were a triumph, also, in matching black-tie evening dress.

Charlotte's photography show was lower key, and the audience, while culled from the same pool, varied slightly. The Submarine Gallery was one of the most popular 'alternative' galleries in London, and catered to much of the underground press and art scene. The people at this show, therefore, were a somewhat more eclectic and unusual crowd. The men changed their dress for individual choices - - Robin a black leather tuxedo, Vladimir a velvet dinner jacket and Paul a silk suit. The women all wore strapless dresses -- Dierdre's again very short, Natalie's again floor-length, and Charlotte's with a mid-calf length full skirt of sheer black lace, and a pair of shimmering spandex leggings beneath.

It could be said that Charlotte's show wasn't the economic success Natalie's had been, but she wasn't expecting to sell her photographs. She was, therefore, somewhat surprised when a number of them did sell -- and to some unusual buyers. Ozzy Osborne bought one, as did Viscount Linley. Just having them at the show would have been enough for Charlotte.

In all, the two women were well-pleased with their nights in the spotlight, and ready to return to work. Two weeks after Charlotte's show, The Animal Liberation Front Benefit took place at Wembley Arena, to a sold out crowd. As the new director of the 'Front', Paul had been thrown into a maelstrom of activity, a large part of which centered on the benefit. His prediction that he and Robin would be working together became a reality as he attempted to understand the alien language of performers and sound- checks.

When the day of the benefit finally came, he was convinced that rock band managers and publicists were agents of the devil (the one he didn't believe in) who had been placed on earth to drive him mad. But with the help of the three women from Hampstead and Robin, everything was running smoothly (at least Robin assured him it was -- to Paul it seemed more like the whole thing was about to fall apart).

At 8 in the evening the first band, *Concussion*, hit the stage. Although the arena was only about half full at this point and the benefit wasn't sold out, Robin assured Paul they would have a good turn out. And by 11 o' clock, when *Experimental Monkeys* was scheduled to go on, Robin's prediction was fulfilled. The arena was filled to capacity with a surprisingly mixed crowd composed mostly of fans of the music who knew little about animal rights and environmentalists who had never heard of the bands involved but wanted to support the cause.

Charlotte positioned herself below the front of the stage with a large camera bag and assorted equipment. Clad in her oldest torn jeans in order to crawl around on the floor, she resembled one of the fans more than a professional photographer. At the edge of the stage, just in front of the wings, Vladimir was in position with a film crew and his own portable mini-cam.

Natalie and Dierdre were standing in the wings, and at a signal from somewhere in the loft, Dierdre stepped out onto the stage. She wore the gown of cobalt-blue tissue faille that Natalie had stigmitized as being only fit for the Academy Awards. The fabric caught the lights as she walked to the center of the stage, and swirled around her ankles in a deep, ruffled flounce that curved up to her knees in the front and was adorned with an enormous bow across the back. In her hair was a spray of blue rhinestones that stood up in the back like an alien's headdress. She stopped at the microphone and took a deep breath. "I hope you enjoyed our two opening acts this evening, Concussion and The Mind Benders. I apologize if the film we showed between the acts upset you in any way -- I assure you, when Robin Herald first brought it to me, it upset me a lot, and when it was first televised on *Below London* we received a great deal of mail regarding the contents, not all of it favorable. A lot of people seemed to feel that we had no right to show the film without warning them about it -- in case they didn't want to see it. We apologize for this, and if you didn't want to see the film tonight, we're sorry about that, also. But we are not sorry we showed the film -- either then, or now.

"Speaking of now, we would like to present our headliner tonight, waiting eagerly in the wings. Please welcome *Experimental Monkeys!*" A cheer went up from the audience as Robin and the band members ran onstage. Robin squeezed Dierdre's hand as he passed her on his way to the microphone. She walked to the wings to join Natalie and Paul.

"Hello," Robin said into the microphone, "And thank you for coming to the Animal Liberation Front benefit. Before we begin playing, I would like to dedicate this song to my friend Jerome, who is no longer with us, except in spirit." He turned to grin at Dierdre, who blew him a kiss. Then the band struck the first chords of the song, and Robin began to sing.

Dierdre looked from Robin into the audience, and was drawn to a man standing at the edge, just below her. He seemed not to be a part of the crowd, and he looked somehow familiar. He was wearing black leather pants and a motorcycle jacket with studs, and when he looked up and met her eyes, he winked. It was Jerome!

She jerked on Natalie's arm and dragged her to the edge of the stage, but he was gone. As she scanned the audience she was certain she saw him moving away from her, towards the exit.

Chapter 45

One Year Later

Robin came dashing up the stairs from the basement and into the foyer, colliding with Dierdre. He was carrying a large cardboard box filled with papers; she appeared to have her arms full of some kind of white, gossamer fabric. The box went to the floor and Robin's papers scattered over the Aubusson carpet. The fabric fluttered down and covered them like a shroud. "Oh!" Robin said, "Sorry, love -- didn't see you!"

"No wonder, with that huge box! Whatever are you doing?" She said this as she carefully gathered up her fabric and attempted to fold it into a semblance of its' former neatness.

"Moving these papers to Nat's house. What's that?" Robin pointed to the fabric.

"It *will* be Chari's wedding veil. Treat it nicely, lover -- embroidered French net, 60 lbs. a meter."

Robin whistled. "Why the hell don't they just go down to the registry office? This wedding is gonna cost a fortune."

"They're only planning on getting married once, so Charlotte wants it to be good. If we ever get married, I can promise you I'll outdo her."

Robin started to pick up his papers and put them back in the box. At this, he laughed. "I have no doubt -- got a date in mind?"

"Don't rush me. Listen, how is it working out, using Paul and Chari's basement as offices? Will it be big enough?"

"Oh, sure. The space is about twice the size of the tiny office they had before, and it can be divided into three large rooms or four adequate ones. Besides, nobody can find the members to arrest them. It'll never occur to the police that the offices would be in the basement of a house you own. Have I told you how generous it was of you to donate the space and pay for the renovation?"

"Yes, but you can tell me again. Got to dash, love -- we have to see if this matches the fabric for Chari's dress."

He straightened up and kissed her. "Have you seen Mudslide today?"

Dierdre nodded, as she turned and headed for the front door. "He's out in the communal garden with John from across the green -- all the dogs and cats are 'helping' him with his roses."

"Oh, lord -- that's a scary thought. See you later." As Dierdre went through the door, Robin lifted up his box again, wishing she had stayed to hold it open for him. He managed to balance the box on one slim hip and get the door open with the other hand. The box started to overturn again and he just saved it. With a sense of relief he went through the door, leaving it open behind him.

Charlotte was beginning to wish she had taken Robin's advice and eloped. How was it possible they had so many friends? At least there was no problem about the garden being large enough for them all, but October was untrustworthy in England, and it would probably rain. Then they would have to go to their contingency plan, and open up all the French doors between the houses.

When Dierdre first decided to have the doors cut into the connecting walls of the reception rooms, Charlotte wondered if that would mean no privacy for any of them. It hadn't worked out that way, however -- none of them ever used the doors except in the case of large parties. Almost by unspoken agreement, they were kept locked most of the time. They had certainly come in handy when one of them was locked out of his or her own house, though -- and that had happened several times.

Paul put his head around the door jamb and made a raspberry at Charlotte. She threw her notebook at him -- the one in which she was attempting to catalogue the wedding gifts already received -- and he ducked back out of sight. "Coward," she muttered, knowing he was already on his way back down to the basement -- his dungeon, she had nicknamed it. Another thing she was grateful to Dierdre for -- Paul's office was right there in the house, where she could make certain no pretty secretaries made passes at him. Then she frowned as she thought of Frieda, the new trainee for The Animal Liberal Front. She was about eighteen, and perfectly leggy and nubile as only Scandinavian girls are. Not Norwegian but Finnish; still the same part of the world as Paul, and she had that amazing pale-blond hair only Northerners come by naturally. Charlotte noticed the way Frieda looked at Paul from under her Mary Quant mascara.

Successfully diverted from her task, Charlotte tossed her notebook onto the coffee table and headed for her darkroom. Conveniently, this was in part of the basement -- the rest of the enormous space had yet to be divided, but her darkroom was already there, underneath the laundry room -- and to get to it, she went through the main room. That afternoon, the front part of the main room was being used for the assembly of flyers and promotional material, while construction continued in the rear. There Frieda was, just as Charlotte had known she would be, stuffing hot-pink flyers into envelopes with the Animal Liberation Front logo on the front. Her shining sheet of pale blond hair hung down over her face as she laughed at something Paul said.

Just as Charlotte reached the bottom of the stairs, Frieda looked up at him with a worshipful gaze. If Paul was embarrassed by this, he didn't let on. He saw Charlotte and grinned at her. "There's my girl! Have you finished your onerous task?"

"Abandoned it is more like. I've come down to work on those photos for you. You know, I'll bet Robin could use Frieda's help next door. He's moving the last of Didi's stuff to their basement."

"He already has an assistant," Frieda replied tartly. She didn't like Robin, because he made sarcastic comments about empty-headed little girls and groupies. Frieda seemed to have the feeling he was including her in both categories.

"Go anyway, Frie -- Robin doesn't seem well suited to the task."

With a flounce of her head, Frieda slid off her stool, allowing Paul a revealing glimpse of her thighs in the process. As the door at the top of the stairs closed behind her, Charlotte started to laugh. "You never discourage her, Paul. Can it be you like the idol worship of your little trainee?"

Paul frowned. "Don't girls that age always get crushes on older men? It seems harmless to me."

"As an 'older man' you barely qualify. Look at the examples she has before her -- thousands of older men abandoned their wives for young girls.""Not before they've married them, I hope?"

Charlotte couldn't hold out against the teasing tone of Paul's voice. "Well, that does seem a little extreme. I guess I can look forward to about ten years with you before you abandon me. By that time Frieda will be too old, and you'll have to find another nymphette."

With a growl, Paul advanced on Charlotte and picked her up, hugging her to his chest and swinging her back and forth. "No nymphettes for this old man! Just one completely absurd, totally twisted photographer!" With this he kissed her, allowing her feet to touch the ground.

Natalie went sliding across the polished floor of her studio, nearly upsetting a table full of painting supplies. She snatched up the telephone on the fourth ring, hoping whoever it was (and let it be Vlad, she prayed silently) hadn't already abandoned her to the dial tone. "Hello!"

"Well, hello, little Russian princess. This is your Russian prince speaking."

"Vlad! Where the hell are you? Why aren't you here? When will you be?"

He laughed. "Even my great intellect will only handle one question at a time. I'm still in Leningrad; that's why I'm not in London; and I should be home in a few days."

"No! Have you forgotten Chari and Paul's wedding?"

"Of course not -- it's not for a week and a half."

"I know you, Vlad -- you'll get caught up in the fall of Communism and never make it back."

"You have no faith in me at all. I'll be there -- this is just too exciting for me to leave without getting it all."

"Vlad, you are safe there, aren't you? I mean, this is a revolution of sorts . . ."

He laughed. "You wouldn't say that if you were here. Most of the people just complain that things aren't happening fast enough for them."

"Then how can it be so exciting?"

"For me, not for them. Forget that -- tell me how everything is going at home. Have you finished that painting you were working on when I left?"

"Almost. I've been pretty busy helping Chari with the wedding."

"I hope you're not planning this kind of a circus when we get married, little princess."

"Oh, even more elaborate. Everything old Russian style."

"Should be interesting. Got to run, honey -- I'm going to film a demonstration for cigarettes."

"What?"

"A protest -- because there aren't any cigarettes. Call you tomorrow -- love you!" And he was gone.

Natalie shook her head as she replaced the receiver. "I'm in love with a man who thinks a demonstration for cigarettes is exciting. Sick, girl -- you're a very sick woman."

"Really? I would have said you were a perfect physical specimen

-- a little tall for some tastes, perhaps." Natalie turned with a jerk and screamed. Jerome was sitting in her overstuffed, cabbage-rose chair.

Chapter 46

He was arrayed in court dress of the early 1800's, and appeared to think there was nothing out of the ordinary in his popping into Natalie's bedroom after a year's absence.

"Jerome! What are you doing here?"

"Aren't you glad to see me? No, I suppose not -- you always scream."

"Don't be silly, I'm thrilled. At least, I guess I am. We figured you'd be reborn by now."

Jerome crossed one satin-clad leg over the other. "Well, all those years I spent as a ghost apparently don't count -- I still have to put in my rest time. Although I think they'd let me come back now, if I put in for an immediate transfer."

"Why don't you? Or maybe you don't want to be reborn?"

"Well, I'm of two minds. I like the afterlife -- the people there are really nice, and there is a lot to learn. But I'm ready to come back -- as soon as I find Alicia."

"Find her? How did you lose her?"

"She's been scheduled for re-birth, damn them!" Jerome scowled, brandishing a fist at the ceiling of the house as if he would like to punch a heavenly computer operator. "Only one lousy year together, and they decide it's time for her to be re-born! Do you believe it?"

Natalie shook her head in sympathy. "I'm so sorry, Jeri. But surely you don't think you're going to find her amongst all the babies being born today, do you? Remember how many people there are in the world, now."

"Remember? How could I forget? That's all the staff talk about, up there -- how you lot are overpopulating the planet and polluting it up so badly there won't be anything left in a couple of hundred years."

"Who are the 'staff'? Are they dead? Is that what people do between lifetimes -- work in Heaven?"

"Yes and no -- the staff are half and half -- what people who believe in religion call 'angels', and souls who have advanced to the point where they don't need to be reborn again. Actually, the angels are just a different type of being to us, and their function seems to be to work at processing souls."

"How strange. I'd love to see them."

"You will, someday. Not for a long time, hopefully. But I have one year to locate Alicia's soul -- if I do, then I can arrange to be reborn somewhere near her. If the year elapses and I haven't found her, I lose my chance. Then I have to just come back randomly and hope to run into her someday. As you said, there are too many people on the earth now for my odds of doing that to be very good."

"A year? Well, that may seem like a long time now, but I don't know if you'll be able to do it. Not without getting pretty lucky."

Jerome reached into the inside of his velvet jacket and withdrew what appeared to be a gold locket, shaped like a heart. He opened the clasp and inside the locket was revealed a tiny ball of light. Natalie leaned over and peered closely at it, but it remained just that -- a very small glowing sphere with no visible power source.

"What is it?"

"A piece of Alicia's soul. She gave it to me just before she left -- and when I find her, the soul will turn pink. Then I'll give her the locket with a piece of my soul inside, and when she grows up, she'll be able to find me."

Natalie's eyes widened. "Do you mean to tell me I'm looking at a person's soul?"

"Only a very small part of one."

"How can you pull pieces off your soul? Sounds painful."

"It is -- very. But necessary, in this case."

"Boy, are you stubborn. You're the only person I've ever known who was ready to fly in the faces of the cosmos in order to be with the person he loved."

Jerome shrugged, snapping the locket closed and putting it back into his jacket. "How many ghosts have you known?"

"Good point. Did you come back for our help, or just to alert us to your renewed residence in our house?"

"A little of both, and at this point it's become houses, hasn't it? Amazing what you people have done in the space of a year."

Natalie laughed. "You haven't seen anything yet. Didi's basement is being converted into offices for The Animal Liberation Front."

Jerome raised one black eyebrow. "Dierdre and her bottomless coffers strike again?"

"Don't scoff, Jeri -- you may need some of the largesse yourself. Don't forget, you're not a rich Earl anymore -- you're just a penniless ghost. By the way, who will be able to see you, this time? And can you leave the house alone? If you're trapped in here again, it's going to be a little difficult to locate Alicia's soul."

"The rules are a little different this time. In fact, to everyone I meet I'm just another person -- they can all see me, and I can go anywhere I want to. But I still have the same powers Jerome the ghost had. I'm not really a ghost anymore, you see, but a soul-in-transition."

"What did you do to convince the keepers up above to let you out for this little quest? From what you told us before I had the impression they're pretty strict about protocol."

"I told them I'd never consent to be reborn. That I'd just hang around for eternity, bothering them. They couldn't wait to get rid of me."

"Only you, Jeri. Only you. So -- I guess this calls for a meeting tonight. Too bad Vlad's still in Leningrad."

"Is he? What's he doing there? Hasn't deserted you, has he?"

"I'd follow him and cut off his balls." Jerome visibly shivered at this macabre thought. "But he's there filming the dissolution of Communism." At Jerome's look of confusion she said, "Never mind -- it was after your time. He'll be home next week."

"If you have an address, I'll go fetch him. No reason why Alicia shouldn't be born in Russia, right?"

"I hadn't thought of that. Good idea -- but keep an eye on him, would you? I don't want him making time with any of those Russian beauties."

"Oh, ho! So I'm to be your gooseberry, am I?"

Natalie stared at him, as nonplussed by this phrase as he had been by the term 'Communism'. "Why would I want you to be a berry? Could you do that, by the way?"

"Never mind, dear girl -- it was before your time! I'll be off then -- as soon as you tell me where your wandering swain can be located."

"No! Not until after dinner -- everyone else wants to see you, too."

"God, how thoughtless of me. Since I can watch you lot on one of the library monitors, I've been keeping track of you. Not everything, mind you -- just the basics."

"Is that supposed to reassure me you haven't been looking into our bedrooms? You're not a voyeur?"

"Actually, that's rather frowned upon in the afterlife. Who's turn to make dinner tonight?"

"We don't do that so much anymore -- we live in three different houses now. But I'll run to Didi's and see if anybody's home. I know Charlotte and Paul are -- he's working and she's trying to get ready for the wedding. She's not very well suited to things like that, our Chari."

"Do you mean to tell me those two aren't married yet? What about the rest of you?"

"I thought you 'kept track of us on the library monitor'."

"Been too busy lately -- usually I just tune in for a minute or so to make sure none of you've been hurt or something bad has happened. You and Vlad married yet?"

Natalie shook her head. "Maybe we will after Paul and Chari. I guess we haven't given it much thought."

"Didi and my wild descendant?" He said hopefully.

"Nope. He won't marry her."

"What!" Jerome was sincerely shocked. "I can see I'll have to talk to that boy. Comprimising the honor of a lady is a serious matter."

"Jeri, you really do have to cultivate a modern attitude about these things. People don't get married anymore unless they want to -- it's perfectly all right for Didi and Rob to live together."

"But does she want to marry him? And why on earth wouldn't he want to marry her? I know he's in love with her -- isn't he?"

"To the first question; I don't really know whether Didi wants to get married again or not. Remember, she is divorced. To the second; Robin won't marry her because he says she's too wealthy. And to the third; yes, he's in love with her. Crazy in love, I'd say. But the thing about all her money always gets in the way."

"Do you mean to tell me the idiot won't marry her because she's rich? Honestly, Nat -- you modern people aren't as clever as you think you are."

Natalie laughed. "I'm not that clever! I'm in the same position Didi is -- divorced and not certain whether to marry again. Besides,

I don't see that it's so very important."

"Getting married, you mean? But isn't it a commitment, of a sort? The ultimate commitment, to the person you love?"

"Perhaps that's the point, Jeri. Are any of us ready to make the ultimate commitment anymore? These days people's lives change so fast, we could all have outgrown one another in five years."

Jerome shook his head. "Alicia waited for me for nearly 200 years, and now I'm willing to postpone my own rebirth to find her. But you lot are worried about 'outgrowing' one another in five years! It's a good thing I decided to come back; you 'modern people' can't manage your own lives!"

Chapter 47

It wasn't difficult to get the remainder of the group assembled in Natalie's reception room once they knew Jerome had returned. Robin even canceled a rehearsal in order to be there -- none of them had imagined they would see their dead friend again. At least, not as Jerome.

Natalie and Dierdre cooked dinner, and Paul made his famous mocha gateau. Charlotte was too grouchy and preoccupied to be willing to cook anything -- she wished she had another month to get ready for the wedding. She never imagined it would be much more difficult than arranging a photographic show; it was even harder than helping with The Animal Liberation Front benefits. Paul kept telling her it would be over soon, and she should relax. But she wanted everything to be perfect, and she was certain she must have overlooked something. Her little sister was arriving in two days to stay with them, and Charlotte enlisted the help of both her friends to entertain her until the wedding.

Now they sat around the table eating Natalie's honey/orange roast chicken with potatoes and wild rice stuffing, spinach salad, creamed onions and celery, and Blush Zinfandel from California by way of Harrods. But for the first time, the food took a back place to the guest of honor.

"I can't believe you're back, Jeri!" Robin swallowed a mouthful of potatoes. "Poor guy -- after all this time, you only get a year with Alicia and they send her back. Sounds like a dirty deal, to me."

Jerome took a sip of wine. "I heartily agree with you, dear descendant. But since they didn't ask my preference before selecting her for reincarnation, they obviously didn't think I was important to the case. It took me a lot of screaming and threatening to get the time to search for her -- it's practically unheard of."

"What did you threaten them with, Jerome?" Dierdre sounded confused. "I mean -- what can the dead use against the people in charge of Heaven? Are they people?"

"To answer your first question -- I told them I refused to come back until they let me look for Alicia."

"If you could do that, why didn't Alicia refuse to come without you?"

Jerome sighed. "It just never occurred to her. You know, women of my day weren't taught to fight authority the way men were. She could have refused -- but didn't realize it. And before I could get to her, she was already gone. This was my only recourse."

Charlotte shook her head. "It doesn't sound too well organized up there. Who are these people who run Heaven? Suicides, like in Beetlejuice?"

"What? What the hell is that? Surely there's no such thing as Beetlejuice, even in the 20th century? I mean, why would anybody want it?"

They all laughed. "No, stupid," Charlotte replied. "It's a movie about the afterlife -- Beetlejuice was a ghost. And in Heaven, or whatever it was, the waiting room was manned by people who committed suicide."

"Cute concept," Jerome said. "But there really are angels -- they're beings and they're alive, but they live in Heaven and when we die they take care of us until we're reborn."

"You mean they live there? They have children, and all that?"

"All that."

"And every one of them works with the dead souls? Our dead souls?"

"All of them -- ours and all the others."

Robin looked over at him suspiciously. "What others? Other countries? Other races?"

"The latter would be more accurate -- other species, I suppose I should say. You didn't really think this was the only planet where there was civilized life, did you? That would be an arrogant assumption."

Paul put his head down in his hands and groaned. "No! I can't take it -- first you blow all Vlad's beliefs in the afterlife, and now you're talking about people on other planets! It's too much to assimilate, Jeri."

"Well, I shouldn't be telling you this stuff, anyway. I'm sure I'll hear about it when I get back. I'm such a blabbermouth."

"What are your plans now?" Paul asked. "Will you be here for the wedding?"

"By then I'll be back. I'm going to Russia to join Vladimir -- I'm going to be Natalie's gooseberry."

They all stopped eating and stared at him in silence. Dierdre shook her head, laughing. "You wanna explain that one, Jeri?"

"Oh, I forgot -- you don't use that term anymore. 'Watchdog', Natalie called it. She wants to make certain Vlad doesn't fool around while he's making his documentary."

"Shame on you, Nat," Robin waved his fork in her direction, "Not trusting Vlad after all this time."

Natalie shrugged. "I figure when you're offered an opportunity, you should take it. Besides, Jeri has to start his search for Alicia somewhere. It might as well be in Russia, right? There are thousands more people in Leningrad right now than there will be at any other time."

"Jeri," Dierdre said, "You should go with Robin when *Experimental Monkeys* go on tour. They'll be gone for six months, and they're covering most of Europe and the United States."

"What do you say, great-great-great-great-grandson? Shall I come along with you? Be Didi's watchdog?"

Robin laughed. "So glad you picked up on that, revered ancestor. You know you're welcome to come along -- maybe we can get some vibrations on that gold heart of yours, and find Alicia."

"Thank you, my friends. With your help, I know I'll beat the one-year deadline."

"If you narrow down the world to one of the Arab countries, you're on your own." Charlotte emphasized her words by swallowing part of a corn muffin. "But before Robin goes on tour, Paul and I are visiting Scandinavia for our honeymoon. You can come with us, too."

Paul started to laugh, and Jerome stared at her in horror. "You want me to come with you on your honeymoon? I realize you and Paul are living together, but I've never heard of having guests on a honeymoon."

"Hey, like you said -- we're already living together. Besides, you're a ghost. You'll be spending most of your time wandering the streets trying to tune in your gold heart, right?"

"I suppose so. I mean, I certainly wouldn't bother you. Paul, what do you think?"

"Who am I to stand in the way of true love? I suppose Chari will be so busy hunting for the soul of Alicia I'll be left on my own." He sighed dramatically, but grinned at Charlotte and clasped her hand.

Chapter 48

When Jerome appeared in Vladimir's hotel room, the film-maker was changing the cartridge in his mini-cam. Jerome's voice behind him caused him to drop the used cartridge onto the wooden floor, where it careened behind a chair and fell on its' side. "Hello, Vladimir," Jerome said in his elegant, calm accent.

"Aaaah!" Vladimir turned quickly, nearly knocking over the table as well as dropping the film cartridge. "Jerome! What the hell are you doing here?"

"Natalie sent me. She said you could help me in my quest."

"Quest? Sure, buddy -- whatever you need. So you saw my gang in London, huh? How is everybody? Are Charlotte and Paul ready for the wedding?"

Jerome bent down and retrieved the film, handing it to Vladimir. "They seem to be, but I've never seen Charlotte so twitty. She's much more upset over this wedding than she ever was about that photographic show she had last year."

Vladimir put the film cartridge on the table, inserted the new one into the mini-cam, and snapped the side shut. "That only goes to show women haven't changed as much as they claim. Weren't they 'twitty' about weddings in your time?"

"Absolutely. Only now they have so much more to do, I thought it wouldn't mean as much."

"Don't you believe it. Have a seat, man. This room isn't much, but it's all I could get. Everybody and his brother are in Leningrad for the dissolution of Communism."

Jerome sat in a shabby armchair. "Natalie mentioned that to me. But why should a change of government be so interesting? For that matter, why should dissolving it be?"

Vladimir laughed, putting the mini-cam and several more cartridges of film into a padded bag. "I can't explain it - - but I'll try while we attempt to find transportation for the day. The car I rented gave up the ghost -- sorry, no pun intended -- and I haven't been able to locate another. Just how did you get back to earth still in your old body, by the way?"

"That's a long story, like the dissolution of government." Jerome removed the gold locket from his jacket. He was now dressed in much the same fashion as Robin, something Vladimir found vastly amusing. He had to admit that both the ancestor and the descendant possessed the legs for tight, black leather pants, however. "It has to do with this locket. I'm on a year-long quest for the soul of Alicia, and Natalie thought as long as you were in Russia, I might as well start here. And she wanted me to check up on you -- be her 'watchdog', she said."

Vladimir laughed. "I should've known. I'm surprised she's held off this long -- listen, there aren't any strange men hanging around the house, are there? I mean, Paul has some people working for him, now -- they aren't bothering Nat, are they?"

"Don't worry, Vlad -- Nat isn't fooling around. And I didn't see anyone trying to convince her to. She probably dispatches any would-be suitors rather well; she could be intimidating."

"Don't I know it. "Well, my dead friend -- shall we sally forth into the streets of Leningrad and look for the soul of your lost love?"

"Lead on, oh chronicler of the world's happenings!"

As the door closed behind them Vladimir said, "I like that title!"

Chapter 49

Vladimir and Jerome arrived back in London the day before the wedding of Paul and Charlotte. Nobody could figure out why they had chosen to marry in October, when the city was in the firm grip of a British autumn. But with the connecting doors between the houses all thrown open, there was enough room to hold three or four hundred people, a sumptuous buffet and live band for dancing. All this would be in evidence, but when Vladimir and Jerome arrived from the airport (where Natalie had picked them up) she warned them that their house would be in a state of chaos, as were the other two.

Jerome thought Natalie had perhaps underestimated the situation in the houses, but he was accustomed to it -- during his lifetime enormous balls had been a regular occurrence, and they always caused a nightmare panic on the day before the event. He managed to calm Charlotte and Paul, convincing Paul to dismiss his staff for the day and thereby reduce the number of bodies in the house that could possibly get in one another's way.

This didn't sit well with Frieda, Paul's assistant, who appeared to be attempting to get in everyone's way. Jerome realized this was her way of monopolizing Paul, and was pleased when Dierdre ousted her firmly from the house. Perhaps someone should speak to Paul about the girl, Jerome thought, and who better than the resident ghost? Strangely enough, he felt as if he had come home again. And now all his friends had offered to help him in the search for Alicia. What more could a ghost want, he thought happily. If he stayed with them long enough, perhaps he could engineer two more weddings during the year allotted to him for the search.

He would be with Robin for six months; that *had* to be long enough. It didn't leave him much time to work on Vladimir and Natalie, but if Robin and Didi set a date, perhaps their friends would, also. He had a lot of work to do, and felt he was up to the challenge. It was almost like being alive, again.

"Jeri, you're sitting on my hat!" Sherrie screamed, and Jerome scrambled off Charlotte's bed, falling onto the floor. "Well, it's not crushed or anything -- you've got to be more careful, not that you have a mortal body again. Have you seen my earrings?"

Jerome stood, brushing off his gray-striped morning trousers. "Over there, on the bureau. Will you get yourself in hand, girl? You'd think it was *your* wedding." He thought how different Charlotte was from her little sister. Sherrie was small, and slender, with dark-brown hair and enormous brown eyes in her little face. She wasn't as pretty as Charlotte, though at twenty there was a good chance she'd grow into her looks. But she was cute as anything, and had accepted his situation the day she arrived in London, apparently seeing nothing strange in a ghost who returned to earth to search for his beloved.

She slid the pearl drops through her ears. "Tell me more stories about London in the early 1800's, Jeri. It'll take my mind off the wedding."

"I doubt if anything will do that, since the event is scheduled to occur in two hours. Besides, I think you've heard my entire repertoire. I think I'd better go see how Paul's doing. Let's hope the male side of his fiasco is in better than the female."

Sherrie sniffed. "Why should it be? Men are never organized. Was your own wedding more smoothly-run?"

"How could it not be, with hot and cold running servants?" Jerome glanced at the disaster of Charlotte and Paul's bedroom, and wondered why Sherrie thought he would be able to see her hat sitting on the bed.

He nearly collided with one of the maids on the stairway, as she struggled to carry an enormous urn of flowers down to the first floor. "Let me help you with that, dear girl," he said, removing the urn from her arms. "Where were you taking it?"

"To the central foyer, sir. But you shouldn't be carrying that -- you're already dressed for the wedding. Aren't you Robin Herald?"

"His cousin, Jerome Kennington. We've been told there's a remarkable resemblance."

"I should say there is, but I see the difference now. You're better looking, I think." Jerome glanced down at the girl as he maneuvered the stairs. She was in her early or mid-twenties, pretty in a robust, farm-girl fashion, with long, auburn braids wound around her head and very green eyes. He hadn't really considered the advantages of having a mortal body again.

"Why, thank you. Where would you like this?"

"On top of that marble plinth."

"Why did you take it upstairs?"

"It needed some water, and the caterers wouldn't let me having any from the kitchen. Right mean, they are, won't help us out at all."

Jerome settled the urn on the plinth. "Oh, really? Let's just go see about that, shall we?"

The girl seemed alarmed. "You don't have to do that, Mr. Kennington! We're managing all right; it's just that they're using every kitchen for different things. The only other water supplies were outside -- and I couldn't find a hose -- or upstairs or the basements. I chose upstairs."

Jerome was becoming more the indignant aristocrat with every step. The maid was becoming afraid of him, but afraid not to follow as well. He erupted into Didi's kitchen with all the arrogance of inbred superiority.

Several people who were working on food look up in surprise. One of them frowned at the sight of Jerome and the maid. "I already told ya', stupid -- nobody but the catering staff is allowed in the kitchen. 'Oo's 'e, then? He can't 'ave no water from 'ere, neither." The man was young and beefy-looking, in his mid-twenties. He had very short hair and his arms were tattooed where he had rolled up the sleeves of his shirt. His cockney accent was so thick it hung in the air around them.

Jerome wondered if any of the Americans had spoken to him, and whether two years in England had enabled them to understand them. "The young lady will have whatever she needs from this kitchen or the others. You will assist her with the remainder of the urns that need water, or you will carry the water out to the urns for her. Do I make myself clear?"

For a moment the young man seemed nonplussed. Then he grinned, brandishing his knife in the air. The other two people working in the kitchen glanced around, then stepped back to clear the room for action. "And 'oo'er you when ye're at 'ome, yer lordship?"

"Absolutely correct -- Sir Jerome Kennington, at your service. For the moment Jerome forget he was supposed to be Robin's cousin. Then he decided there was no reason Robin couldn't have a cousin who was also a lord.

"Well, I don't care 'oo ye are, ye're bloody lordship -- clear off outta the kitchen. Me boss said nobody was allowed but the catering staff." Jerome dodged around the island in the center of the room, avoiding the carving knife. He was as well-trained as any aristocrat of the British Regency period, better than some due to his time in the army. But he didn't expect what came next. What should have been only a glancing blow to dislodge the knife from the man's hand sent that object flying with such force it embedded itself in the pale rose paint of the wall. The 'prep' chef blinked, but recovered enough to take a swing at Jerome's head. The other man's hand shot out and intercepted the blow, and with what appeared to be very little effort, Jerome lifted him off his feet and threw him bodily over the cooking island. He landed with a crash against the wall and subsided, unconscious. Jerome frowned. He knew he had used very little effort -- this shouldn't have happened.

He realized the rest of the people were staring at him with awe and fear, including the little maid.

"Your friend will no doubt have a terrific headache when he awakens. One of you will assist this lady with her task. If your boss wishes to speak to me, I will be available." With a bow to the maid, he turned and left the kitchen.

"And it was as if I had super-human strength -- I threw him across the room with no effort at all. Although in my time I was noted as something of a Corinthian, I never could have done that. In fact, I've never seen anyone who could, apart from some film characters."

"Is my tie straight?" Robin turned to Jerome, who adjusted his silk bow-tie. "I think we look like a lot of monkeys, in these damned suits. It seems as if the 'afterlife guardians' have given you some unique powers in order to safeguard your stay on earth. I mean, what would they do if you died again, during the search for Alicia?"

"Well, it was never discussed. But what should I do about it? Do you suppose the caterer will sue?"

Robin laughed. "I sincerely doubt it -- Didi hired him. Most people understand her social standing, and are reluctant to cross her. Did you know she was invited to have tea with the princess?"

"Diana?" Robin nodded. "She hasn't yet; I don't know if she ever will. Not exactly her style. But it's a sure thing nobody wants to offend her. Have you seen my handkerchief?"

But as they were descending the stairs, they heard yelling coming from the kitchen. "Now what?" Robin muttered, turning toward the sound.

Jerome's little maid erupted from the kitchen, crying and clutching her apron in her hands. She was followed by a very large, very bald man, who seemed to be berating her for something. He stopped short at the sight of Robin and Jerome. Frowning horribly, the man forgot his quarrel with the maid and concentrated on Robin and Jerome. "Which one of you 'ad a dust-up with my Will?" He asked belligerently.

"I did," Jerome replied, at his haughty, drawling best. "Your assistant has appalling manners. And so do you."

"You near cracked 'is skull fer 'im -- you don' look so bloody strong ta me. I should sue you lot -- nobody but me own people comes into the kitchens when I work."

"I suggest you take yourself off, then," Robin replied. "Go back into the kitchen, and if I hear anymore talk of suing, you won't cater another wedding or so much as a birthday party for a cat in London again. And anyone who wants to come into *my* kitchen can do so -- remember that, or Jerome might do the same to you he did to Will."

Jerome crossed to the little maid. "You look worn-out, poor thing. Don't work anymore today -- come into the garden and have a glass of lemonade. I'll make certain you're paid anyway."

He led her away, still sobbing. Dierdre came dashing down the stairs, wearing a pale pink satin robe. Robin could see the flash of peach-colored stockings and a silk teddie underneath, and hoped nobody else had. "Don't just stand there like a lot of dolts," she screamed. "It's starting to rain!"

Chapter 50

Epilogue: A Wedding

"We're ready, Rob -- go get the band started, would you?" Dierdre was glad Charlotte and Paul had decided on a late afternoon wedding. Once the rain started, it continued in a steady, miserable drizzle for the remainder of the day. Fortunately it wasn't bad enough to keep any of the guests away, but it definitely precluded an outdoor wedding. They were prepared for this, and everything was designed so it could be quickly disassembled and brought inside. Even the white wicker gazebo in which the wedding couple would stand had been reconstructed in the foyer of Charlotte's townhouse.

The animals thought the whole thing was a party being given particularly for their amusement. It was difficult having three adolescent cats and dogs who were accustomed to the run of three houses -- they did their best to get in everyone's way. Finally they settled down in the basement room of Natalie's house, where she placed all their favorite blankets and toys, and the enticement of special food treats.

The caterers kept trying to close the door down into the basement, which meant Natalie would keep dashing back to open it and scream not to do it again.

Dorinda, their East Indian maid, was now in her last year of college. She was still their housekeeper, and had given up her other clients in order to take care of all three townhouses. This suited her just fine; it was the right amount of hours to allow her to do homework and have a social life. The day of the wedding she was in charge of the extra maid help, and had brought her boyfriend along to assist. He was a very shy Indian man, probably in his mid-twenties, and they had been relieved to note he wore Western dress without what Charlotte called 'head diapers'. That meant he wasn't a Moslem -- they knew Dorinda was Hindu, and hoped Rashid was, also. He took the organization of the wedding very seriously, and appeared to be more nervous than any of the major participants.

There would be no minister, since Charlotte disliked all patriarchal religions pretty much equally, and Paul didn't care one way or the other. His parents and one of his brothers had come to England for the wedding and a short vacation, and were staying in Charlotte's townhouse. His mother seemed rather upset that their ceremony was so unorthodox, but she didn't say much. In fact, her English wasn't too good and she seemed overwhelmed by everything that was going on around her. So she just sat on the couch in Charlotte's living room and talked as best she could to an array of early guests, dressed in a very attractive dark- rose silk dress that Didi had help her buy.

Experimental Monkeys started playing a love song they had written for the wedding, and Robin's clear voice floated through Charlotte's reception rooms into the other houses. The French doors were all open, and the huge urns of roses were everywhere. Dark pink roses, pale ones, and cream- colored with rose tipping. Paul, his brother as best man, Vladimir, and several of their friends were standing around the gazebo, all dressed in the grey morning suits with matching gloves and top hats. The ceremony was being performed by a television psychologist from Didi's station, who had become ordained in the Unitarian church just for occasions like this one. The mother and father of the groom were seated on a pink velvet loveseat situated nearby.

The procession began with a flower girl, though it had been difficult to find any friends with a small child. This had been solved when Dorinda volunteered her youngest sister. Now the eight-year-old walked solemnly down Charlotte's staircase and toward the reception, carrying her basket of baby roses. Her black hair and dark skin and eyes were dramatic against the pale pink silk dress, as if a doll had come to life. Her hair hung straight down her back, crowned with a wreath of baby roses, and she wore tiny pink lace gloves.

There was no Maid of Honor, because Charlotte refused to choose between her friends and her sister. Instead there were six women (Sherrie, Didi, Natalie, another photographer and two models who were friends of Charlotte's) all dressed in identical dark pink silk. The dresses were very simple, fitted sheaths with scalloped necklines, v-backs and long sleeves that puffed at the top and tapered narrow at the bottom. The only ornamentation were satin bows at the bottom of the 'v' and the top of the slit, in the back. They wore matching suede high-heeled pumps, one rose in their hair, and short satin gloves. They each carried one long-stemmed rose.

Charlotte's dress was strapless, of white organza over taffeta. It had a very full skirt ornamented with pink silk roses. She wore pink satin ballet slippers, long pink lace fingerless gloves, and carried a cascade of the cream roses tipped in pink. Her hair was loose and foamed around her back, topped with a coronet made of roses. Jerome was her escort. She was wearing the antique engagement ring Paul had given her. She told him she didn't want another ring, and they decided not to wear wedding rings. Instead of exchanging rings during the brief ceremony, they read poems each had written for the other.

The reception was in Didi's house, while Natalie's had been reserved for those who wanted to dance. Another band played while Paul and Charlotte cut the cake and photographs were taken. The cake itself was a little different in that both cake and frosting were chocolate -- the couple had agreed neither of them liked vanilla in any shape or form. It was five layers tall and decorated with a cascade of real roses -- they didn't like frosting flowers, either. The table with the cake and two for gifts were located in the foyer; in the small reception room were three buffet tables, and smaller tables and chairs were in the large reception room.

Jerome watched them pass out pieces of cake. Both had warned the other of severe repercussions should a food fight ensue, but noticed they were surreptitiously trying to get cake on one another without being touched themselves. It made him think of his own wedding, so long ago and so very different, except for the men in gray morning suits and the bride in white. Cloud and Ebony came to where he was sitting on the stair case and vied for his attention. He lifted the locket out of his shirt and showed it to them, petting them and allowing them both to jump into his lap. "What do you think, little friends? Can I find her in a year? Natalie's right, you know -- it doesn't seem like such a long time when you consider how very large the world is."

Cloud, who had a perpetually serious look on her little face as if she was contemplating the mysteries of the universe, picked up the locket in her paw. Lifting it so she could rub against it, she allowed to fall back into his shirt. "Thank you, sweetheart -- with your blessing, how could I go wrong?"

He heard a lot of yelling and laughing below him, and stood with both half-grown cats in his arms. Charlotte was coming towards the stairs, carrying her bouquet. "I'm going to toss the bouquet now, Jeri -- go down into the crowd." As she came up even with him, he smiled at her. Ebony tried to bat the cascade of roses out of her hand. "No, Eb -- you can't be the next married. You're too young!"

"I'll stay up here with you, lovely lady," Jerome told her. "I'm not likely to be the next to wed."

She grinned at him, and he moved back so she could position herself near the banister. Turning her back to the crowd below, she threw the roses into the air. Charlotte was more athletic than most women, and it sailed straight over the crowd and landed in Natalie's arms as she was trying to serve cake to some small guests.

Every one laughed, and Charlotte turned to look down. "Tried to escape, did you, Nat? Can't get away from Fate!" Natalie saluted Vladimir where he was taking photographs of the event. They both grinned.

Robin ate a bite of cake and asked Didi why she hadn't tried to catch it. "It's not our turn, yet. When it is, the bouquet will come to me as it did to Nat. I didn't get any cake, you know." He fed her some of his own.